THINKING FAST

Slocum found the remaining pair of rustlers near the end of the line, staring, with hands on hips, at a wet, trembling gelding. "Hell, somebody didn't cool out his horse, that's all," the nearer one remarked to Slocum. "I sure ain't gonna do it for him."

"There's a skittery one over there that bothers me," Slocum said, inventing this as he pointed to the far side of the picket line.

Turning to look, the rustler who'd spoken put himself in perfect position for Slocum to clip him behind the left ear with the long, steel barrel of his .45 Colt. He dropped like a stone, and his partner found himself gawking down the round, black hole to eternity.

"Don't make a sound," Slocum cautioned. "It would be a shame to spoil all this good work."

DON'T MISS THESE
ALL-ACTION WESTERN SERIES
FROM THE BERKLEY PUBLISHING GROUP

THE GUNSMITH by J. R. Roberts
Clint Adams was a legend among lawmen, outlaws, and ladies. They called him . . . the Gunsmith.

LONGARM by Tabor Evans
The popular long-running series about U.S. Deputy Marshal Long—his life, his loves, his fight for justice.

LONE STAR by Wesley Ellis
The blazing adventures of Jessica Starbuck and the martial arts master, Ki. Over eight million copies in print.

SLOCUM by Jake Logan
Today's longest-running action Western. John Slocum rides a deadly trail of hot blood and cold steel.

JAKE LOGAN

SLOCUM AND THE GHOST RUSTLERS

BERKLEY BOOKS, NEW YORK

SLOCUM AND THE GHOST RUSTLERS

A Berkley Book / published by arrangement with
the author

PRINTING HISTORY
Berkley edition / November 1994

ISBN: 0-425-14462-3

BERKLEY®
Berkley Books are published by The Berkley Publishing Group,
200 Madison Avenue, New York, New York 10016.
BERKLEY and the "B" design
are trademarks belonging to Berkley Publishing Corporation.

PRINTED IN THE UNITED STATES OF AMERICA

10 9 8 7 6 5 4 3 2 1

1

Curiosity got Slocum into it. That and a long, hard winter that had given him a terrible case of cabin fever. With the painfully slow retreat of the snow, eight feet on the level at one time, and the inexorable appearance of thin, green shoots of new grass, came rumors out of the Texas Panhandle. At first, Slocum scoffed at them.

Invisible cattle rustlers? No such thing. Then the rumors acquired substance when men Slocum knew and respected began speaking in hushed tones about the unseen night riders. Ranchers in the area bounded by Canyon, Texas, in the north and Tulia in the southeast had been losing cattle. *Lots* of cattle. No one had ever seen the rustlers, their horses left no tracks, yet the wide swaths cut through the new prairie grass by the stolen cattle all led to the upper end of Palo Duro Canyon.

Now, Slocum knew that Charlie Goodnight still lived in the bottom of the canyon, near the middle, and operated a successful ranch there. But old Charlie would never run a wide loop. There were some who said that in his young and restless days, Charlie Goodnight had run as many cattle with questionable brands as those bearing his own. There'd been that herd he had made history with by driving the critters north to Colorado by way of New Mexico Territory and through Raton Pass. In the days that had been done, it constituted a grand adventure.

So Slocum gave in at last to his gnawing curiosity and saddled up Sugarloaf, his brindle-colored half-Arab stallion, threw a packsaddle on a mild-mannered roan gelding, and headed for Fort Worth. On the way he contemplated the possibilities presented by what the unlearned and superstitious called "ghost rustlers." After a brief visit with former associates, he made good time riding northwest out of Fort Worth. The air was moist, sweet, and warm, coming up out of the Gulf. Slocum took pleasure from drawing it deeply into his big barrel chest and letting it ruffle his earlobe-length black hair.

From the added height advantage of his greater than six-foot-one frame, he gazed far over the prairie. He did so with clear, sharp green eyes that danced with the laughter he did not release as he thought of those ghostly cattle thieves. There had to be some practical answer. Right then, with the sun warm on his broad back, John Slocum decided that he would be the one to rob the rustlers of their protective cloak of myth.

With him thus committed, his stomach, rather than his mind, took note of the savory odor of frying meat. A plaintive growl reminded him he had not eaten since gnawing on a biscuit and some jerked beef half an hour before sunup. His only consolation at the time had been the strong, hot Arbuckle's coffee with which he had washed down the Spartan fare. This tempting aroma beckoned to Slocum, and he cast his gaze over the terrain in an attempt to locate the source.

Nothing showed. Only the gradual rise in the plain ahead, this narrow road stretching westward beyond Childress, along the Prairie Dog Town Fork of the Red River. A day beyond lay Palo Duro Canyon, and before it the town of Happy. Who, he wondered, had settled in this forsaken place? The grade turned out to mask a deep, wide coulee with a clear-water creek meandering through the middle.

Slocum's keen green orbs picked out several structures that proved more than a casual camp. He angled toward them, the packhorse on obedient tow, and the distant objects resolved themselves into a large, sturdy lean-to, a brush lodge, and four large canvas tents. Stick figures of four men moved among the permanent encampment. At fifty yards, Slocum reined in. He removed his weather-beaten Stetson and waved it over his head to attract attention.

"Hello the camp!" he called pleasantly.

"Howdy y'rself. You alone, mister?" yelled back a portly fellow in blue wool trousers that had once borne white pin-stripes, and a red long-john top.

"I am. I'm friendly."

"Ride on in."

Fast on his feet for one of such girth, the greeter met Slocum a dozen strides outside the setup. "Name's Carter. Stub Carter I'm called," he advised.

"Slocum," the tall, muscular, sun-browned man allowed.

"Welcome to Paradise." At Slocum's odd expression, Carter rushed on. "That's what we named this place. Me 'n my partner. Hey, Finney, c'mon out here. We got a visitor."

A tall, skinny scarecrow of a man, in the white shirt and the apron of a bartender stepped from the largest of the tents. He held a towel in one pale, long-fingered hand. Arms akimbo, he assumed a gawky stance and blinked ice-pale eyes.

"Who—uh—who we got here, Stub?" he asked. His slurred, imprecise speech made him sound like he'd crossed the river and left half his load on the far bank.

"This is Mr. Slocum, you idjit!" Stub snapped. "Now, you remember your manners and offer Mr. Slocum a drink. Step down, an' light a spell, Mr. Slocum."

"Uh—uh—what's yer pisen, Mr.—uh—Slocum?" Finney asked.

Slocum revised his opinion of the campsite. A road ranch, no doubt about it. He shuddered inwardly at the thought of that gray-streaked towel wiping the glasses from which customers had to drink. "Do you have any beer?" he asked, opting for the least of possible evils.

"Sure do. Got some o' them hinge-gate bottles straight outta Saint Louie," Stub enthused.

"I'd be obliged," Slocum allowed.

"Oh, no obligation about it. First one is on the house; the rest you gotta pay for," Stub informed him. "We whip up some mean victles, too."

"I'm sure you do," Slocum stated dryly. Then he caught a whiff of the roasting meat. "Smells like you're cooking up something open-pit."

"That we are. Expectin' some thirty fellers along later, an' we done stuck a hind leg of beef over the coals. Got some hickory, white oak, an' applewood. Ought to make it re-e-eal tasty."

Slocum's stomach agreed. He dismounted and entered the tent into which Finney had popped a moment before. Six large vinegar barrels had been set up along the wall to the left, with rough-sawed planks on top to form a bar. For a backbar, one of the entrepreneurs had taken an old pigeonhole mailbox form and knocked out some of the dividers to provide high enough spaces for whiskey bottles. Some of those, no doubt the pricier potables, wore thick coats of dust. One, of clear glass, with a worn cork, held a caustic-looking liquid that Slocum gauged to have been colored with cut-plug tobacco. A wooden tub on the floor held cool creek water and some two dozen pint-sized brown bottles.

Finney retrieved one of these and snapped open the hinged, heavy-gauge wire apparatus. The white ceramic stopper, with its red rubber gasket, released with a distinctive *pop!*, and a curl of blue-white smoke rose off the brew inside. Slocum could smell the rich hops-and-barley-malt aroma. At least they had good taste in beer, he concluded.

"Duh—you—uh—want a glass?" Finney asked.

Suppressing a grimace, Slocum answered, "No. I like it straight from the bottle."

Twenty minutes later, with his hunger still unabated, Slocum watched as three cowhands trotted up and dismounted outside the tent saloon. They entered, laughing and talking together. One patted a hard, flat belly.

"Sure beats hell outta draggin' around a cold sandwich in yer saddlebags, now, don't it?" a lank, youthful ranch hand declared to his friends.

"'Special one what Cookie done rustled up," the tall, blond cowboy on his left agreed.

"It ain't so much the bread's all dried out," the third hand contributed, then chorused with the others, "It's that the meat's so danged tough."

"Beer."

"Beer."

"Beer," all three ordered.

Someone else who knew better than to risk exposure to the utensils of the establishment. Slocum acknowledged their presence with a nod. The tall, blond one studied him with open curiosity.

"Yer new around here?" he challenged.

Slocum took time for a long swallow before answering. "Just ridin' through."

"You lookin' for work? Our boss is hiring."

"Thanks, no. I already have a job," Slocum stated casually. "Heading for Happy to start it now."

"Hummm. Happy, huh? That's where them ghost rustlers are operatin', ain't it?"

"So I've heard," Slocum acknowledged indifferently.

"You're being nosey, Spence," the youngest of the trio cautioned.

Spence eyed Slocum closely: his wide, well-worn cartridge belt—each loop filled with a shiny clean .45 cartridge—the low drape of the open holster, the smoothly worn grips of the big .45 Colt Peacemaker that rested in it, its safety loop slipped free. "The ranchers up that way hiring fast guns to ride around their herds?"

"Not that I know of," Slocum said truthfully. Then he unloaded a whopper. "I'm going to be working in the general mercantile."

An eyebrow sailed toward a leonine widow's peak on Spence's high forehead, and his eyes narrowed. "No offense, mister, but you ain't no store clerk. Not the way you wear that iron."

"They come in all sizes," Slocum gave back calmly.

"What? Gunfighters?" Spence prodded.

"No, store clerks."

Sensing that he was being made fun of, Spence jumped from friendly badgering of a stranger to shingle nail–chewing mad in an instant. His face went a deep red, eyes wide and shiny, glazed with the hunger for a fight. Before he could carry off his intentions, Slocum reached out with a huge, hard hand and balled the front of Spence's shirt. Without the slightest sign of effort, he lifted the young cowboy off his boots.

"Son, you're in over your depth," Slocum advised calmly. "I reckon that meat is about ready to have us make a fuss over it. I know I plan to take on quite a lot. Why don't you boys order your meal and settle in to enjoy it?"

Temper flared again. "I ain't no boy," Spence grumbled, though the fire had gone out of it. He didn't like hanging in midair.

Stub appeared then, carrying a platter piled high with juicy slices off the big round of beef, and edged with blackened, pit-baked potatoes. "Here now, Spence, you knows the rules," the proprietor stated fussily. "Ever'body gets along or those what can't get their butts booted out. This meat's smokin' hot, an' you'd best wade into it fast. There's spuds, some onion relish, an' fresh-baked bread to mop up the juices. Settle down now an' enjoy."

Smiling, Slocum released Spence and turned back to his beer. "I'll take a plate of that, too," he announced.

"Reckoned you would," Stub concurred. "So I brung you one, heaped high. You want to find a table?"

"Here's fine," Slocum declared, ready to stand awhile after two days' long ride.

"Suit yourself."

Spence had joined his friends and looked up now from his plate, mouth full of good beer. "No offense, mister. Only I was curious. Gunhands get better pay than cowhands. Thought I might apply, too."

Slocum shot him a smile. "It's a free country. You're welcome to try. Only, like I said, I don't know of anyone hiring." That wasn't entirely true. Concealed in a leather folder, wrapped in a neckerchief, Slocum bore the five-pointed star, stamped out of a silver peso, of a Cattlemen's Association range detective, the same one worn by the Texas Rangers.

"You're right welcome to use the lean-to," Stub Carter told Slocum shortly after nightfall. "That's what this here hospitality station of arn's all about."

Evening had brought more of the local trade and three other travelers. All made use of the accommodations, ate, and drank. A man and woman who had arrived together paid a dollar for use of one smaller tent for the night. The other male sojourner opted for the lean-to and spread his blankets at as much distance from Slocum's as the cramped space allowed. It had cost them fifty cents each for the privilege of keeping the dew off their faces.

Rather a stiff tariff, Slocum considered. Though when one had the only game in town, price would not be an issue. He had dined again on the roasted beef and potatoes, although he avoided the "onion relish," which turned out to be made mostly of chopped raw chili peppers. He washed it down with another bottle of Anheiser's Special Malt Lager.

Then he saw to his horses and turned in early. He wanted to be on his way at sunup. Sleep came quickly, despite the loud voices from the tent saloon and the twang of a guitar. By near midnight, the last drunk had been extinguished along with the lights. Slocum's slumber deepened. Another hour passed.

A sudden sound jerked him awake on a nearly moonless night. For a moment, Slocum could not get his bearings. He heard the noise again, a soft footfall on the sand-crusted soil. Slowly, Slocum raised his head. Faintly he made out three dark figures bent over his neighbor in the lean-to. A soft hiss resolved into whispered words.

"Go slow. Don't want to wake him."

"Shoulda clunked him on the head first thing," came the airy reply.

"He coulda made a noise and woke the other one. We wanna get him, too."

Not so, Slocum thought to himself as his fingers sought and closed around the use-worn grips of his .45 Colt Peacemaker. Ever so slowly he eased the seven-inch barrel from leather. The feather-light search of his roommate must have gotten heavy-handed. The traveler uttered a grunt and snort and reached upward with a groping hand.

"Dammit, cut his throat," the middle one hissed.

Starlight glinted blue off a knife blade. Slocum eared back the hammer and triggered a round in a smooth, single action. Yellow flame speared the darkness and illuminated the trio of ne'er-do-wells who had earlier been introduced as the swamper, hostler, and cook. The latter gave a short, sharp cry of pain, dropped the knife, and fell face-first across their victim.

"Ohmygod!" the small, rangy hostler blurted. He spun toward the source of the blast, his hand seeking the Smith & Wesson .32 in his waistband.

Slocum let the man clear his trousers with the diminutive revolver before he pinwheeled him with a hot .45 slug to the belly. Doubled over, the livery attendant dropped on the squirming man who shared the lean-to. An explosive curse burst from the fellow, who now had two dead men lying on his torso and legs.

"Gawdammit, get them off me," he yelled.

"Hey, mister, hey, jist a minute," the saloon swamper bleated. "Don't shoot me. I didn' do nothin'. We was only funnin'."

"Show your hands," Slocum snarled. "And they had better be empty."

Reluctantly, one hand came into view, raised above the nervous thief's shoulder to be silhouetted by the frosty light of the starfield behind him. Left-handed, Slocum tugged up his trousers and fitted boots to his bare feet. All the while he kept the prowler covered. Satisfied with his wardrobe, Slocum came to his knees.

His prisoner decided the time had come to take back the initiative. From behind his back, he produced a short-barreled .44 Merwin and Hulbert and squeezed the double-action trigger. His bullet cracked past Slocum's head, close enough for him to feel the wind. Untroubled by the need for haste and stealth, Slocum had better aim.

His big, blunt-nosed .45 bullet smacked into flesh in the miscreant's left shoulder. Squealing like a pig, the feisty swamper indexed another round. He was no slouch as a gunhand, and his slug cut hair from the right side of Slocum's head. The raven strands fell tickling on his bare chest. Again he lighted the interior of the lean-to with a belch of flame from the Colt. The brightness had not faded when a red splotch appeared around a .45-size black hole in the breastbone of the swamper.

From beyond the lean-to came a pitiful wail in the voice Slocum recognized as Stub Carter's. "Oh, lordy-lord, that Slocum done kilt Lonny, Burt, an' Kerbs."

"Duh—uh—wha' you wan' me to do 'bout it, Stub?" his more stupid partner asked.

"You stupe, Finney," Stub groused. "Use that gawdamned shotgun."

Stub's last word was not entirely out of his mouth when Slocum hit the ground fast. He rolled to where his companion traveler had extricated himself from the bodies.

"My god, you're fast," the breathless drummer gulped out, meaning the gunplay.

"It helps keep me alive," Slocum informed him dryly. "Now, stay low. They've got a shotgun out there."

"They who?"

"Our congenial hosts." Buckshot pellets ripped through the brush wall of the lean-to and ended further conversation.

Slocum moved again, this time to the front of the shelter. He made out the shambling gait of Stub Carter, his shoulders hitching up and down with each step, as the road ranch proprietor hastened away. Then he heard movement from the side of the lean-to where the shotgun blast had originated.

"I think—duh—I think I got 'em, Stub."

"Well, make sure, idjit!" Stub yelled from a greater distance.

Finney showed himself around the edge of the lean-to and gaped in surprise when he saw Slocum crouched in the entrance. He jerked up the barrel of his 10-gauge L. C. Smith and yanked hard on the trigger. The inevitable happened—the muzzles rose on the double-gun—so that Finney ventilated the leaves of a cottonwood instead of Slocum's hide. Quick for a man so slow-witted, Finney broke the shotgun and inserted two fresh cartridges. The brass shells clicked noisily as he slid them home and snapped shut the breech.

With speed and clearheaded accuracy, Slocum put a figure-eight pair of holes two inches above Finney's navel. The reed-thin beanpole gaped disbelievingly and produced a barely visible frown as the enormous pain began to register. Slowly the arms holding the L. C. Smith drooped. It clattered loudly on the ground when Finney released his grip. Sure of his kill, Slocum came to his boots and headed off in the direction taken by Stub Carter.

He found Carter hastily saddling a gray gelding in the small makeshift stable. "Turn around, Stub," Slocum commanded.

Stub stiffened and darted a quick glance over his left shoulder, and his full, greasy lips formed his mouth into an "Oh" of resignation. All the fight drained from him then, if indeed he had every possessed any. But he had not surrendered his craftiness. Using the stirrup fender—upraised to allow access to the cinch—to hide his movement, he eased his right hand toward a saddle holster.

"Now—now, we can work this out, Mr. Slocum. Yessir, indeedy do we can. Only a misunderstanding."

"Do you rob and kill every stranger that comes through here?" Slocum asked conversationally.

"No. No, sir, Mr. Slocum. Only—only those what look like they've got a good stake with 'em and won't be missed by anyone," Stub babbled.

"A discerning piece of scum," Slocum observed. "How long's this been going on?"

"Long enough," Stub Carter replied, the fingers of his right hand closing on the grips of the old Colt Dragoon he carried on his saddle. "Long enough to know all the tricks," he went on as he whipped the big cap-and-ball pistol clear and spun to use it on Slocum.

Slocum shot him between the eyes. A stunned expression froze on the face of Stub Carter. He wavered, his rotund body melting slowly to the ground. A final gasp of surrender came as his chest struck the hard soil.

"What is it? What's happening?" the frightened voice of the woman traveler called from the tent she shared with her husband.

"Now, Martha, it's none of our business," her mild-mannered spouse tried to calm her.

"No. I heard shooting, Hiram. What is going on?"

"Nothing, ma'am," Slocum responded to her. "Just Mr. Carter and Mr. Finney celebrating their retirement from the road ranch business."

2

Only a single kerosene lamp glowed a soft yellow in one corner of the small shack on the outside of Happy, Texas. Two men stood in its rays, facing a third, who remained in deep shadow. All that could be discerned of him was a large black hat, its front brim turned down over an invisible face, and a cape-style leather duster of the same color. Discomfort registered on the weathered faces of the pair dressed in denims, flannel shirts, and vests. Their boots had the scuffed, worn appearance of working cowboys', and big, shiny spurs weighted the heels. The larger of the two stiffened slightly at the first words to come from the shadowed figure.

"Kelso, I want you to step up your activity. We need to move more head."

"That ain't gonna work, Boss," Herman Kelso protested. "Things are getting a bit hot out there. Some of the bigger spreads are hiring fast guns."

"Butch, has that ever bothered you in the past?" the Boss asked in a cajoling tone. "I looked you up because you are one of the best. Your suggestions improved my plan until it became brilliant. I have every faith in you."

Butch Kelso was not to be swayed by flattery. "There's talk the Association is bringing in some agents from Fort Worth. Those boys carry Ranger badges, and they're every bit as mean as the Rangers. I say we should lay low for a while. It's just plain too hot out there."

Unseen by his visitors, the Boss narrowed his eyes. His voice took on a rough, threatening tone. "If you think this is hot, would you like to go back to New Mexico Territory?"

Paleness spread over Kelso's sun-browned features. "No— no, Boss, I . . . uh . . . I sorta prefer Texas for the time being.

Lot more comfortable, if you know what I mean."

"Very well, then. I expect to see an increase by half over the next month. I trust I can rely on you to produce satisfactory results." Without waiting for any response, he terminated the meeting by turning on one heel and exiting through the rear door.

"Shit!" Butch Kelso exploded. "I got a bad feeling about this."

Sugarloaf crested a rolling ridge in the Panhandle prairie and there it lay, spread before the eyes of Slocum. Happy, Texas. He had selected this as a starting place since it lay to the south of Palo Duro Canyon. If stolen cattle disappeared into the canyon, reason dictated that they had to come out somewhere. If he found the final destination of the missing livestock, he stood a good chance of getting a line on who had taken them. Perhaps someone in Happy might provide an answer.

With his packhorse tagging along, Slocum started down the reverse slope toward town. His course intersected another road where he overtook and passed a buckboard bearing a family to town. A dour-looking man in blue denim drove stoically. His wife, in a paisley print dress, sat at his side, face shaded by a large sunbonnet. Three towheaded children, barefoot, the boys in bib overalls and shirtless, the girl in a flour-sack pinafore, rode at the tailgate, legs dangling over the edge. The girl's bare legs were as sun-browned as the boys exposed shoulders and arms. They waved shyly as Slocum trotted by.

Nice folks, Slocum thought absently as he gained on the lumbering wagon and its team. A small sign proclaimed in bold black paint, "HAPPY Pop. 245."

Slocum walked Sugarloaf past it and entered the residential fringe of Happy, Texas. The town was located in Swisher County, Slocum recalled from his briefing in Fort Worth, which had so small a population that it shared its law enforcement with neighboring Wadall County, with Canyon serving as its county seat. The sheriff's name was Harlan Butcher. Not an auspicious handle for a lawman, Slocum considered. Immediately he entered the village of Happy, he began to notice that it was abnormally quiet for a Saturday afternoon.

Half a dozen young boys, bare as the day they'd been born, splashed in a placid pool formed by Dennison Creek, near the bridge. Yet they were inordinately subdued. Their activity lacked the usual raucous shouts and laughter. Even the dogs seemed unnaturally calm. Only two raised their muzzles from their front hoofs and snorted disdainfully as he ambled past. None burst forth in uninhibited barking.

When he reached the main business section, a sparse half dozen spring wagons and buckboards waited in a fan-shaped cluster in front of the general mercantile. Eight head-hanging cow ponies lined the tie rail outside the largest of three saloons. Four small boys played a desultory game of marbles in the dust under a stout old cottonwood, which must have been young when the Spanish came through the area. Seven women, all accompanied by their furtive-looking spouses, went about the business of shopping. None turned an eye toward Slocum.

Puzzled, Slocum made more than his usual careful scrutiny as he picked his way through the ruts and mud holes of the main street. He noted a big sign, black again, that indicated a hotel. A light touch on the reins sent Sugarloaf in that direction.

Slocum stepped down from the saddle and did a loose tie over the crossbar. He would arrange for stabling later. Dust bloomed in a cloud as he smacked his chaps, vest, and shirtfront with his sweat-stained, pearl-gray Stetson. Satisfied for the moment, he climbed the two steps that cut obliquely across the angled front of the hotel boardwalk. He entered through ornate, stained-glass French doors.

Predictably, heavy burgundy drapes kept the lobby and sitting room area in perpetual gloom. A small, pulpitlike desk occupied a prominent place at the foot of a curved staircase that led to the second floor. Behind it, a young man only a scant few years beyond acne stood in shirtsleeves, long, black sleeve protectors on each forearm. A green visor shaded his eyes. He glanced up as the door closed audibly behind Slocum.

At once he arranged his face in a disapproving expression of rejection. Such a fine establishment did not cater to saddle bums. Slocum crossed the short expanse to the desk and worked his face into a smile.

"Howdy. I'd like a room, second floor at the back, plenty of light."

"I'm sorry, sir, we are entirely booked up," a prissy voice answered him.

He might have expected it, Slocum thought, resigned; it went with the job. He fished in a pocket of his soft, plyable leather vest and produced a three-dollar gold piece. He let an auric ray of sunlight, that entered through a circular window in the wall at the stair landing, strike it for a moment.

"I'm sure you can arrange something, now, can't you?"

Eyes fixed on the coin, the clerk all but simpered. "Yes, yes, perhaps I was hasty. We may have a cancellation. Mister . . .?" The gold piece disappeared between nimble fingers.

"Slocum. Nice town you have here."

"Newcomer? Or just passing through?" He began to write in the large registration book.

"I'm traveling. Business in Amarillo," Slocum said to evade the question.

"Your profession?" the clerk pressed.

It was none of his damned business, but Slocum answered him. "Cattle buyer."

The clerk's face underwent a remarkable transformation. Beaming, he blurted exactly what he had on his mind. "Oh, well, then, that would explain—"

"My scruffy looks?" Slocum prodded. "I've covered a lot of ground the last couple of days. Do you have a bath available?"

"Yes, sir. Only there's some other guests—ladies, quite a few in fact—who are monopolizing our four tubs. I am sorry. There's the barbershop. Woodie Webber has a washhouse in the rear," the clerk offered helpfully.

"Thank you."

"You have luggage?" the clerk asked, offering a room key.

"Mostly trail gear. I'll store it at the livery."

"Quite all right, Mr. Slocum. Anything you need, just ask, yes, sir. I'll be happy to accommodate you."

"You've been a prince," Slocum said dryly as he headed for the stairway.

Slocum took only his saddlebags, a pair of slightly larger parfleche envelopes, and a narrow, rectangular wooden case from the packsaddle to his room. There, he unpacked, selected a fresh change of clothes, and left, locking the room behind him. In the street, he forked the brindle stallion and rode the two blocks to the livery stable.

"Two, three days," he told the hostler. "I'll pay in advance."

"Won't be necessary. I got your horses, don't I?" A mischievous sparkle filled his eyes.

"I'd like to store my camp gear. Do you have a cupboard that can be locked?" Slocum asked.

"Sure enough. What with no stage runnin' through here, I get a lot of calls for that sort of thing. Now," the old man reviewed, "you want to grain the packhorse once a day, the stallion twice? Fresh bedding straw and plenty water. That'll be two bits a day for the one, thirty cents for the other."

"Done. I'll unsaddle and get everything packed away, then get out of your way."

"Oh, I don't mind company any at all. D'you happen to play checkers?"

"I've been known to," Slocum answered thoughtfully. "I might be a bit too busy while I'm here, but you never know."

"Fine with me. Just in case, I'll keep the coffee hot and something set aside to sweeten it with."

His task completed, Slocum left the livery ten minutes later, his spare clothes over one shoulder. He found the barbershop and entered to the tinkle of a small bell over the door. An unctuous little man with pigeon breast and prominent Adam's apple greeted him.

"Howdy, howdy. Come right in, mister. Two chair, no waiting." He peered at Slocum through half glasses, out of pale, watery blue eyes.

"I'll need a bath later. You have plenty of hot water?"

"Oh, yes, sir. Now, hang up them duds and sit yourself down." He patted the chair farthest from the shop front.

Slocum took the one nearer the window. He wanted to study the goings on in Happy while the barber worked on him. His action earned him a nervous, uncomfortable expression from the tonsorialist.

"I . . . uh . . . I . . . uh . . . think you'd find this chair more comfortable," the discomfited barber suggested hesitantly.

"Oh?" Slocum's query fell just short of a growl.

"Well . . . well, you see, I have a customer favors that chair and he's due anytime now."

"I like this one. He can use the other for once," Slocum prodded.

"I . . . I really think it would be better if . . ."

Sudden anger flared in Slocum. "If I what? If I crawled on my belly like you seem to favor doing? I don't know who this fellow is, but if he's a reasonable man, he'll either wait until I'm finished or take the other chair."

"He's . . . he's not very reasonable," Silas Webber muttered, mostly to himself.

Slocum adjusted his position in the chair and leaned back. "I'll take a shave and trim. Not too short at the back."

Trembling visibly, Webber draped the cloth over Slocum's body and secured it at the back of his neck with a thin metal clip. His small hands worked agitatedly to whip up the lather. With uncertain jerks he spread a thick coat over Slocum's leathery, tan face. He had finished the last dab when the door swung open with a bang. Three men entered and stopped short.

"Hello, Woody." A gravelly voice greeted Webber.

"Good day, Mr. Kelso. It'll be just a minute. I have another customer to tend to."

Butch Kelso's eyes narrowed and his face flushed. "Ain't gonna be any minute, Woody-boy. Tell him to move over and wait. I'm ready for my weekly trim."

Webber's eyes grew wetter yet, and his receding chin wobbled as he spoke. "He . . . uh . . . he said he wanted this chair. I tried to tell him, Mr. Kelso."

"You didn't try hard enough," Kelso growled as he closed the distance between the doorway and the chair. "Now, stranger, get out of my chair."

"Yes, please, sir," Webber agreed. "Perhaps you should take the other chair and make yourself comfortable while I attend to Mr. Kelso."

Slocum eyed both of them. Calmly he formed the words. "No, I don't think so. Let him wait his turn."

"I will like hell," Kelso exploded. He backed his demand with a huge hand which flashed forward and balled the barber apron and the front of Slocum's shirt.

At once the fight exploded.

From seemingly nowhere, Slocum planted a big, hard fist under Kelso's left eye. The callused knuckle split skin, and blood flew in an instant. Rocked backward, Kelso took the cloth covering with him. His vision blurred, he failed to see the low-slung holster and its well-used Colt.

"Linc, Johnny, get him," he ordered.

With a roar, one of his companions, Johnny Tulip, snatched up a long-bladed pair of barbering scissors and leapt at Slocum.

Slocum stopped him with a solid kick to the crotch. The scissors dropped, Tulip's face turned bright red, and he puckered tightly to suck in his breath in a porcine squeal. Numbly he sat, spraddle-legged, on the floor. Still, the younger of the pair of sidemen held back. Slocum turned his attention to Butch Kelso.

Kelso waved and faked a couple of punches, and caught Slocum's hard, straight left flush in the mouth. Lips mashed, he made growling, gagging sounds and rocked backward a moment.

Then he came on.

Arms windmilling, Kelso moved in on Slocum, who perforce had been backed against the barber chair. Slocum slipped a couple of blows off his shoulders and tapped Kelso on the torn spot of his left cheek. Kelso put a fist solidly into the center of Slocum's chest, and he sprawled backward in the chair.

"Gidd 'im, Linc!" Kelso mush-mouthed.

At once he and his other friend closed in. Blows rained onto the supine Slocum. He tasted the salt-copper flavor of blood in his mouth and blinked to keep his vision clear. Overconfident, Linc Parsons got in a bit too close.

Slocum gathered his legs under him and flexed them. Powerful muscles propelled him upward, and he rammed Linc under the chin with the top of his head. Parsons uttered a soft groan through teeth clopped suddenly shut, and went over backward. He rammed into the wall-long mirror, shattering it, and rebounded. His head made a hollow gourd sound when it struck the floor. That left Slocum a clear shot at Butch Kelso.

He came off the chair with both arms pistoning. Heavy blows to Kelso's midsection drove the blustering town bully backward. Vaguely Slocum could hear the frenzied bleats of the barber. Slocum followed his advantage, set his feet, and powered a right to Kelso's nose. He felt cartlage give and the greasy flow of blood.

Kelso backpedaled crazily and collided with the coat tree, which broke in half. Blinded by pain and rage, Kelso swatted with both paws at Slocum. The big man who had been both a lawman and a longrider fended them off easily. He waded in, working Kelso's fat paunch again. Each punch brought a grunt from the six-foot, 230-pound Kelso. He managed a ringing smack to Slocum's left ear and a glancing blow to the face that drew blood. By that time, Johnny Tulip had recovered enough to come to his feet. Unsteadily he advanced on Slocum.

From the corner of his eye, Slocum saw the still-aching Tulip make his move. This time sunlight through the front window glinted off the straight razor in Tulip's hand. Slocum shot a left-right-left combination to Kelso's head and followed through with a roundhouse kick to the groin.

Kelso went down howling. Slocum slipped the big .45 Colt Peacemaker from its holster in a blur. Johnny Tulip saw it and went white. The razor slipped from his grasp, and he raised both hands in surrender. Slocum stepped into him, eased off the hammer, and then slammed the seven-inch barrel into the side of Tulip's head.

He crashed into the narrow shelf of barbering tools, ripped it from the wall, and went down like a slaughtered steer. Shiny implements skittered across the floor. Kelso stirred and Slocum reholstered the six-gun. Kelso looked up through his misery to see the big, hard-fisted man standing over him. Slowly he marshaled his thoughts to form panting, slurred words.

"It ain't . . . ain't over . . . yet . . . mister."

"Yes, it is," Slocum told him. Then the rocklike right fist that had held the Colt an instant earlier slammed down, and sturdy knuckles rammed into the forehead of Butch Kelso.

Kelso's eyes crossed, then straightened. He tried a kick, only to be rewarded by a whistling left to the point of his jaw. A bright white light erupted in Kelso's head, followed by the swift, all-enveloping spread of blackness. With a soft, pink-frothed sigh, he toppled over backward.

"Look what you've done," whined the voice of Silas Webber. "Look what you've done to my shop. It's ruined." He stopped, gulped, and stared at Slocum. "I've never in my life seen such brute ferocity. You tore into those three like a grizzly."

"They were the ones to open the dance," Slocum observed, not even winded by his efforts.

"Yes, but . . . *that* was Mr. Herman Kelso, and two of his best guns."

"I reckon I don't impress easily," Slocum stated flatly, then added, "I'm ready for my shave now."

He settled back in the chair while Webber dithered over the damage done his shop. It had been rather thoroughly trashed, Slocum was forced to admit. A rabbity squeak came from the barber when he discovered the shattered remains of his soap mug. Shaking it accusingly, he approached the chair where Slocum waited.

"What will I ever do? Who is going to pay for all this damage?" He retrieved his razor, and Slocum observed the trembling of Webber's hands.

Slocum snatched the towel from the waist-bound apron the barber wore and wiped away the lather. "I've changed my mind on that shave," he announced.

Looking relieved, Webber literally wrung his hands in despair. Slocum rose from the chair while Webber repeated over and over that he was ruined, out of business for certain. Slocum stepped to the unconscious hardcases and went through their pockets.

From each he extracted all but a single dollar of their cash funds. The accumulation he handed to Webber, whose watery eyes grew wide behind the thick lenses of his spectacles. "This ought to cover it," Slocum told him.

Then he bent and grabbed Kelso and Tulip by the shirt collars and dragged them out onto the boardwalk. He returned and repeated the task with Parsons. That accomplished, he re-entered the chair.

"Not too short on the back," he reminded the flustered barber.

3

While the unnerved Woody Webber snipped away at Slocum's untidy raven locks, he managed to recover his composure. Then, true to his profession, he became downright loquacious. His prim tone of voice did not improve with his newly settled demeanor.

"Let me tell you, Mr. . . . uh . . . Mr. . . . ?"

"Slocum."

"Let me tell you, Mr. Slocum, those are mighty dangerous men you locked horns with. Butch Kelso came to town some three months ago. No one knows for whom he works. That goes for those gunslicks he pals around with, also. Bit by bit they took over the town. In all honesty, I have to say that you've made some powerful enemies. That is if you are intending on staying any length of time?"

"I might be. What about the local law? Doesn't the marshal keep Kelso's kind in line?"

Webber answered quietly, his faint heart betraying him again. "The marshal is not in town. Hasn't been for quite a while."

Slocum decided on a different tack. "So Kelso showed up here about the same time the ghost rustlers began their work?"

He sensed the shiver of fright that passed through the barber. "Mr. Slocum, it doesn't pay to speculate along that line. Butch Kelso has been seen in town at times when the . . . uh . . . mysterious rustlers have been in the act of taking a herd. There appears not to be any connection. Certainly none I would care to inquire into. Surely you don't intend to pursue that line of questioning?"

"No. Only curious."

"Why's that? You being a stranger and all?"

"I'm a cattle buyer. Naturally when my clients have their herds go missing, it is of interest to me. Of course, it's not any of my direct concern. My need is to deliver cattle to the packing houses in Chicago."

"And, naturally, you don't particularly care from whom you buy them?" Webber prompted slyly.

"Did I say that?" Slocum snapped in a hard tone.

"Oh, no. No, of course."

"Then I would suggest that it not be repeated. To anyone. Clear?"

Webber cut his eyes to the unconscious forms on the boardwalk. "Yes, sir, Mr. Slocum. Yes, indeed."

"When you are through diddling around with my hair, I could use that bath."

"Quite right. In a minute, just a wee minute," Webber babbled on.

Slocum winced and wished there were another barbershop in town, or another barber.

Steam rose in whisps from the soap-scummed hot water in a high-back copper tub, supported by four clawed feet that held marble balls. Slowly the stiffness and soreness from days on the trail, and the fight with Kelso and company, eased out of the corded muscles of John Slocum. He had scraped his own chin and cheeks clear of ebony stubble by the light of a small glass oil lamp. Now dirt and sweat peeled off of him in rolls of lather. His thoughts drifted over the information from the Cattlemen's Association in Fort Worth, scraps of data he had obtained from Silas Webber, and his own evaluation of Kelso.

"Curiouser and curiouser," he murmured aloud.

Before his speculation could go forward, the rear door to the barbershop slammed open to reveal Butch Kelso, Linc Parsons, and Johnny Tulip. They had returned for round two. In the first quick, surprised glance, Slocum saw that they had brought help along.

Each clutched a hickory ax handle. With low growls, they leapt at the man in the tub. Water and soapsuds sloshed up over the steep sides as the trio began to smash their clubs into

Slocum's torso. They made soft, meaty smacks—a butcher tenderizing a recalcitrant steak.

All Slocum could do was cover his head with his arms. He took stinging blows on both forearms, and his left biceps went suddenly numb when Kelso landed a solid smash to the deltoid muscle. At first he could do nothing to recover, let alone retaliate. Embattled and jangled by incessant new pain, Slocum's body endured terrible punishment. Strangest of all, a corner of his jumbled mind recorded, was the silence.

No shouts of triumph, no threats or brags. Only swift, determined, quiet abuse. At last Slocum got his body in motion. He slammed his upper torso from side to side until the tub began to rock. Harder, he willed himself. Harder still. The copper vessel rose precariously on two legs. One more time.

With a powerful lurch the polished marble balls gave way on the soap-slickened floorboards and the tub went over. A cry of anguish came from Johnny Tulip when the rim of the tub slammed into his shins and pinned him to the floor, inundated by a wall of steaming water. At once, a naked Slocum exploded through his assailants and dove across the slippery floor in the direction of his cartridge belt.

Relentlessly, Butch Kelso and Linc Parsons followed him. He covered his head as well as possible, avoiding a knock-out blow, while he scuttled through their gauntlet of hickory clubs. It seemed an eternity before his outstretched hand closed around the butt-grips of the .45 Peacemaker.

Slocum's Colt came free. Three ax handles froze in mid-swing. Three mouths opened in dismay. One throat ripped raw with a shriek of agony when the hammer fell and Slocum put a .45 slug through the thigh of Johnny Tulip.

"You get the next one right between the eyes, Kelso," Slocum grated out over his pain.

Tulip flopped around on the wet floor like a fish in the bottom of a boat. Blood spurted from the through-and-through wound. Slocum nodded in his direction. "You'd better get him out of here and to a doctor fast. He'll bleed to death if you don't."

Butch Kelso looked at his sideman and then Johnny Tulip. "You take his shoulders, I'll take his feet."

"The top half's the heavier," Parsons pouted.

"It also won't be kicking. Now, do it before he leaks himself dead." To Slocum, over his shoulder, voice and face choked with rage: "We're not through with this. You'd best dry off, dress, and get out of town."

Hell, Slocum thought after they had departed, they don't even know my name.

For all his youth, Jason Harper had had the reputation of a trustworthy hand, one able to do his job and always "ride for the brand." Entirely on his own, he had taken his half day off on Saturday afternoon to follow a hunch. He had worked for the Bar-J ranch north of Happy for three years, which constituted almost his entire work experience. Two nights earlier, the Bar-J had lost seventy-five head of prime young steers.

Harper drifted northward on his day horse, drawn by the wide swath of bent and crushed grass that marked the route of the stolen cattle. With him came the scruffy little mutt that had adopted him when the dog first wandered onto the headquarters place of the Bar-J. "I'm right," Jason said aloud to the dog. "I can feel it in my bones, Brandy. Those cattle are somewhere in the big canyon. All we've got to do is look around real good and we'll find them." Brandy responded with a sidelong glance of liquid brown eyes and a puzzled expression. He gave a short bark of interrogation.

"What I mean, I can get that herd back, save Mr. Greerson a lot of grief."

Jason Harper rode on in companionable silence with his favorite cow pony and Brandy. To his right front, the cleft that marked the upper end of Palo Duro Canyon became more prominent as he progressed. The trail led right toward the Prairie Dog Town Fork of the Red River. When he was close enough to see sunlight sparkling off the ocher water of the river, the wide swath turned eastward and headed directly for the canyon.

"I knew it! I knew it! We're gonna find those cattle."

Enthusiasm driving him, yet with caution born of experience, Jason Harper rode on into the bottom of Palo Duro Canyon. The canyon was a deep gorge cut in the otherwise rolling prairie in prehistoric times by a much more vigorous

Red River, and its colorful walls revealed the aeons of time and the epochs of life that had existed when alternately the region had been clear land, or part of the floor of a gigantic sea.

Jason Harper marveled at the alternating bands of pale yellow, thickly encrusted with ancient sea shells, and darker layers of silt, soil, sandstone, and limestone in a variety of colors, from palest white to nearly black. In no time, the walls towered above him. Deep shadows concealed the openings of side canyons. Cottonwoods, accompanied by their cousins the aspins, vied with bristlecone pines, all stunted by foreshortened periods of sunlight in which to grow.

A faint tingle of uneasiness traveled along Jason's spine. He had to remind himself to keep his eye on the signs left by the recent passage of the Bar-J cattle and not gawk at the mysteries of the past. Accustomed to hunting down strays that had wandered from the herd, Jason found his tracking task as simple as if arrows marked the way.

The signs led to a narrow side canyon. Jason reined in and dismounted. He tied off his cow pony to a lower branch of a gnarled cottonwood. Instinct prompted him to proceed on foot. In a stern whisper, he commanded Brandy to remain behind.

Minutes later, he congratulated himself on his forethought. The passage he entered meandered along the course of a tributary stream to the Red. It widened as he went, and Jason soon found out the cause. He had encountered a box canyon, into which the creek entered by way of a waterfall. He also found the cattle.

Excitement clutched Jason as he worked his way through scrub brush toward the grazing, softly lowing beasts. They seemed entirely content in their new pasture. Then, back near the base of the waterfall, Jason spotted a thin stream of smoke rising. Instantly, he dropped to his hands and knees. One dominant thought assailed him.

He was all alone. What would he do if the rustlers discovered him? How many were they? The questions spawned by his new knowledge swam in growing number in his head as Jason eased his way through the placid animals. Suddenly he found himself on the edge of the brushy meadow, not fifty yards from a small campsite.

Flattened on the ground, Jason Harper stared in wonderment at the three figures he saw before him. He recognized all of them. His eyebrows rose together to crowd his full head of light yellow hair. The one with the bulky bandage on his leg, who walked with obvious pain and the aid of a pair of crutches, was Johnny Tulip. And with him was Yancy Hake, another hanger-on of the third man . . . Butch Kelso.

He was by far not a stupid man, and it all came clear for Jason Harper as he stared at the trio. The mysterious rustlings had begun shortly after Kelso and his hardcase friends came to town. They obviously did not work for any local rancher. They rarely left Happy for any reason. Not long after Kelso arrived, the marshal had taken a prolonged leave of absence. He had said something about going south for his rhumatiz.

That had been three months ago, in the dead of winter, and no one had thought there was anything significant about it. Kelso sort of moved into the vacuum left behind. He and his bully-ragging companions held sway over the town. They intimidated the townspeople and the ranch hands from nearby spreads. Now, if he could believe his eyes, they had turned out to be the invisible rustlers who had been so busy stealing cattle all over the county and north into Wadall County.

Not a trained investigator, Jason Harper nevertheless made careful note of everything he saw in the camp. From a tree limb hung a series of running irons and brands. Many calves and yearlings not as yet caught up in the spring roundups would be unbranded. An unusually heavy period of rains had delayed that annual event. It all played into the hands of the rustlers.

Jason also noted a tarpaulin-covered stack that must contain supplies for a long stay. Johnny Tulip could not ride with the rustlers, so he must have been set up as camp guard, someone to tend the stolen cattle. That made sense to Jason Harper. He also saw a large tent spread out and ready to erect. They felt mighty sure of themselves, he thought. Maybe too sure. If he could bring his boss here, some of the boys, maybe from other ranches, too, they would have proof enough to string up the rustlers on the spot.

No, that wouldn't do, Jason thought. The law would have to take its course. He would ride to the home spread, notify his boss, and go on to find the sheriff and report it. Carefully

Jason reviewed by sight everything he had witnessed. Then he began to ease himself backward into the milling cattle.

One steer sighted him, stiffened, and raised its head to bellow a interrogatory warning. Jason lay deathly still. He dared not even breathe. When the voice reached him, it sounded to be right on top of him.

"Damned cows," Butch Kelso grumbled. "I'll be glad when this is over with an' we can go spend our money someplace so far away that when you say the word 'cow,' the folks ask, 'What's that?' " Laughter answered him.

"Now, Butch, you don't want to go bitin' the hand that feeds us," Yancy Hake teased.

"Only way I want to bite one of these critters is cut in a two-inch-thick steak, slow cooked over hickory wood," Kelso muttered. "Well, Johnny, me 'n' Yancy had best be gettin' back."

"Naw, Butch. Wait awhile. We've yet to pop a cork on the first bottle of whiskey you brung me."

"Umm. Now, that's a fact, Johnny. Don't see why not we get to that right away."

Softly sighing out his relief, Jason Harper continued his cautious departure. Fortunately, most of the steers ignored him. He weaved his way through the herd in order not to create a straight-line ripple of movement among those who did shy out of his way. At last he reached the taller growth and stood upright.

He had best hurry, he decided, if he was to catch the three of them with the missing cattle. Jason set off at a fast trot through the narrowing passage of the canyon. On his fourth stride, his boot sole came down on a pile of loose shale. The brittle rocks clattered noisily as they slid down the bank into the small creek. Jason froze in a moment of indecision, and then, certain the outlaws would have heard the noise, he sprinted in desperation for his horse, unmindful of any more noise he made.

Butch Kelso stopped in a rigid pose while pouring whiskey into a tin cup. Faintly, but clear enough to identify, he had heard the rattle of rocks. They had not fallen of their own accord. He knew the canyon well enough to discount that possibility. Something, or someone, had disturbed them.

"Boys," he said softly, "I think we have had company. Or are about to get some."

"A couple of the others?" Johnny Tulip suggested.

"Nope. Weren't no other sound but them rocks being knocked a-flyin'," Kelso maintained. "Yancy, get your horse and take a swing around these critters. See what you can see."

"Sure, Butch. But with all them rains, stuff will be fallin' outta these walls for half of summer."

"Just do it, all right?"

It took Yancy only ten minutes to find Jason Harper's bootprints. He hollered his discovery to Butch, who went at once to his horse and tightened the cinch. In the saddle, he joined Yancy. Over his shoulder he called back to Johnny Tulip.

"Hold the fort, Johnny. We're gonna go find whoever it was got a look at us."

They rode out into the main canyon five minutes later. Heavy hoof impressions, wide apart, marked the speedy departure of the unknown observer. Butch pointed to them.

"Those are gonna lead us to whoever it was saw us together with those steers."

"And then what?" Yancy Hake asked.

"What do you think?" Kelso set off at a fast trot.

Out on the flats, he and Hake spotted the small, dark, distant figure at the same time. They urged more speed from their mounts. Slowly the distance narrowed. Once, as they drew nearer, the fleeing man looked back. He set spurs to his pony's flanks and broke into a gallop.

Kelso and Hake did likewise. Butch drew his six-gun, a finely engraved Merwin and Hulbert double-action, tilt-top revolver. At a range of thirty yards, he tried a shot. It cut air six feet to the side of the thoroughly frightened Jason Harper.

Powerful chest and haunch muscles drove Butch Kelso's horse forward even faster. The animal, like that of the man they pursued, became heavily lathered. It retched and grunted with each pounding forehoof. Gradually the distance began to close again.

At twenty yards, Kelso tried again. His slug clipped Jason Harper's left shoulder. The young cowboy cried out in pain and pounded his spurs harder into his pony's sides. Kelso and Hake got in even closer over the next three minutes. Again, Harper looked behind him in panic.

A grinning Butch Kelso leaned forward and to his right and looped a brawny arm around Jason Harper's slender waist. With a powerful yank, Kelso stripped the youth from the saddle. Reining up in a cloud of dust and bits of turf, Kelso dropped Harper unceremoniously to the ground.

"Wha-what are you gonna do now?" Jason Harper asked, befuddled by fear and the punishment of the chase.

"Simple, kid," Kelso told him as he redrew the Merwin and Hulbert. "I'm gonna kill you."

A loud, sharp blast from the .44 was the last thing Jason Harper heard.

4

Those who knew him, even slightly, could attest to the fact there was no back-down in John Slocum. Slocum had been born in Calhoun County, Georgia. Calhoun County was in the Allegheny Mountains, and the country was all V valleys, softly rounded hills, and bad roads. It was into this isolated hill-country setting that John Slocum had been born in the late 1840s, the second son of William and Opal Slocum.

Although most of the hill farmers owned a few slaves, Slocum's father, William, never did. He worked his land with the help of his sons, Robert and John. All the hours of drudgery on ground that, as the legend went, "best grew rocks," still left time for the boys to get into plenty devilment. And, by the time John reached thirteen, there wasn't a bear wallow or a buck rub within twenty miles that he and his brother didn't know.

They fished and swam the creeks, hunted the hills, and trapped for fur. Before the age of fourteen, John was a fair plowman, teamster, dairyman, shepherd, logger, and one whale of a Saturday night scrapper. The Slocum who showed his face on the streets of Happy, Texas, in early evening was a natural marksman. He'd first gained his prowess on an old flintlock that his daddy had carried in the Mexican War. He had improved on it ever since.

Slocum also had a taste for champagne. He had acquired it on July 21, 1861, after the Battle of First Manassas. In the late afternoon, when the Yanks had broken on Jackson's Brigade, a powder-stained, confused John Slocum had come upon fellow Confederate cavalry looting a general's provisions wagon. This Yankee general had brought cases of Monopole champagne for a victory celebration. The real victors drank it beside the stream—no more than a creek, really—the water

29

full of bobbing bodies and blood eddies along the banks. Slocum never forgot the tingling, tantalizing taste of that champagne.

Later he served as a sharpshooter, potting imprudent Yankee officers along the front lines. His skill with a gun grew. By the end of the war, he could hold his own with any long or short gun known to man. All he needed was a couple of rounds to learn where and how the weapon shot. That talent had served him well in the years since. After the attacks by Kelso and his bully boys, Slocum had a strong suspicion it might benefit him again this night. With that in mind, he set out to find a thick, rare steak and some potatoes.

People along the boardwalk gave him startled, uneasy looks as he ambled down the street. Small town, Slocum thought dismissively. Word gets around fast, and mightily distorted at that. In the middle of the second block of the business district, he saw yellow light spilling into the street from high, wide windows, the lower halves of which were shrouded by chintz curtains. A sign, jet black as all the others in town, advertised it as the "VIRGINIA HOUSE."

Pleasant odors wafted from a large stovepipe that extended above the roofline at the rear. Slocum eagerly headed in that direction, guided by his rumbling stomach, and walked cat-footed to the door. It opened onto the soft, pleasant murmur of friendly conversation. A young woman in a high-necked, lace-trimmed gingham frock stood beside a large, brass crank-handle cash register near the door. She held hand-printed menus in one shapely hand.

"Good evening," she said warmly.

"I'm looking for some dinner," Slocum stated simply, eyes fixed on long, graceful waves of burnished auburn hair and a fair complexion that was saved from being pallid by a flush of the juices of life.

"A table, sir? Or will you sit at the counter?" a lovely contralto voice urged.

"Table. Off to the side, please," Slocum answered automatically.

She led the way, which gave Slocum a delightful view of a firmly rounded bottom that recalled longings too long suppressed. She reached an empty table near the divider to the kitchen and turned with a rustle of skirts. Slocum ignored the menu extended in her hand.

"Will this do?"

"Uh . . . yes. Just fine." Belatedly he took the use-worn sheet of paper. She had the deepest, bluest eyes he had ever seen.

He seated himself and ordered without looking at the bill of fare, his eyes locked on her loveliness. "Steak, thick, rare, only hot through, with potatoes and onions, fried just soft."

"Yes, of course," she said, as though, she'd been expecting exactly this order. "We have corn."

"What?"

"Cut corn comes with the meal."

"Oh, yes. Sure."

"Something to drink, Mr. . . . ?"

"Coffee."

"Your name is Coffee?"

"No. My name's Slocum. I'll have coffee to drink."

"Shall I bring that right away?"

"Yes, please," Slocum continued, still in an apparently mesmerized state. "The owner?" he pressed, fighting to make small talk, to keep her there at any cost. "Is he from Virginia?"

"No, I'm not. I'm Virginia Stuart, this is my place. I'll bring you your coffee, Mr. Slocum." She left swiftly, unable to contain a small trill of laughter.

Virginia did not return with the coffee for three long minutes. She had to interrupt her mission to take money from a stout, middle-aged couple who had finished their meal. She made change for them, then disappeared into the kitchen. Slocum had almost given up when she appeared at his side with a steaming crockery mug.

"Sorry this took so long. My only girl is out with a sick child, and I'm waiting tables for her," Virginia explained.

"Cashier and waitress both. That must keep you busy," Slocum opined lightly.

"It certainly does, considering I'm also the cook."

Slocum blinked at her. Either business was bad, which he doubted from the savory aromas coming from the kitchen, or this small, insular town had not entirely taken to Virginia Stuart. At least not enough to be willing to work for her. Most eateries of this sort still had male cooks. Usually fat, sloppy men with grease-shiny faces and dirty aprons. Had Virginia Stuart taken exception to this rule?

Virginia smiled, and light laughter colored her words. "In answer to the questions written all over your face, I am new in town, I took over this cafe from Opie Fallon, who got too fat and sick of smelling cooking food to want to go on. I couldn't find a cook who wasn't working for one ranch or another. So, having put my life's savings into the place, I had to run it myself." She paused, and a puzzled expression ran across her lovely, regular features. "I don't know why I'm telling you, a complete stranger, all of this."

"I have a kind face?" Slocum suggested.

Virginia studied him for a moment, shook her head. "Rugged, handsome, yes, kind . . . we-ell, I'll withhold judgment on that. Potatoes are already on. I'll have your steak up right away." She whipped around the partition into the kitchen before he could reply.

"Steady, now," Slocum cautioned himself aloud. He found he wouldn't mind spending more time with the owner of the Virginia House. The early supper crowd had begun to thin ten minutes later when Virginia approached the table with his meal.

Still smoking, the enormous steak lay on a platter, red juices oozing from the top. A mound of potatoes and fried onions accompanied it and a scatter of golden kernels of corn. A thick slab of homemade bread, lightly grill-browned on one side, also came with it. Slocum accepted the platter gratefully and gestured to the chair opposite his.

"The rush seems to be over. You're welcome to that chair to take a breather."

Virginia accepted with genuine gratitude. "Maybe this way no one will notice me for a while and I can really get some rest."

They talked lightly of trivial matters while Slocum methodically cut strips of steak and chewed them with relish. Eventually, Virginia must have worked herself around to feeling familiar enough to broach the topic that had been number one throughout town, judged by her customers, for the whole day.

"I understand you met our charming Mr. Kelso this morning."

"Ummm," Slocum responded, his mouth full of steak and home fries.

"Poor Silas Webber seems to have lost his entire shop as a result. At least he spent the whole of the noon hour in here telling anyone who would listen that he had."

"He got paid for it," Slocum commented flatly.

"By you?"

"Nope. Kelso and his friends contributed. Though they didn't know it at the time."

Virginia laughed lightly. "You're something, Mr. Slocum. How long had you been in town when all this happened?"

"About half an hour . . . the first time," Slocum responded.

"*First* time? You mean there was another donnybrook?" A small, vertical crease appeared appealingly between her dark copper brows.

"Yes. I was . . . discommoded . . . er . . . in the bath, when the gentlemen returned to continue our conversation."

"My goodness, what happened then?"

This high-flown language had begun to get to Slocum. "They beat the hell out of me with ax handles, so I shot one of them."

Virginia's fascinating cobalt eyes went wide and round. Her words did not match her expression. "Good for you! It's about time someone had sand enough to stand up to those scum."

This took Slocum by surprise. He covered his imbalance with a light chuckle. "You sound the regular Texas hardscrabble farm girl."

Those fetching orbs narrowed, grew decades of degrees colder. "And what if I am? I grew up on a farm, but I grew out of it, too. I went to the big city, took schooling as a nurse—now, don't laugh. Yes, it was in a convent school, and the sisters are every bit as strict with and mean to the postulants as everyone hears."

Fascinated, Slocum pressed for more. "What happened then?"

"When I decided that I was not cut out to be a nurse, let alone a nun, I left," Virginia stated simply. "I worked at different jobs: seamstress, waitress, companion for small children. But I put aside my stake. I dreamed of someday having a business of my own. To be my own boss and set the rules. When I had enough, I started looking around. That's how I came to find out this place was available. But we've talked entirely too much about me, Mr. Slocum. What brings you to Happy?"

"My given name's John, but most people call me plain Slocum. No Mister." He decided on sticking with the story he had used so far. "I'm a cattle buyer. Curiosity about these ghost rustlers brought me here."

Virginia's eyes went wide again. "That's a dangerous inquisitiveness to have in these parts, Slocum," she said throatily.

"That depends," Slocum continued inventing. "It could have a bad impact on my business. It wouldn't do to unknowingly buy stolen cattle. A man's reputation, you understand."

A twinkle returned. "I think I do, Slocum. In your business, a good reputation is invaluable. There's some who lump cattle buyers with used buggy salesmen." Her tinkling laughter took the sting out of it.

Slocum had worked himself halfway through his steak by that time. He framed a jesting reply and had started to deliver it when the double front doors crashed open with enough force to shatter the glass in one side. Over the ringing notes of falling shards, a voice Slocum had come to recognize brayed to the stunned customers.

"Everyone clear out. I got something to settle with this tinhorn."

Kelso had come back.

After killing Jason Harper, Butch Kelso and Yancy Hake rode directly to Happy. There they learned from Linc Parsons that the troublesome stranger had not taken their advice to leave town. Instead, Parsons asserted, he had spent the late afternoon visiting various businesses in town, and cooly sipping a beer in the Panhandle Paradise saloon.

"What's more," Linc concluded, "I heard he was bangin' everyone's ears about us."

"Where is he now?" Kelso demanded.

"Over at Miss Ginny's, eatin' his supper," Linc Parsons informed his boss.

"Well, boys, since this gent is such a slow learner, I think we need to personally escort him out of town."

Forking their mounts, Kelso and his henchmen rode down the main street of Happy, to the front of the Virginia House. They dismounted, and Linc Parsons got a fit of the giggles thinking about the fate of the hard-faced stranger. Kelso led the way up the steps and kicked open the double Frenchy-style doors with enough force to shatter the pane in one when it banged off the inner wall.

"Everyone clear out," he snarled. "I've got something to settle with this tinhorn."

Faces paled around the room, and the diners made hasty efforts to remove themselves from the cafe. Virginia Stuart glared her frustrated anger at Kelso and his underlings and remained seated at Slocum's table.

"Go on, sister, that means you, too," Kelso growled.

"This is my place; I'm not leaving. And I want you trash out of here now." Virginia bravely defied him.

"You'd be wise to go, Virginia," Slocum advised quietly.

"Not even these scum would hurt a lady," Virginia sneered at them.

"At least get clear of this table," Slocum commanded a little harsher than he had intended.

"All right, Slocum," Virgina said with a sigh. "If that's what you want. But watch them. They're snake-mean and underhanded." She edged away from the table and entered the kitchen.

"*Slocum,*" Kelso prodded nastily. The name set off a tiny warning bell in the back of his head, though not strong enough to deter him from his purpose. "What kind of a name is that for a *real* man?"

Slocum fixed his level green gaze on the trio. "A proud enough one to folks from Calhoun County, Go'gia." The soft purr of a Southern accent had entered Slocum's voice, as it often did when he got good and angry.

"Georgia, huh?" Kelso brayed. "Well, this is Happy, Texas, and it's my town. Around here, folks do what Butch Kelso tells them to do. And I say get the hell out." To his sidemen, Kelso added, "Spread out, boys."

Linc Parsons sidestepped to the counter, eyes locked on Slocum at the table. Yancy Hake oozed toward the opposite wall, which put him directly in line with Slocum. Kelso's burly frame filled the center aisle of the small eaterie. Slocum took it in and shook his head sadly.

"I'll leave when I am good and ready," he answered flatly.

"No more of your lip, *boy*," Kelso shot back. "Any talk from you is gonna come from that six-gun you're so handy with. You done shot an unarmed man today. Around here, that calls for a killin'. We tried to wear down your cockiness, make you see reason. You shot m'friend Johnny for our efforts. Now it's time for Sam Colt to make the decisions."

"That would be a terrible mistake," Slocum suggested, his green eyes unwavering.

Kelso went bright scarlet, white flecks of froth at the corners of his mean, down-turned mouth. "I'm tired of hearing you run that mouth, I said. I'm tired of seeing your face. You've got one minute to clear outta here, then your gun's gonna do your talkin'."

"I *am* getting tired of all these interruptions," Slocum allowed with a heavy sigh.

Tension became a palpable thing while the octagon-faced Monitor wall clock loudly ticked off the seconds. A small tic developed at the corner of Kelso's left eye. His thick fingers hovered over the butt of his Merwin and Hulbert. At last the long, black minute hand jumped forward a notch and the cafe exploded into action.

Kelso's draw came swift and sure. Triumph shined in his face as he brought the muzzle upward toward a line level with the center of Slocum's chest. Then the tablecloth blew outward, followed by a shower of splinters, and Kelso's six-gun went flying. Howling in pain, he gripped his bullet-punctured right forearm with his left hand.

Instantly, Slocum brought the Colt out from under the table. Linc Parsons and Yancy Hake had their weapons halfway out of leather when Slocum swung his .45 Peacemaker to the right and put a slug in Parsons. Much earlier, Slocum had gauged the gun-handling ability of all three. He had judged by the way they walked and stood, the set of their six-guns, and the amount of wear on the holsters.

Kelso, he had decided, might be an idiot, a loudmouth, and a bully, but he was by far and away the most accomplished gunhand. Yancy Hake he saw as a punk, but a dangerous one. Slocum knew he could do him anytime. Linc Parsons was snake-eyed and silent. He hadn't said anything during the previous encounters and had remained quiet this time.

At least until Slocum shot him low in the right side. Now he thrashed on the floor and wailed in misery. The bullet must have clipped his hipbone, Slocum reckoned.

"Get him, Hake! Goddammit, get him!" Kelso shrieked, blood welling between his fingers.

Slocum swung the Peacemaker toward Hake, only to see all three men freeze at the ominous clicks of twin hammers on a 10-gauge Greener shotgun at the counter. Those clicks were *loud,* Slocum thought.

"Don't do it," Virginia advised in a hard, no-nonsense voice.

Hake dropped his revolver as though it had suddenly caught fire. His eyes had cut from his intended victim to the deadly black holes of the Greener's muzzle.

"Does the marshal have any deputies in town?" Slocum asked calmly.

"No," Virginia answered. "And he took his winter vacation down south. Hasn't come back yet. But you know that, Slocum. So what do we do?"

Slocum resisted displaying his badge. "I guess we'll just have to take these three to jail ourselves," he suggested.

He rose silently and made a thorough search of the trio. He disarmed them of a variety of guns and knives and shoved Kelso toward the door. It looked to him as if this would turn out to be a long night.

5

"We need to get a doctor for these two," Slocum advised as he bent to examine Linc Parsons's wound.

"I have to close the place, then I can help you take them to the jail," Virginia responded.

Slocum considered that a moment. Parsons had not been hit in the hip, and could walk. Among the items removed from all three had been, unexpectedly, short lengths of rope called "piggin' strings" by cowhands. They were used to tie the two hind legs and one front leg of a calf together to facilitate branding. Kelso was a gunhawk, plain and simple, not the type to have the tools of a working cowboy on his person. Whatever, the strips of lariat would make it possible to take them alone.

"If you'll let me borrow that shotgun, I'll take them there myself," Slocum told Virginia. "You shut the cafe down and go for the doctor. You can meet me at the jail."

Virginia produced a brief, uncertain smile. "Done."

Slocum tightly bound the hands of Kelso and his henchmen behind their backs and roughly pushed them toward the door. With his Colt back in leather, Slocum relieved Virginia of the Greener and prodded the barrels into Parsons's back when he faltered.

"Take it easy!" the gunman wailed. "You done shot me, ain't that enough?"

"You won't be able to ride, so we'll walk. Which way is the jail?"

"Go to hell," Kelso grumbled.

"North a block," Virginia told Slocum from inside her cafe. "A little stone building across the street from the city hall."

"Thanks."

With another prompting from the shotgun, the three hardcases started off in a shambling walk. Each muttered a low string of curses, peppered with dire promises of unlikely and obscene things they would do to Slocum at their next meeting. Whimpers of pain also came from Kelso and Parsons. Slocum ignored them and instead took note of the town's reaction.

Turtle-like, shop clerks and merchants working late popped their heads from doorways to stare unbelievingly at the spectacle. Few could credit that they actually saw what appeared to be going on. Word spread faster than on an army post. Slocum became aware of a gaggle of small boys who appeared out of nowhere to stand along the main street. They jeered and made faces at the prisoners.

One gutsy lad stooped, picked up a fresh, moist road apple, and hurled it at Kelso. He scored a perfect hit on the center of the bully's chest.

"You li'l bassart!" Kelso roared, horse manure dripping from his shirtfront. "I'll cut yer nuts off for that."

"Not you, *Mr.* Kelso. Not in jail you won't," the mopheaded ten year old chirped in scorn.

"I shoulda done for your Paw right proper, instead of jist blowin' off a kneecap," Kelso growled.

Sharp pain exploded in Kelso as Slocum jabbed him in the kidneys with the Greener. "Shut your lip and move out a bit faster," the big, raven-haired man demanded.

At the jail, Slocum located a large ring of keys on a wall peg behind a desk that wore a thick layer of dust. He locked Kelso, Parsons, and Hake in separate cells, had them back up to the bars, and untied the piggin' strings. By that time, he heard voices and the clump of bootheels on the stoop outside. He left the cellblock and greeted Virginia Stuart and a portly man with graying hair, a button nose, and a twinkle in his soft brown eyes, which robbed his face of age.

Virginia did the honors. "Dr. Morton, this is Slocum. He's the one who took down Kelso and two of his rat pack."

"Well, I must say I am pleased to meet you, Mr. Slocum." Dr. Morton had a light, breathy tenor voice. "We have had more than our fill of Mr. Kelso and company."

"Watch that mouth, you pill-rollin' barfly, or I'll kick your butt up between your shoulder blades," Kelso snarled from his cell.

"I . . . uh . . . I went for the doctor first," Virginia said to cover the embarrassing moment. "I really do have to get back and cover that broken pane and close for the night."

"I'll come by and see you home after," Slocum offered gallantly.

"Thank you, Mr. Slocum, I'd . . . appreciate that," Virginia replied, coloring slightly.

"Two of them are shot some, Doc," Slocum began after Virginia left. "One could be serious."

" 'Serious' is *dead* in my business, Mr. Slocum," Dr. Morton tut-tutted. "When it comes to this sort, I'd as soon it *was* serious."

Slocum nodded sympathetically. "I understand, Doc. I'll keep a gun on them so they don't bring you any grief."

Morton sighed. "I appreciate that, Mr. Slocum. Shall we begin?"

"I suppose you'll want water?" Slocum prompted.

"Oh, yes."

"Is there a town well? Seems no one has been in here for a while."

"Yes, but the marshal has his own well and pump in a small room back of the cellblock."

"Good enough," Slocum said.

Nearly an hour later, Slocum locked the front door of the jail and marshal's office behind him and walked the now-silent street back to the Virginia House. Miss Stuart waited for him inside, a single kerosene lamp flickering low to dispel the deepest shadows.

"All taken care of?" she asked.

"Yep. They aren't going anywhere for a while. Uh . . . here's your shotgun, Miss Virginia."

Virginia flashed a warm smile. "My friends call me Ginny. I'll put this away and we can go."

A late moon had risen, nearly three-quarters full, a large yellow disk with swirls of pinkish orange around it. Ginny slipped her arm through Slocum's and matched his long stride.

"It's lovely tonight," she said in an effort to dissipate images of the confrontation in the cafe. Slocum made no reply. Determined to draw him out, she returned to the subject she least wanted to air. "You handled that gun rather well for a cattle buyer."

"It's a lonely, dangerous job sometimes, Ginny. A feller has to be able to take care of himself." Slocum disliked deceiving her, but the nature of his assignment dictated it.

"So I . . . noticed. You never did answer my question before those lowlifes interrupted. Will you be in town long?"

"Two, three days."

"Most talkative man I've run into in months," Ginny teased. "Seriously, I suppose you grow terribly tired of hotel rooms and restaurant-cooked meals."

"That's true," Slocum allowed.

"There's a basket supper and cakewalk at our church tomorrow evening. I know this is terribly brazen, but I would be pleased if you would accompany me."

Not since the gangly, awkward teen years of his youth had John Slocum been invited to a church social. Ginny's ingenuous request had him instantly off balance. He started to stammer a refusal, then took his own good advice and remained silent.

"Everyone will simply be dying to meet the man who treed Butch Kelso," Ginny added encouragingly.

"I . . . I'm not exactly eager to get the notoriety," Slocum said, easing himself away from accepting.

"Oh, Slocum, you amaze me. I'd think you'd be eager to meet the local ranchers. They'll want to talk to you. Most have been afraid to leave their spreads to arrange sale of . . . what stock hasn't been stolen."

It would give him a chance to question those men who had personal experience with the ghost rustlers, Slocum considered. That, and the sensation of stirrings that had long been suppressed, brought on now by Ginny's delightful presence, caused him to relent.

"All right, I'd be obliged to escort you to the supper, Ginny."

Beaming up at him, her head all but resting on his broad chest, Ginny smiled sweetly. "I thought you might be." Then her aerial mood dissolved as she pointed ahead down the narrow side street. "There it is. My dear little house. It came with the cafe."

Slocum followed her pointing finger to a small, white clap-board house that could not have contained more than three rooms, seated quarely on a modest lot. Almost as an after-thought, he took in the inevitable whitewashed picket fence and the rosebushes climbing toward the front windows.

"Until tomorrow, then?" Ginny asked shyly.

"I'll see you for breakfast, you know."

"Oh, of course," Ginny answered breathily. Then she stood on tiptoe and kissed him lightly on the cheek. "Good night, Slocum."

After she had disappeared into the tiny house, Slocum confronted his situation eyeball to eyeball. He breathed out slowly. "Well, I'll be damned."

Moonlight spilled liquid silver over the pastureland on the O/S ranch of Ozzie Simpson, five miles west of Happy. Briggs, Granger, and Thompson walked their horses slowly around the herd, half-drowsing. The spring gather had been completed despite the excessive rains. All that remained now was to keep the herd together until the branding could begin Monday morning.

Unless a thunderstorm brewed up, their nighthawk shift would pass in peaceful boredom. Briggs dreamed of a tall, fat schooner of beer with which he would wash down a smoky shot of rye. Granger's mind held the tantalizing image of the smoothly rounded bottom on that dusky gal, Salina, in the Panhandle Paradise. Thompson thought of his buxom, pixie-faced wife and two small young'uns, waiting for him in the small shack next to the bunkhouse. None of them had taken into consideration the plans of others.

Seven men waited in the deep shadows cast by a clump of paloverde trees. Only their eyes and heads moved as they kept watch on the three cowboys riding the ten-to-four shift. When the last of the trio had ridden silently by, one lean, lanky hardcase reached up to scratch a bristly chin.

"I don't like doin' this without the boss bein' here," Pete Lang complained.

"We've got a job to do an' we're gonna do it," Griff Quinn hissed back. "You like them greenbacks get laid in yer hands after each haul, don'tcha?"

"Oh, sure, no complaint there. Only we ain't never done a herd without the boss bein' along."

"Well, he ain't here, Pete. So shut up an' put that flour sack over your head an' let's get on with it," Oliver Utting snapped.

"Hump you, Ollie," Pete bitched. He put on his hood, though.

"Pete, you, Griff, an' me will take care of them riders," Ollie announced, taking charge. "The rest of you boys take the swing and drag and start that herd moving. Head them toward the Frazier spread. We can't make the canyon before daylight. We'll hold 'em in that big arroyo and start off again late tomorrow."

"Good thing it's gonna be Sunday," Griff Quinn observed. "Won't be a lot of folks out and about."

"That's the way the boss planned it," Utting stated, ending discussion. "Now, let's be quick about it."

"We gonna klonk 'em on the head an' take their horses?" Pete Lang asked.

"That's the usual way, ain't it?" Utting snapped back.

With a minimum of noise, the seven rustlers moved out of their concealment and went to their assigned tasks. Pete Lang caught up with Vince Briggs first. He gave a muffled howdy and moved in closer on the unsuspecting cowboy. Then something went terribly wrong for Briggs.

"Hey, you ain't one of the reg'lar hands," he challenged.

"Nope, I can explain." Pete stalled as he rode in closer. He kept his right hand in plain sight, empty, in the moonlight. His left held a stone-headed Kiowa war club he had traded for some years ago.

"There's something wrong," Briggs persisted. "I can't see your face." Alarmed, he went for his six-gun.

Instantly panicked, Pete Lang beat him to the draw. His own Colt Frontier model flashed fire and spit a .44 bullet that ripped into Vince Briggs's chest and ended all thoughts of a cool beer.

"Briggs, you idiot, you'll stampede the cattle," Hank Granger called in a singsong, steer-soothing tone from nearby in the dark. "What's the matter?"

They'd done kicked over the thunder mug, Griff Quinn

thought as he approached Hank Granger. He fisted his Smith American .44 and lined the sights on the cowhand's head. Granger sensed his menacing approach and whirled in that direction. Quinn tripped the trigger and sped a hot slug into Granger's open mouth.

At once, the cattle began to mill restlessly, and a few bellowed in protest to the loud, startling noise. "Aw, shee-it! You've done did it now," Utting raged as the steers came splay-legged to their hooves. Half a dozen bolted away in fright.

"Hold it right there," Brad Thompson commanded as he made out Ollie Utting's silhouette in the moonlight.

Utting twisted his way and shot Thompson through the breastbone. Without even time to think of his widow and the orphans he was leaving behind, Brad Thompson slumped forward over his horse's neck. Instantly the herd erupted into frenzied life. Bellows of outrage goaded them to greater confusion and speed.

"Head 'em up! Head 'em up, gawdammit!" Utting howled at the other rustlers. "They gonna run every ounce of fat offin 'em."

In a maddened swirl, the herd thundered past the fallen O/S cowboys and off into the distance, northward by accident more than design. The boss, Ollie Utting thought as he tried to bring some order out of the chaos, would have a blue-haired fit over this.

Butch Kelso paced the floor of the small shack on the outskirts of Happy. Pale dawn light came through a dust-grimed window as his face turned a dark scarlet from self-induced rage. He tried to organize his thoughts to offer some justification. From the start he knew he would come off second best in the battle of words.

"It ain't my fault. I didn't have nothin' to do with what happened. I was locked in that stinkin' jail all night."

"You are paid to make sure these sort of things don't happen, Kelso," the Boss snapped, his face obscured by a full-faced black mask. "We didn't hire you to try to tree every stranger who rides into town, like some pimple-faced, juvenile punk."

"Now, dammit, that ain't fair. This . . . this Slocum was makin' a challenge to our control of the town. Somethin' had to be done."

"Not last night, it didn't," the Boss grated. "What happened last night was stupid. Careless and stupid. What's worse, after all our careful planning, this . . . this *underling* of yours makes a complete shambles of it. Everyone knows that 'ghosts' don't put bullet holes in people. Utting and those other two simpletons with him have left behind some very tangible clues that those cattle are not simply walking away on their own."

Kelso looked helplessly at the angry, faceless man before him. "It's only the first killings. Maybe nobody will connect it up to what we're doin'," he suggested lamely, thinking miserably of the young cowboy he had killed the previous afternoon.

"You are right; they are the first. And they had damned well better be the last."

Fire in the words of the Boss should have warned Butch. But Kelso's smart lip could not let it go. "Listen to me, for once, Boss. Those night drovers are gettin' edgy. The boys done what they had to. If you don't like the way I'm runnin' this outfit, you can get someone else."

"You cretin!" the Boss thundered. "I *don't* like it, and you're in no position to walk away from it. Three men were killed. Perhaps the U.S. marshals in Santa Fe would like to learn the whereabouts of Butch Kelso? It could happen if you don't use some savvy."

Kelso washed pale. "Now, Boss, that's not a white thing to say."

"I mean it. There will be no more murders. Keep those two-bit gunhawks in line, if it means killing one of them to impress the importance on them."

Disbelief registered in Kelso's bleak expression. "That ain't exactly gonna be easy. What with what happened last night, these boys ridin' night herd are gonna be on the prod. They'll shoot and ask questions later. Like I said before, might be we should lay low for a while."

"No, Mr. Kelso. We will not 'lay low,' as you so colloquially put it. We have commitments to meet. You can make that happen for us by bringing in more cattle. I didn't stand bail for the three of you to listen to you whine and snivel about how difficult the job is going to be. I got you out before you ran into some hardhead who asked the right questions. And to get more beeves pushed through the funnel. Is that clear?"

"Y-yes, sir. I reckon it is. Might be I'll have to deal with this Slocum. Word is he's a cattle buyer, but he's got moves like a gunfighter."

"Forget Slocum. Tend to what you're good at and let others take care of sideline irritants. Now, good day. I want to see you producing results by tomorrow night. And no more killings."

6

For all its trappings of what Slocum disgustedly called "civilization," he found himself enjoying the church social. He had picked up Ginny at four in the afternoon, surprised that the event would start in daylight. The Virginia House had been open only three hours in the morning, as it was every Sunday. Slocum had barely managed to get in before the final call for breakfast. Ginny told him when to be at her house at four. Now he found himself shaking hands with the mayor, Arthur Canby.

"My . . . my, the word has certainly gone around about how you handled that Butch Kelso and his associates, Mr. Slocum," the medium-size, potbellied politician purred.

Slocum had seen the balding, portly man glad-handing his way through the crowd in typical politician fashion and asked who he might be. When informed of the identity of the Texas good ol' boy, he thought it a good time to do some direct probing about the rustlings.

"Thank you, Mr. Mayor," Slocum said softly. "You know, in my business, we hear a lot of strange stories. Can you tell me anything about these so-called ghost rustlers?"

The mayor's pale gray eyes, behind thick spectacles, went wide. "Oh, my dear no—no, not at all. There have been some cattle missing lately," Canby added cautiously. "Since I can hardly imagine what use a ghost would have for live steers, I find it hard to believe in such beings."

"My thought was that they might be a little more material than ghosts," Slocum suggested to set up the mayor. "Has anyone mentioned the possibility that, since the rustlings started shortly after his arrival in town, Butch Kelso might have something to do with them?"

"Dear dear, the thought has never occurred to me," Canby responded, looking distracted and uncomfortable. "Nor, I imagine, to anyone else. Mr. Kelso is simply a phenomenon of isolated frontier communities, I'm afraid."

Slocum's green eyes turned hard and bored into those of the mayor. "Are you sure, Mr. Mayor? Or is that wishful thinking?"

"See here," Canby blustered a moment, and then pursued a new line of speculation. "This isn't any sort of official inquiry, is it?"

"No," Slocum denied. "Nothing of the sort. Only . . . idle curiosity. As I said, such things affect my business. I came here to see if there was anything to it."

"But—accusing Mr. Kelso . . . without proof . . . ," the mayor spluttered.

"Could be an unwise thing, I understand," Slocum said to conclude the conversation. "Excuse me, I want to get a look at those food baskets. Figure out which one I want to bid on."

"You'd be wise to pick Miss Ginny's. She's the best cook around," Canby advised, then looked stricken. "Don't tell my wife that," he hastily added.

Laughing, Slocum parted company with him. He quickly found himself lionized by a circle of cackling, middle-aged ranch wives. They, too, believed he had done the community a great service. With greater tact than his usual, he managed to extricate himself from their bubbling praise.

"There you are," boomed a tall, slender man with hair combed straight back from a pronounced widow's peak. "The Reverend Thackery, Mr. Slocum. I want to tell you how uplifted my flock was this morning, when news spread of your accomplishment. Jailing that riffraff was a godsend for our small town."

"Everyone seems to hold the same opinion, Reverend. But I don't see how I did so much. Anyone could have put those lowlifes in jail."

"Not in Happy, Mr. Slocum. Sadly enough, not in Happy. Although as a man of the cloth I must take a position of condemning violence, I must say I am disappointed in our marshal. Had he taken a firmer stance, rapped this Mr. Kelso over the head with a nightstick the very first day and dragged him off to jail, the people would not have lived in fear these past three months. Instead, he closes his office, pleads health reasons, and flees to Galveston to take a warmer climate for the winter."

"Is the marshal a member of your congregation?"

"What? No—no, he's not," Reverend Thackery answered distractedly, as if not entirely certain the reason for that question.

Slocum gave him a bleak smile and turned away. The reverend wasn't finished as yet. "Mr. Slocum, although like I said I am unalterably opposed to violence, in light of your success, would you perhaps consider settling in Happy?"

"No, Reverend," Slocum told him with a straight face. "The first day I'm in town I get in a fistfight with three men, then get the tar beaten out of me with ax handles and wind up in a gunfight. Happy's far too violent a place for me."

Reverend Thackery blinked, took in the width of Slocum's shoulders, his height crowding close on six-two, and his big, scarred-knuckle hands. "Somehow," he said in a small voice, "I find that hard to believe."

Ginny rescued Slocum then and dragged him over to a group of men, obviously ranchers judging from their dress, who were in serious conversation. "I thought you'd want to hear about this," she prompted him.

Their talk was about the most recent rustling. "Three men killed, too," one cattleman stated. "That's the first time for anyone being hurt."

"I'm afraid it won't be the last, Herb," another burly rancher opined.

"Why do you say that, Joe?"

"These rustlers are growing bolder. They don't seem to care what they do, have no fear of the law, what little we have around here," Joe said.

"You're right about the law, Joe," Herb put in. "You know, I'm thinking that considering what happened yesterday, we ought to get ahold of Arthur Canby and bring him over. Have him appoint Mr. Slocum here as chief deputy marshal. That might put the fear of God in those rustlers."

"No, thank you, gentlemen. I've never taken to the idea of wearing a badge." True enough. In the many times Slocum had served as a lawman, he rarely wore the tin star on his shirt. Made too good a target, he told everyone.

A tolling hand bell prevented any more conversation. "Listen up, folks. We're about to start auctioning off the supper baskets," Mayor Canby announced. "Now, all you single men who have a special lady you want to share a tasty meal with had better get down front. You'll want to pick 'em out and bid 'em up so's to be sure you get your choice."

The unmarried bravos began shuffling through the crowd in eagerness. Slocum hung back. He'd have no trouble identifying Ginny's basket, and he felt certain no one would bid too aggressively against him.

By scrupulously avoiding the cakewalk, Slocum had a great time at the social. He and Ginny ate her basket supper with gusto, walked around the small park next to the church, and later danced to the music of two fiddles, a guitar, and an accordian. The festivities ended shortly after sundown. Buckboards, buggies, and spring wagons whisked away many of the folks, while others strolled the quiet, empty streets of town.

With Ginny comfortably on his arm, Slocum started off in the direction of her tiny clapboard house. "Thank you," he said simply.

"What for, good sir?"

Slocum tried to explain. "You've given me back a piece of life that was once very dear to me."

"I feel I should be the one thanking you."

"Ginny . . . there's something . . ." Slocum wanted very much to tell her that all was not as it seemed. Years of cautious living prevented it.

That, and two of Ginny's shapely fingers, which she impulsively laid against his lips. "Not now, Slocum. This is a time for enjoying life, not for serious looks at what we might have been—wanted to be."

Driven by a similar impulse and his rising desire, Slocum kissed her fingers. At once, Ginny stiffened, then she rose swiftly on tiptoe and replaced her fingers with her lips. It grew into a long, deep kiss. Ginny broke off, gasping.

"Oh, Slocum, I'd thought . . . hadn't really hoped . . . do you—do you feel it?"

A gentle smile played on Slocum's lips. "Yes, I . . . definitely feel something."

Ginny looked around her and got her bearings as though for the first time. "It wouldn't do to go to my house. If only there was somewhere—" She let it hang.

Slocum had a hard time believing this change in fortune. Amid all that had happened in one short day—Kelso's unreasoned aggression, the ghost rustlers, the killings—how had this alluring young woman gotten to him so completely? Not something to question, old son, he chided himself.

"There's a back stairway at the hotel," he suggested.

"Oh, yes—yes, let's go there," Ginny urged.

They retraced their steps to Main Street. Ginny took Slocum by the hand and led the way to the alley that extended along one side of the hotel. They turned in and walked with exaggerated quiet to the rear of the building. Slocum tried the door and found it unlocked.

Quickly they entered. Ginny removed her shoes and Slocum walked on the balls of his feet. Fortune smiled on them. They encountered no solitary wanderer, and not a stair tread squeaked. Slocum fished the room key from his vest pocket and unlocked the door. They entered, and Slocum closed the door solidly behind them.

Ginny tittered like a schoolgirl sneaking away for her first kiss. She ducked low to soundlessly set her shoes on the floor, then she was in Slocum's arms. Her own encircled his neck as they kissed. Fires, long banked, flared in both of them.

When their kiss ended, Ginny drew back her head so she could gaze into Slocum's eyes. "Oh, Slocum, that was wonderful. Shall we try again?"

His full, firm lips found hers and tasted of her sweetness. This time they clung together much longer. The urgent movement of their mouths became amorous, then blazingly passionate. With deft, experienced fingers, Slocum began to undo the long line of buttons on the back of Ginny's dress.

At least, Slocum thought as he surrendered to his ardor, he would not have to interrupt the proceedings to turn out the lamp.

•　•　•

A thick wall of roiling powder smoke concealed one side from the other. Yet soldiers screamed and died all around Sergeant John Slocum. Bright yellow flashes of exploding artillery shells hurt his eyes. His throat was raw and scratchy. No one, least of all Sergeant Slocum, knew which side was winning. In the ragged terror of battle, no one really cared. Sergeant Slocum lay on his back in a ditch, down by the crossroads church, and tried to count the number of men he had left in that Hell-come-to-Earth called Antietam.

Slocum woke with a start, bathed in sweat, a scream trying to tear up out of his chest. Calm returned at once, borne on the sweet scent of Ginny Stuart's subtle perfume on the pillows, and the delightful memory of a satisfying night. Slocum swung his feet out from under the thin sheet that covered his nakedness.

He rose, padded to the washstand, and poured water to bathe his face. He studied his craggy jawline in the small wooden-framed oval mirror and decided he could do with a shave. With spring well established, no fire burned in the potbellied stove, so he had to seek out hot water.

Slocum dressed, slid on boots, and took the back stairs to the hotel kitchen, where he fetched a tin bucket of steaming water. He removed his shirt, added a drop to his mug, and whipped up a lather with the brush. Images from the pleasant nighttime hours kept interfering with his silent plans.

He had yet to check out Canyon, Texas, where the complaining ranchers had the office of their local association. Slocum sensed that he had gleaned all he could get from the residents of Happy. He favored another enjoyable tryst with Ginny, yet he had come here with a purpose, and time dictated he do something about that.

Ginny had left shortly after four in the morning, and he would see her again at breakfast. That opened the door to one unpleasant event. He didn't like the fact that some unnamed person had hurried a judge into town and gotten bail set on Kelso and his vermin. That could bring on a repetition of Saturday night. Slocum decided to run the situation in Happy past the association's men in Canyon. Maybe they had some insight on who might have been eager to free Kelso.

With the last of the whiskers and lather scraped away, Slocum abandoned that line of thought and gave his attention to gathering his few possessions. He packed them in saddle-bags and the parfleche envelopes. These he sat by the door, and then he left his room to get breakfast.

He would eat, saddle Sugarloaf and the packhorse, and return for his possibles and to check out. Then on to Canyon.

Ginny looked up expectantly from the cooking range when the tiny bell jingled over the door. Her flattering blush and quick smile reassured Slocum when he entered. She had found the night as marvelous as he. A gawky girl, all legs and sharp angles, mousey hair pulled back and tied in a bun, waited by the cash register. She offered Slocum a menu and showed him to a table.

Before she could bring coffee, Ginny joined Slocum where he sat. "Good morning," she purred.

"Good morning to you. I see your sick waitress has recovered."

"Yes. Actually it was her child that was sick."

Slocum raised an eyebrow. "She's hardly more than a child," he observed.

"True enough. We hardscrabble Texas farm girls tend to marry young, you know," Ginny teased. Then, "Anyway, she was here first thing this morning. That's all right, Dora," Ginny told the girl when she approached with the coffee. "I'll take this gentleman's order."

Frown lines creasing her high, smooth brow, the waitress retreated to her place beside the money box. Ginny eyed her and spoke with genuine sympathy. "I feel so sorry for her. She's well into marriageable age, seventeen now, but . . . so plain. None of the young men around here show any interest in sparking her."

"I thought you said she married young."

"That's a kindly fiction created by Reverend Thackery," Ginny said, dismissing the topic, her eyes fixed on the checked tablecloth.

"Maybe she should go to the big city and take up nursing?" Slocum teased.

"Slocum, that's . . . unkind."

"Yes," he admitted. "You could never have been 'plain.' Now, then, how about a slab of ham, three eggs, potatoes, biscuits?"

"We have grits."

Slocum nodded enthusiastically. "Them, too."

"Sounds like you have a big day ahead of you."

"I do. I have to ride to Canyon."

Ginny's disappointment flared on her face. "So soon?"

"Business, I'm afraid. I'll be back, though. Nothing could keep me away, truth to tell."

Ginny covered a radiant smile with a small hand. "That's encouraging. I'll miss you, John Slocum."

"I'm not too happy about it, myself," he allowed.

"When are you leaving?"

"Right after you fix me breakfast, woman, so you'd best get at it," Slocum informed her with mock gruffness.

Before the sun had climbed an hour into the sky, Slocum left Happy, Texas. His parting with Ginny had been better done publicly, he admitted. And he would, he vowed, come back to see her again.

Carl Hartson came into Canyon, Texas, at mid-morning. Outside the brick bank building on Sutter Street, he left his lathered mount at the tie rail with an angry wrap of the rein over the crossbar. He took the wooden stairs up the side of the two-story structure, banged through a door and down the hall with an angry thud of bootheels.

Without a knock, he entered the office maintained by the local Cattlemen's Association. "Gawdammit, my Bar-C has been hit by those rustlers!" he bellowed loud enough to be heard out in the street.

"You're in good company, then, Carl," Bob McClure of the Running Snake responded as he glanced up from the Amarillo newspaper on his desk. "Now, why don't you calm down some and tell us about it?"

"The cattle were taken sometime in the early morning hours. One hand killed outright, another dragged and not expected to live and you gawdammit want me to calm down?"

"Easy, easy, Carl," Bob cautioned. "Everything is being done that is possible for us."

"Is it? Where's that lazy, stupid, fat-assed sheriff of ours?"

"Yesterday he left town for Amarillo. He'll be back around noon."

Carl's crimson face turned darker. "He's always some other place when a herd gets run off. Too damn convenient if you ask me."

"I'll inform the sheriff the minute he gets back," McClure promised.

"You do that. And while you're at it, you can tell me what in hell is going on down at Fort Worth. Why hasn't the state done something about this?"

Bob McClure rose and crossed to a rosewood sideboard. He poured three fingers of bourbon in a cut crystal glass and handed it to the furious Carl Hartson. "Relax, Carl. The state *is* sending someone."

"How many someones?" Hartson demanded suspiciously.

Uncomfortable with the answer he had to give, McClure said quietly, "One."

Hartson blew his anger out in harsh, jerky movements. "One? *One!*" he exploded, then gulped down the whiskey and threw his hat on the floor. "Now, gawdammit, Bob, that's bullshit! One man. These damn ghost rustlers are making a shambles of ranching hereabouts. Four good men killed, another at death's door, too. And our association big shots send us one man."

"You know the old saying, Carl," Yates Harkness put in. "One riot, one Ranger."

"We need a company of Rangers, by god," Hartson growled.

He glared hotly at Yates Harkness. He had never come to like the outsider. Harkness ran a big spread up by Amarillo. Of an age with Hartson and McClure, in his early fifties, he had hard, blue eyes and fleshy lips that had always given him a sinister look, Carl thought.

Bob McClure ran long, thick fingers through his graying hair. "Not possible, and you know it, Carl. We have to settle for what we can get."

"No. I won't settle for it. I want action and I want it fast. I'm thinking of arming my hands and going hunting for those misbegotten rustlers in the Palo Duro."

Yates Harkness and Bob McClure joined in disabusing their colleague of that plan. "Carl, Carl," Bob said soothingly, an arm around Hartson's shoulder in comradely fashion. "You can't go off half-cocked like that. Think it through, man. This is something beyond us. Leave it up to the professionals."

"Bob's right," Harkness added. "We're only lucky these demons aren't hitting up around Amarillo. If it will help, I'm willing to offer a reward, dead or alive, for the rustlers."

Carl looked at Harkness, did a quick revision of his opinion of him, and let the rest of his steam bleed off in a long sigh. "That's mighty white of you, Yates. We'd only finished the spring gather and I'd be hard-pressed to come up with the same. My hand that was killed, he was a family man. His widow and young'uns will be grateful, too."

"Well, then," McClure said and breathed easier, "that's settled? No uncoordinated action. We wait for the man the association is sending."

"When's he gonna be here?"

"Within the week," Bob McClure answered imprecisely.

"I'll wait that long," Carl Hartson agreed. "But then, hell, I ain't got anything left to lose."

7

Slocum leaned back in the saddle, eased his legs. He had covered better than half the twenty-six miles from Happy to Canyon in good time. The sun rested warmly on his shoulders and back. So far he had seen not another person on the narrow, rutted road. Not that he would have welcomed company. Better that he didn't have to invent reasons for being there. While he flexed his shoulders, Slocum let what little he had learned circulate through his mind again.

His biggest problem, he acknowledged, was that he didn't have proof of anything. No identifiable connection between Kelso and the rustlers, nothing that indicated the absent marshal had some involvement with Kelso or the rustlers. Worse, not the least idea of the identity of those who profited from the stolen cattle. If he had that, Slocum decided, he would have the answers to the other unknowns.

Ordinarily cautious and alert, Slocum showed no surprise when his packhorse whiffled an announcement of the presence of other horses. "I know," Slocum said aloud. "They've been back there for the past quarter hour."

Some fifteen minutes earlier, Slocum had become aware of two riders behind him who held on the edge of his range of vision, neither coming closer nor lagging back. In the last five minutes, they had closed in by enough for the sorrel gelding to catch a whiff of fellow horseflesh.

They had, Slocum judged by the sudden sound of rapid hoofbeats, been joined by a couple of friends. Might as well drop the pretense of ignorance. He looked over one shoulder in time to see a faint flash and spurt of smoke from a rifle held to the cheek of one of his pursuers.

A split-second later the bullet cracked past his head. "We'd

better move out, Sug," Slocum observed as he touched the
blunted rowels of his Texas Star spurs to the horse's golden-
brown flanks.

Sugarloaf jumped to a fast trot, which Slocum encouraged
into an all-out run. Beyond his back, he heard a shout and a
speed-up of the four riders. Another glance behind revealed
that they wore flour sack hoods over their heads. The rifle spat
another slug, which moaned off a rock ahead and to the right
of Slocum.

Damn, this was getting him nowhere, Slocum reasoned.
A powerful, speedy animal, Sugarloaf was held back by the
packhorse. Slocum broke free the dally around his saddle horn
and cast the gelding off to fend for itself. At once the distance
widened between him and the quartet chasing behind. Two
shots sounded almost as one, and the rounds snapped past
uncomfortably close.

To hell with this, Slocum decided. He had no love of being
chased. Especially by hooded men. When he topped a steep
rise and dropped out of sight of his pursuers for a moment,
Slocum cut hard to the right and reined in. His .45 Peacemaker
filled his hand in an instant. Then the first rider showed over
the crest.

Slocum shouted his demand. "Haul in and put up your
hands."

Instead, the masked gunman tried to change direction and
shoot at the same time. Slocum blasted him from the saddle
with a solid hit in the chest. By then the second and third of
the hardcases had come into view, riding side by side. Each
carried a rifle, and they fired only a split second apart.

Hot lead burned air over Sugarloaf's hindquarters and
kicked up dirt behind Slocum. Coolly he triggered another
.45 cartridge, which sent its slug to drill a neat hole in the
belly of the nearest assassin. Without even time for a grunt
of pain, Slocum's third bullet hit the same man in the chest
and spilled him out of his saddle.

Return fire from the remaining gunhawk cut through the
loosely hanging leather of Slocum's vest under his left arm.
Too damned close, big, raven-haired Slocum thought as he
raised his Colt and pumped a bullet into the off-white cloth
bag that covered his assailant's face. He had neither need nor

time to check results, because the fourth rider burst upon him from an unexpected direction.

A rattle of loose stones and the retching of a severely jolted horse swung Slocum in the saddle. Almost too late, he faced the fourth gunhand, who had ridden wide and came on him from behind. The .44 Remington in the hooded killer's hand bucked and spewed flame and smoke. The slug smacked noisily into the cantle of Slocum's saddle and burst through the wooden frame with a shower of slivers.

Hot pain bloomed in Slocum's lower back, three inches above his lean buttocks. It affected his aim as he squeezed off another .45 round. An anguished cry came from his attacker as the sizzling lead cut a path across the top of his right shoulder. The stranger bit back his misery long enough to raise and cock his smoking Remington. Slocum proved faster, sending a fatal messenger into the chest of the would-be killer. Struck twice, the last a mortal wound, he reined in and still tried another shot. Slocum, dizzy with his own injury, cut down the stubborn gunhawk with a final, decisive bullet in the brain.

Reeling in the saddle, the dead man dropped his revolver, blinked once from reflex, and slid off sideways, onto the ground. Slocum sucked in a deep gust of air and felt gingerly along his back. He found the bullet mashed into mushroom shape and wedged between two badly deformed cartridges. Giddy with relief, Slocum realized that the stout casings, and his thick cartridge belt, had stopped the nearly spent slug.

It took him a while to tidy up. He had four excited, nervous horses to round up, in addition to his pack animal. Then, wincing from the daggerlike shafts of pain in his back, he had to load the corpses onto their uncooperative mounts. Slocum rested when he had accomplished that, drank deeply from his canteen. Curious, he roused himself and went to the skittery horses to peel off their lifeless riders' hoodwinks.

All turned out to be strangers, except for Linc Parsons. His deep-set, cold, pale blue eyes stared wide open at eternity. Parson's broad, rubbery mouth would speak no more insults or intimidating threats. But Slocum recognized him, from the long, greasy, yellow locks to the tiny patch of small-pox pits on his left cheek and the tip of his nose.

Linc Parsons, freshly bailed out of the Happy jail, Slocum

thought darkly. No doubt this had been an attempted grudge killing, spawned in the twisted mind of Butch Kelso. Well and good, Slocum thought. He would deal with Kelso when he returned to Happy.

Prodded by the attempt on his life, Slocum decided to detour past the entrance to Palo Duro Canyon before riding into the town of Canyon. From a great distance, he could see the large flocks of birds circling in the sky. They had been attracted by the abundant water in the Prairie Dog Town Fork of the Red River, which in ancient times had carved out the spectacular canyon. Cottonwoods, paloverde, and blackjack pines lined the shore, making a wide ribbon of green through the red-brown barrens that surrounded the watercourse.

Long before Slocum drew near to the winding, verdant belt, he began to see broad swaths of crushed and browning grass. Long tracks had been worn bare by repeated erosion from the hooves of heavy animals. No game trail, this, Slocum well knew. These pathways came from several directions, all pointing unerringly at the upper entrance to the canyon.

When he came nearer, Slocum found fresh sign, some not more than eight or ten hours old. Clear impressions of the split hooves of cattle began to appear. Oddly, though, he noted not a single hoofprint of a horse. Experience told him that grazing animals did not keep in such a tight cluster when left to themselves. *These* cattle had been driven through here. And by someone who left no tracks. Even most sign of the livestock had been scuffed over and blurred out. Kelso and piggin' strings, stolen cattle and no sign of horses. Somehow he was missing an element that kept it from adding up.

Puzzled, Slocum rode on, headed westward toward Canyon.

A brazen sun had slid halfway to the meridian when Slocum walked Sugarloaf down the main street of Canyon, Texas. The four body-draped horses behind him drew immediate attention. Gawkers acquired immediate vitality, and word of the train of corpses sped along ahead of him. Two men with badges waited for Slocum outside the sheriff's office.

"You a bounty hunter?" a big, fat man demanded. Hard,

gray-green eyes glared at Slocum from above a large, gray-streaked walrus mustache.

"Nope," Slocum answered. "Just a man who got jumped by road agents."

Slocum decided to offer the least detail possible when he observed the man's belly sagging over a cartridge belt that held a brace of holsters filled with matching Smith and Wesson American .44s. There were food stains on his white shirt and the lapels of his rumpled black suit. Such a slovenly demeanor, Slocum had noted before, often marked an unkempt manner of thinking.

The untidy man introduced himself. "Harlan Butcher. I'm the sheriff." He waited with obviously bored anticipation for Slocum to reply in kind.

"Slocum." He didn't have to be cordial, but he did have to get along with Butcher.

"Who are they?" Butcher asked with a nod to the bodies.

"Don't know. Strangers to me."

Butcher's eyes narrowed. "Why'd you kill them?"

Slocum had trouble believing that. He chuckled lightly. "Because, Sheriff, they were trying to kill me."

Suspicion curled Butcher's thick lips into an ugly sneer. "I thought you said they were road agents."

"I assumed they were. Actually, I didn't have time to ask. They opened the dance without any warning."

"There ain't a scratch on you," Butcher accused as though disappointed.

"Turned out I am a little better than they were," Slocum gave him dryly.

"You a hired gun?"

"No. Not at the present."

"What's your business here, then?" Butcher demanded.

"I'm a cattle buyer. Maybe these fellers knew that and thought I had a lot of money on me."

"Do you?" Butcher probed, still searching for some sensible answers.

"No, Sheriff. We don't conduct business that way anymore. It's all done by bank draft." Then Slocum added a shrewd probe of his own. "Do you recognize any of them, Sheriff?"

Butcher strolled along the lineup of corpses, lifted heads,

peered into faces. "No, can't say that I do," he answered sparingly.

Not even Linc Parsons? Slocum thought to himself. Odd bit that. With Kelso, Parsons, and the others on the prod in Happy, it seemed only reasonable that the sheriff would be aware of their identities. "What about you, Deputy?"

"I'll ask the questions around here." Butcher interrupted any response from his deputy with a snarl. "You figure to be here long, Mr. Slocum?"

"A few days. I'm on the backside of my swing, headed north again," Slocum invented.

"Well and good, Mr. Slocum. Uh—don't plan on leaving Canyon until your story can be checked out."

Slocum raised his hands from the saddle horn, palms turned up. "In that case, I have no intention of going anywhere for a while, Sheriff. Where do I take the bodies?"

"Leave them with me. We'll take care of that," Butcher snapped.

"I'll be at the best hotel in town, in case you need me," Slocum advised and turned Sugarloaf's head away from the lawmen.

There turned out to be only two hotels in Canyon. One consisted of large, open rooms on both of two floors, without any attempt at privacy. The other had narrow rooms that reminded Slocum of jail cells, with the outside wall of the building dominated by a single, stingy window. Twenty-five cents a night, with washbasin and thunder mug, outhouse and bath out behind. Baths were five cents extra.

Slocum paid willingly. Following instructions given him at Fort Worth, he settled in, then spent a comfortable half hour washing away trail dust. Refreshed, Slocum set off to follow the usual routine of a traveler. That brought him to the Branding Iron saloon. Over a beer, he made acquaintance with several local ranchers. Their talk, although guarded, revolved around the rustlings.

"I tell you it ain't natural," one burly, red-faced cattleman declared to a round of nodding heads. "Ain't anybody who can go around and not leave some sign of bein' there."

"Then you subscribe to the 'ghost' theory?" Slocum prodded.

"There's been some killings lately. Certainly in those cases something was left behind."

"What do you mean by that?" the florid-faced rancher demanded.

"Ghosts don't need to use bullets on anyone. They can't be hurt, most times can't be seen. At least that's what I was taught about them," Slocum responded.

"All right, sure, I agree. There's men behind this. Only no one knows who they might be," another ranch owner, named Simms, allowed.

"No idea at all?"

"Nope. None," the first man responded. "So far I ain't lost a head. Not that that means it can't happen tomorrow."

Sheriff Butcher entered the Branding Iron a moment later. By mutual, unspoken agreement, the topic of conversation was changed. "How much are you offering?" Simms asked Slocum. "Now that we've got the spring roundup out of the way, we're ready to sell or drive north."

"Forty dollars a head for prime steers, at the railhead. For range cattle, twenty to twenty-five."

"We can make more takin' 'em overland to Dodge City."

"Not for much longer," Slocum said. He felt grateful for the briefing he had been given by the Cattlemen's Association. "Already the Texas and Pacific and the Katy have lines into Fort Worth. Cheaper and easier to take your herds there."

Simms's friend snorted. "The Kansas-Missouri-and-Texas ain't got half the stockcars we'd need."

Butcher downed his second shot of whiskey, grunted in disgust, and left the saloon. The batwings flapped in his wake. Slocum looked speculatively after the sheriff, conscious of the way the ranchers had switched subjects when the lawman had entered. Did they suspect something, and if so, how could he get it out of them?

"I'll be in touch before I leave town," Slocum injected into the flow of talk. "Tell me, you got interested in selling your cattle rather quickly when the sheriff entered. Any reason?"

Both men shrugged. "Nope," Simms stated. "The sheriff's doing what he can, I suppose. Only we didn't want to sound like we're criticizin' his effort to find the rustlers."

Slocum nodded and strode out onto the boardwalk. Raucous voices from the street corner drew his attention. Looking that way, he saw a young woman, who appeared distressed, surrounded by three gangly young men. Their voices, slurred by liquor, rose again.

"C'mon, pretty lady, how 'bout tellin' us which saloon you work in?"

"I told you, I do not work in a saloon. Now, if you please, let me pass and be about my business."

A stubble-chinned saddle bum wheedled. "Hey, sweetie, how about givin' ol' Dusty a great big smooch?" A big, dirty-nailed hand settled on her shoulder.

"Take your hand off me!"

Slocum had heard enough. In five long, fast strides he reached the altercation on the corner. He spoke from three feet away. "I believe the lady wishes to be left in peace."

"Butt out, saddle tramp," one of the trio growled.

Slocum clapped a big hand on the shoulder of the rude-mouthed drover, spun him, and slammed a cocked left fist into his exposed cheek. Staggered, the man put up his hands to ward off further blows. They came, now to his midsection, and doubled him over, retching. Slocum clubbed him on the back of the head and drove him face-first into the boardwalk. By then, one of the bleeding man's companions had leapt at Slocum.

Hard knuckles met the attacker. Slocum drove his fists alternately into a vulnerable chest. They made sounds like dull drumbeats. Surprise registered on the drifter's face. He made a futile effort to brush aside the punishment, then settled for a knee to Slocum's groin.

Expecting such a tactic, Slocum pivoted slightly and popped a hard right to his opponent's nose. Blood squirted, and the crunch of cartilage sounded clearly. The last of the trio wanted nothing to do with those powerful fists. He went for his gun.

Slocum beat him. The hammer fell on the Peacemaker, and a .45 slug ripped through the shooter's arm, an inch above his right elbow. Screaming, he dropped his cocked weapon, which discharged into the street. His eyes refocused, the second rowdy spat blood and a curse and hauled his six-gun free of leather.

With a quick step closer, Slocum swung the seven-inch barrel of his Colt and slapped it against the side of the drunken brawler's head. Rubber-legged, the man went down. The young woman gasped and turned away in rejection of the violence.

By that time, face shiny with sweat from the block-and-a-half run, Sheriff Butcher lumbered onto the scene. He had one of his Smith Americans out and pointed it at Slocum.

"I'll take that gun, Slocum," Butcher growled.

"No need, Sheriff. I only shot one of them, and that in the arm."

"I won't deny it, I don't like you, Slocum. You have a way of attracting trouble."

"This—this was not his fault, Sheriff," the pleasant-faced young lady interrupted. "These unsavory men accosted me and made improper suggestions. This gentleman came to my aid. They started the fight."

Not entirely true, Slocum thought. He appreciated her help, but felt uncomfortable about requiring it. Butcher eyed him askance.

"That right?"

"Essentially, yes," Slocum responded.

Sheriff Butcher lowered the hand he had extended for Slocum's revolver. He touched the other to the brim of his hat. "I'm right sorry this happened in my town, Miss . . . ?"

"Billingsley, Sheriff."

"Ol' Pete's li'll girl?" Butcher asked, stupified.

"The same."

"You've . . . uh . . . grown some in the last two years," the gaping lawman blurted.

"Have I, Sheriff?" Her laugh lightened everyone's mood.

Butcher turned to Slocum. "I'll let you off this time, Slocum. Though you are prone to drawing violence, I must admit any right-thinking man would have stepped in on the behalf of a fine lady like Miss Billingsley."

"Thank you, Sheriff. I'll be on my way." Always the gallant, Slocum tipped his hat to her and politely said, "Sorry to have made your acquaintance under these circumstances, Miss Billingsley."

"Considering . . . the pleasure has to be mine, Mr. Slocum. Perhaps we'll meet again."

A wide, white grin spread on Slocum's face. "Yes, perhaps we will."

8

They met that evening for an early dinner in the hotel dining room. Clarissa Billingsley had dressed in her Eastern finery and drew admiring glances from every man in the room. Her long, blond sausage roll curls and fair, glowing complexion set hearts to smoldering. Slocum had changed into twill trousers, a white shirt, tie, and cloth vest. The wife of the hotel's proprietor seated them at a small table in front of red velvet drapes. A candle, in a tall glass chimney, flickered on the white linen covering.

"This is not as elegant as what you are accustomed to back east," Slocum said in apology.

Clarissa smiled quite brightly. It caused her button nose to crinkle. "I think it's delightful. I grew up eating in this dining room every Sunday afternoon."

"There's pig knuckles, sauerkraut, and mashed potatoes on the nightly special," the gray-haired hostess suggested. Slocum made a face. "We also have roasted bison, and antelope steak, corned beef, or ham."

"I'll take the bison," Slocum said, thinking of the rich, sweet flavor.

"It's all on the buffet. Help yourself."

"I'd like the brace of pan-fried pigeons in that delicious champagne sauce. Do you still have that, Mrs. MacGruder?" Clarissa Billingsley asked.

Mrs. MacGruder's face slid into a beaming smile. "I sure do, honey. When we heard you were coming home, I made sure we had plenty of your favorite."

"Oh, thank you. I haven't had anything quite so good . . . since I left to go to school."

Slocum and Clarissa talked of inconsequentals until a waiter in black trousers, half-apron, and white shirt brought Clarissa her soup. Slocum had to get his from the buffet table. It was bean soup, thick and quite delicious.

"Do they have wine by the bottle?" he asked between bites.

"I believe they do. Not a large selection, but suitable for Canyon," Clarissa replied.

Slocum ordered a bottle of claret. The waiter came with it five minutes later, wiped dust from the shoulders and neck, pulled the cork, and offered a taste to Slocum. Uncertain of the wine ritual, Slocum took a sniff, swallowed a little, and looked blankly at the waiter.

He described the wine. "Marymount. It's from Missouri. Not like New York state wines, but the reds don't travel well."

Slocum supposed so. In fact, he didn't have the slightest idea. It tasted all right to him—bold, rich, and almost vinegary dry. When they had finished the soup, Slocum went back to the buffet and loaded a plate with a slice of bison roast, a slab of ham, and some corned beef. He added boiled potatoes, a wedge of cabbage, and green lima beans. Clarissa's eyes widened at the pile of food.

"Long day's ride. I'm hungry," Slocum explained, a tinge of pink in his cheeks.

"You didn't take any of the relishes," Clarissa observed.

"Rabbit food," Slocum said dismissively.

"Have you visited my father, about buying his herd?" she asked.

"No, I only got to town today." It pained him to carry out the pretense with this charming young woman.

"He's had some cattle stolen."

"A lot of people have lately," Slocum said to sum up the situation.

A hot light came to Clarissa's eyes. "I'd like to get my hands on them. I'd swing them from the nearest cottonwood."

"Here now," Slocum teased. "That doesn't sound like the model Eastern educated young lady."

"Out here, I'm not a lady. I'm my father's daughter. I ride and I shoot, and—and I've even chewed tobacco."

"I'm aghast." Slocum kept up the lively banter.

Clarissa's light laughter and barbed remarks made the evening vigorous. When they had finished, with generous servings of peach cobbler for desert, Clarissa became serious again. "Will I see you another time?"

Slocum raised an eyebrow, tried to keep it light. "Bold is the style in the East now?"

Clarissa's tinkle of laughter drew more longing looks from the unattached males in the room. "Brazen is more like it, I'm afraid. But I do want to see you more, Slocum. Please pay a call at the ranch. I know Daddy will welcome someone to talk to."

"You're going there tonight?" Slocum asked.

"A buggy will call for me tomorrow morning. I'm staying here at the hotel."

"Then may I ask for your company at breakfast?"

"I accept," Clarissa said with enthusiasm.

"I'll see you to your room."

"Thank you, sir. Then I suppose it's off to your manly pursuits of whatever nature?"

Slocum contradicted her. "Off to sleep, I assure you. I am tired."

Outside the door to her room, they paused. "Sleep well, Miss Billingsley," Slocum offered.

"It's Clarissa, please. And I shall," she added with a coy smile. "I will have the most wonderful dreams." Then she was gone and the door closed tightly between them.

Later, after the town had settled down for the night, Slocum left his room and went quietly down the rear stairs to the alley behind the hotel. Following the directions given him in Fort Worth, he traversed the alley to the junction with another. That placed him along one side of the two-story brick bank building. Walking with heels elevated, Slocum went past the wooden stairway to the second floor and out to where he could see the front of the building.

Sure enough, a lamp glowed low in the corner window of the upper level. He was to meet two men there—Bob McClure, whom he had met in Fort Worth, and Yates Harkness. Satisfied, Slocum moved quietly to the staircase and climbed the weathered treads to the landing at the top.

His hand rested for a moment on the knob, then he turned it

and swung the door inward. At once, a brilliant flash momentarily blinded him and the hot sting of a bullet burned a line across the top of his left shoulder. Instinct took over and he dropped flat to the floor.

He heard the uncertain shuffle of boots as his vision slowly cleared. His right hand found the grips of his .45 Peacemaker, and he drew the Colt silently. Two darker figures gradually materialized against the background of light that spilled through the glass partition of the office Slocum was to visit. No way to cock his weapon without noise, so Slocum did it with speed, and the Peacemaker barked loudly.

His bullet struck the center of bulk in the nearer assailant, and the man went to the floor with a soft grunt. With only a moment's pause, Slocum fired again, and a cry of pain came from the darkness a fleeting second before the other unknown assassin slammed past him and out onto the stairway. Slocum considered going after him, then hesitated.

Something didn't fit right. He took note that the men whom he was to meet hadn't come into the hall to see what had happened. They hadn't even called out a question. Suddenly alert, his body tense with apprehension, Slocum came to his feet and walked to the Association office door. Colt at the ready, hammer eared back, he turned the knob and opened the door.

Bathed in yellow from the guttering lamplight, Slocum saw Bob McClure, alone, with his head on the desk between outflung arms, surrounded by a pool of blood. Slocum did a quick check of the room, sucked in a deep breath, and crossed to the desk. As he bent over the dead body, bright lights exploded in Slocum's head and he fell to the floor unconscious.

Fuzzy images wavered over him, and the light had grown a lot brighter. Slocum squinted and tried to make out who the figure above him was. New pain throbbed in his head, and he groaned. With great effort, he moved his hand to the area of pressure at the back of his head. His fingers came away with blood on them.

"Get up. You're goin' with me," a gravelly voice boomed and echoed inside Slocum's aching skull.

"Wha—who?" Slowly Slocum fixed his uncertain gaze on

the face of Sheriff Harlan Butcher.

Butcher bent down over him, features contorted into rage. A big hand reached out and balled the front of Slocum's shirt. Butcher heaved Slocum up off the floor. In spite of his best efforts not to, Slocum yelled at the enormous agony in his head.

"Go easy. I got hit on the head."

"Hit yourself, you mean," Butcher growled.

"No. There were two men. Out in the hall. There's a body out there, Sheriff."

"You mean you killed another one?"

"Wh-what do you mean, 'another one'?" Slocum asked, his mind muzzy.

"Who else did you kill beside Bob McClure?" Butcher barked, face inches from that of the disoriented Slocum.

"I—I didn't kill McClure. I found him dead, at his desk."

"You can drop your lies, Slocum. I know exactly what you did." He held Slocum's Peacemaker by the muzzle. "You snuck out of your hotel, came up here, and murdered Bob McClure. Then you smacked yourself on the head with this gun to make it look like you had nothing to do with it."

With tremendous effort, Slocum rallied his thinking. He stared blankly at his Colt. "Then—then why is there no blood on that gun? Whatever gun hit me would have to have blood on it. I didn't bleed all over that carpet from my nose."

"Maybe you cleaned it off," Butcher suggested indifferently. "There's two spent casings in your gun, and McClure was shot twice. Case closed, as far as I am concerned."

"I don't believe you, Sheriff. Cleaned my gun off *after I was unconscious*? Come on."

"There's only you to say you was knocked out. Coulda been playin' possum."

"Don't you know anything about collecting evidence, Sheriff? I had a meeting here tonight with McClure and Yates Harkness."

"Mr. Harkness ain't even in town. He's got a ranch up by Amarillo," Butcher contradicted. "You'd better come up with something better."

"When I came in through the door to the stairs, someone took a shot at me. I returned fire, hit him dead center, then fired at the man with him. There should be a bullet hole in the door, and blood on the carpet in the hall."

"There is a hole there, Harlan," one of the deputies said from somewhere out of Slocum's sight. "And there's blood on the carpet."

"Coulda been put there anytime. And what's to say Bob McClure wasn't shot out there and drug in here? No, we've got our man right here. Slocum, I'm arresting you for the murder of Robert McClure."

Butcher's deputies manhandled Slocum into a cell and locked the door. The sheriff made no offer of medical attention. A twinge from his shoulder reminded Slocum of the shooting in the hall.

"Give me a minute, Sheriff. Look at this," Slocum urged as he pulled his shirt aside to reveal an angry, red welt. "The bullet that struck the door put a crease on my shoulder. If I did *that* to myself, where's the powder burns?"

Butcher shrugged. "You probably got that when you killed those poor cowhands this afternoon."

Stunned, Slocum held in his breath and checked his anger before answering, "Now those highwaymen are 'poor cowboys.' Where do you get the solutions for your cases, Sheriff? From that book by the Brothers Grimm?"

Butcher looked blank. "Who are they? Did they write about crime and detection?"

"No. The book is *Grimm's Fairy Tales,* Sheriff."

Fury darkened Butcher's face, and he launched his heavy body at the bars. Then he checked himself and spun on one boot heel. "That smart mouth of yours is gonna get you hung, Slocum."

"I want to see a doctor."

"Suffer. They say it's good for the soul."

"You'd never know, Sheriff. You sold yours a long time ago . . ."

With a blasphemous curse, Sheriff Butcher slammed through the door that separated the cellblock from his office.

"To someone, right?" a voice completed Slocum's expulsion from the cell next door. "Oh, that's so true, young man."

Slocum looked in the dim light to his neighbor. He was

small of stature, with a bookish air, a suit rumpled and torn, his face narrow and gaunt. A scholarly type, gone too seed. He smelled of more than too much whiskey.

"Allow me to introduce myself," the wretch grandly announced. "Everet Dudley Denny, Ph.D., LL.D., and of late, professor of classic literature at a university that shall remain anonymous. I loved your bit about the Brothers Grimm. Fit to a tee."

"Your sheriff does seem a little single-minded and simplistic," Slocum observed.

"Our sheriff, as you so unfortunately named him, is a horse's ass," the drunken Denny stated with utter dignity. "And corrupt. Utterly, totally corrupted by someone. I know that for a certainty. I can smell it. The nose knows, you know." Denny delivered this earnestly, then broke into a fit of giggles.

Suddenly tired of it all, his head throbbing, Slocum said in a bored tone, "They call them alliterations."

Denny seized on this. "A-ha! A man of letters, no doubt."

"No. Only finished a year of upper school. But I did pick up a little here and there."

"Ah, yes, the untutored prairie philosopher," Denny rhapsodized.

"If you please. My head feels like a mule kicked it; I'm sore and tired. Can we carry this on tomorrow?"

"Why, certainly, young man. I'll be here a few days. A little matter of some potent firewater I consumed but was unable to pay for. Good night to you."

"Good night, Professor Denny," Slocum answered with unfelt politeness, eager to crawl with his misery into darkness.

At the sound of the cellblock door creaking open, Slocum looked up from his bleak contemplation of the previous night's events. Try as he could, he found it impossible to piece together exactly what had happened. He had gone to his arranged meeting, he had been shot at. He had shot back, one man escaped, he had stepped over the body on the hall floor and entered the office.

Slocum remembered seeing the corpse of Bob McClure, head and arms sprawled on the desk. Then blankness and pain, and awakening with the sheriff standing over him. Slowly a clearer image evolved as the jailer neared his cell. Someone had to have come back and removed the body before Sheriff Butcher got there.

Butcher was untrained in law enforcement methods, and stupid, opinionated, all of that . . . "Brung you some eats," the jailer interrupted Slocum's train of thought. "An' a visitor."

Slocum focused then on the corridor outside his cell. Standing beside a man he had not seen before was a tearful Clarissa Billingsley. Something akin to embarrassment and remorse washed over Slocum. He made a curt gesture.

"You shouldn't be here," he told her.

"I heard the awful things they're saying you did. I had to come. Don't worry, Joh—Mr. Slocum, my daddy will have you out of there in no time."

"There's no bail for people accused of murder," Slocum advised dully.

"But you didn't do it. I know it. My daddy's got lots of influence. He'll get you out. Please believe me," Clarissa stated with assurance.

"You'd better go now."

Clarissa looked at Slocum, and her eyes filled with tears. "If . . . if that's what you want. But I'll talk to Daddy first thing. He'll do everything he can. He'll get you out, wait and see." She fled, a sob only partly stifled in her throat.

Somehow, Slocum didn't feel like eating.

Two days passed before Peter Billingsley appeared at the jail. Full of fuss and bluster, he demanded that the municipal justice, in the absence of the circuit judge, set bail. His demand was, as Slocum expected, denied.

"I can't understand that man," Pete Billingsley complained to Slocum. "I put him in office, put Wade Mannors on the circuit bench, too. They owe me one. Now, young man, my Clari says you didn't do it, an' that's enough for me. I'll do all I can for you. Get you a good lawyer—if there is such a thing. From what you've told me, they don't have a case. It'll only be a short while."

After he left, Everet Denny sidled up to the wall of bars that separated his cell from Slocum's and cocked a dubious eye. "What do you think?"

"I need to know more about Sheriff Butcher before I decide," Slocum responded.

Denny cackled. "Then you've got something else in mind besides trusting to the law to free you? Remember *Henry the Sixth;* 'First we hang all the lawyers.' Shakespeare." He paused, wiped his thin lips. "Harlan Butcher is somewhat of an enigma. He's not from around here. Just elected last term. A stranger to the county." During Denny's pause, Slocum recalled that the lawman had a slight Eastern accent. "Butcher's main office is here, in Canyon. But he divides his time between this office, Happy, and Tulia. He spends three days a month in each of the smaller towns of the county.

"It's said," Denny told Slocum in a hushed, conspiratorial tone, "that Yates Harkness, an Amarillo rancher, put up the money for Butcher's campaign. During the election, the two of them were thicker than thieves. Since then, they've not passed a dozen words between them."

Slocum considered the source and discounted that. "When is he away?" he asked.

Ev Denny, who had only started to dry out, licked his lips again, and scratched his balding head. "I can't recall exactly. I think I overheard mention of Happy being next. But it won't be for three or four more days."

"Ummm. Then it has to be now."

"What does?"

"I need to get out of here, and a breakout is the best way. To do it, I'll need your help."

Everet Denny gaped in utter disbelief at the big man with the dark hair and intense green eyes. "I'll be damned," he gasped.

9

At ten o'clock that night, eleven men rode soundlessly over the prairie outside Canyon, Texas. The herd they were going after was a big one. Like most of the outfits, the Lazy Y had completed its spring roundup, and held over nine hundred head in pasture close to the headquarters. This would be the largest single rustling so far.

Every one of the hooded riders knew it. They looked to their boss for control and the right decisions to make it work. Even though they would not be able to take all of the cattle, their share of the booty would be fat indeed. Nothing like a stack of double-eagles to generate excitement and dedication to the task. They reined in a half mile short of the herd.

"We'll need something to happen to get their minds off the herd. What say you two boys cut around wide and set fire to that big ol' barn Young has on his place? It'll take all but a few hands to fight the fire, keep it from spreading."

"Good idea, Butch," Pete Lang agreed.

"The rest will spread out and hit the herd. Don't let anyone get in your way and don't let anyone see you. If they do, you know what's to be done," Butch Kelso stated harshly.

Twenty minutes went by while the rustlers maneuvered into position to take over the herd and drive it off. Night riders had been doubled or tripled on most ranches since the step-up in raids. That meant they would no doubt have to kill one or more of the cowhands. To their credit, some of the cattle thieves objected to that. They would exert every effort to avoid bloodshed.

By careful, hidden approach, the more reluctant ones managed to clear three of the hawks from their saddles without giving the alarm, or being seen. A fourth man went down with only a short grunt. Then the sky to the south turned orange and reflected firelight flickered off low, scudding clouds.

At once the alarm sounded and the herd guards became dangerously alert. Cautiously the rustlers withdrew into the shroud of darkness. When the barn became fully engaged, not even that could hide them. The two remaining drovers spotted them at the same time.

"Over there—riders," one shouted.

"And there. They're all around," his partner replied.

Butch Kelso coolly shot one through the chest with the Merwin and Hulbert in his left hand. He silently congratulated himself for spending the money on enough ammunition to make him proficient with either hand. He also cursed Slocum for shooting him in the right arm.

A flat report sounded from the other side of the herd and took his mind off that. Good, he thought, the other drover's taken care of. At once he gave a sharp whistle, the signal to move the herd, and the gang started out.

Slowly at first, the reluctant cattle began to mill and circle, until the natural leader stepped out and headed off to the east. They had only a few miles to cover to the safety of the canyon.

Behind them, Clarence Young looked up from fighting the fire in his barn. His face was blackened with soot, showing dark red where sweat had washed clear lines. He had heard the shots and knew what must be happening.

"Leave the barn, boys," he shouted to his hands. "We can keep it from spreading now. Saddle up and go after them damned rustlers."

"You mean the ghost rustlers?" one big-eyed youth asked.

"Ain't any ghosts usin' six-guns," Young snapped. "They're live enough, least until you catch up to them. Now, get movin'."

Twenty men broke off firefighting to catch up horses from the spring gather ramuda and throw saddles over their backs. They jolted out of the ranch yard only twenty minutes behind the stolen herd. They had high hopes of catching up soon.

Unconcerned with keeping weight on the animals, the rustlers lined them out and constantly pushed to increase the pace.

Like typical trail drivers, however, the tough men of the Lazy Y thought in terms of a slow-moving herd of stupid cattle. So confident were some of them that they fashioned hangman's knots of their lariats as they rocked along at a fast trot.

It would have been foolish to streak forward at a gallop. Tired horses and winded men would not have had a chance in a pitched battle to recover the herd. This added to the advantage held by the rustlers. When the cattle leaned into a fast lope, Kelso gave the signal to ease back and hold at that.

Half an hour went by without incident. The first head had entered Palo Duro Canyon when three Lazy Y riders appeared on the horizon behind the gang. Wisely they refrained from firing random shots. Instead they pressed onward with determination. Seven more soon followed, with the main body only a quarter mile behind.

Always cautious, Kelso kept meticulous watch on their backtrail. He saw the riders in the moonlight along the crest of a swell. His men and the herd passed through a broad pool of shadow. Sharp whistles signaled to the gang to leave the herd to the drag riders and header. Silently the eight outlaws faded into the darkness.

They well knew what to expect. Kelso had drilled them on it often enough. When the eager pursuers rumbled into range, they opened up with a rapid fusillade that cleared three men from the tops of their horses and spread confusion. By maintaining rapid fire, the rustlers soon drove off the first arrivals.

Disorganization then changed into panic among the balance of the Lazy Y hands. Long-range rifle shots from the crest they had so recently deserted finished the task. Concerned as much about scattering the herd as facing the guns of the rustlers, they agreed to hold back and the next day go after the men responsible.

Laughing when he figured out their intent, Kelso remarked to Ollie Utting, "Well, the ghosts done scared off another batch of no-sand cow nurses."

"I swear to Ya-hew, this stuff tastes as bad as it did when my sainted mother used to wash out my mouth for experimenting with the more colorful aspects of the English language," Everet

Denny declared, his face screwed into a mask of disgust.

"Stop talking or you'll swallow it," Slocum advised.

Breakfast had been served a short while earlier, and with no sign of Sheriff Butcher, Slocum had decided to put his plan into action. To do so called for considerable sacrifice on the part of Everet Denny. It also leaned heavily on his acting ability, Slocum worried.

"Should I get started now?" Denny asked, his mouth ringed with foam and bubbles.

"Might as well."

Denny groaned mightily, then again. In a hollow, mournful voice, he called out in apparently fatal misery. "Ooooh! Turn-key, help! Help me. I—I think I'm dyin'."

A small portal opened in the cellblock door. "Shut up, Everet. You're just dryin' out, that's all."

"No! No, it's not. I—I g-got foam running outta my mouth. Help me!"

Daylight cut off as the small door closed. Then the thick oak entrance door swung wide. The flabby, moon-faced jailer waddled down the corridor. The key ring had been hung over the butt of his revolver. His eyes widened as he drew nearer.

"M'gawd, you are sick. I'll go for the doc."

"No—wait, help me now. Oh, god, I see them. They're everywhere," Denny raved on, frothing at the mouth. He pointed to the ceiling, the back wall of his cell, then over the turnkey's shoulder. "Look! See them? See them all slimy and wriggling. Oh, god, snakes! I ca-a-a-an't sta-a-and sna-a-akes!"

Terrified of snakes, the jailer turned halfway around. Slocum's arms shot from his cell in the same instant, and his big hands closed around the neck of the guard. With carefully applied pressure, he throttled the struggling man.

"Get the keys," he snapped at Denny.

Timidly, Everet Denny did as he'd been told. He gingerly handed the keys through the bars as Slocum lowered the unconscious jailer to the stone floor of the cellblock. "Here. Good fortune go with you. Where are you headed?"

"It's better you don't know," Slocum told him as he reached through and fitted the key into the lock. The bolt turned smoothly, and Slocum stepped out into the aisle.

He dragged the lawman into his vacated cell and secured the door on him, after carefully removing his six-gun. Slocum gave Denny a jaunty wave and started toward the office. He paused at the main egress to the cells and listened. No sound from beyond. He unlocked the door and eased into the outer room.

Slocum found it empty and quickly located his Peacemaker. Oddly enough, he found his saddle gun and the gear from his room stacked in a cupboard. Gathering it, he returned to the cellblock and locked the door behind him. Then he went to the rear door, opened it, and stepped through. Slocum secured it from the outside and started off along the alley.

Half a block from the jail, he tossed the keys into a rain barrel. Tension mounted in Slocum while he worked his way toward the livery on the south end of town. There were two in Canyon, the other serving the town from the west side. Slocum had paid for three days and now owed for two more. He was grateful, though surprised, to discover his money untouched. He'd been willing to bet Butcher had cleaned him out. Half a building length shy of a major cross street, Slocum pulled up short at the sound of voices.

"If I was him, I'd find a way to bust out of that jail and get clear the hell an' gone outta Texas." Slocum immediately recognized the voice of Pete Billingsley.

"Oh, Daddy, why would you want a think like that?"

"Because Butcher is determined to fit a rope around your friend Slocum's neck even if he has to buy witnesses to lie on the stand," Billingsley told his daughter.

"But he's the law," Clarissa protested with Eastern naïveté. "He's supposed to work within the rules."

"People like Butcher make their own rules. Or whoever owns him makes 'em for him," Billingsley snapped. "But enough of that. Let's find your Aunt Bertha and head back for the ranch."

Slocum waited in apprehension until their footfalls faded. Taking a deep breath, he stepped out of the mouth of the alley and crossed the street with a purposeful stride, looking neither right nor left. He breathed freely again when he entered the narrow sanctuary between two buildings.

At the livery, he paid the charges due, and added a five-dollar gold piece. "That is for you, if you have difficulty remembering I was ever here."

The elderly liveryman eyed Slocum levelly. "Hear you locked horns with Butcher. You ask me, he's as full of stuff as a Christmas goose. Anyone on the outs with him is all right by me. I never seen you, don't know nothin' about you. Y'all take care of yourself, hear?"

Grinning, Slocum rode off into the early morning with a lighter heart.

Slocum traveled south out of town, making no attempt to hide his tracks. He turned east a mile below Canyon and still left a clear trail. Two miles eastward, he turned north. He continued, leaving ample sign behind until he angled onto the road to Amarillo.

Careful to watch his backtrail, he proceeded along the main road, the marks left by Sugarloaf and the packhorse blending into those of other travelers, until he reached a bridge over a shallow creek. The plank floor left no trail to follow. On the far side, Slocum halted and dismounted. He led his animals to the bank of the stream and tied them off to a branch.

From a saddlebag, he took a curry comb and brush. With these, he meticulously rubbed out every mark left by horses or his own boots. At the water's edge, he urged Sugarloaf and the roan into the water, stepped in himself, and disrupted the remaining imprints. Satisfied, he put away the tools, mounted up, and continued southeastward toward the Prairie Dog Town Fork of the Red River.

His disappearing act, like that of the ghost rustlers, should have given fits to anyone in pursuit. Well aware of the danger of overconfidence, however, he remained in midstream until the creek joined the river. When he had estimated a mile's distance toward the mouth of Palo Duro Canyon, Slocum kneed his mount to the right-hand bank and up out of the water.

Slocum stopped the animals on a slanted rock slab. Dismounted again, he fished in his shirt pocket for his makings and rolled a quirley. He went through two hand-rolled brown tubes of Bull Durham, and then decided the creek bank had dried enough to wipe out the tracks in the mud.

In the saddle again, Slocum didn't have to think twice about his destination. Palo Duro Canyon waited straight ahead.

The Boss and the two men with him sat down at a table in the comfort of a back room of the Branding Iron saloon in Canyon. After a mustached and aproned waiter delivered a bottle of Old Overhold rye and three glasses, the Boss slammed his open palm on the table.

"Dammit, Slocum is gone. Totally disappeared. No one is to blame. He's clever, tricky, and dangerous. But I'll take care of that later this morning. To make matters worse, Butch Kelso is getting out of hand."

"You're right about that. First thing I heard this morning was that five more men had been killed last night. And a barn burned at the Lazy Y," the man to the Boss's left grumbled. "You don't keep people thinking they are fighting ghosts with things like that."

"He's nothing but a two-bit killer," the third man agreed. "I'd say he's doing things his way out of spite." He eyed the Boss accusingly.

"We agreed that I was to tell him to lay off on the killings. What he chose to do is out of my hands."

"Not necessarily," the second man pressed, palm raised to quell interruption. "We could arrange to have him removed."

The Boss sighed and studied his associates. "No. I think that simply jailing him for a short while ought to be lesson enough."

The others nodded agreement. They downed their drinks and rose to leave. The third man, closest to the door, spoke quietly on their decision. "I'll arrange for Kelso to be put back in the Happy jail."

A few minutes before eleven in the morning, Yates Harkness rode into Canyon. He called to men he knew and urged them to meet him in front of the sheriff's office. A crowd quickly gathered. When the numbers had increased sufficiently, Harkness stepped up on the boardwalk and raised his hands for quiet.

To an intent gathering, he revealed news that angered and surprised them. "Men, I've only learned something this morning I thought important enough to ride down here and tell you. The man that was held in this jail for the murder of Bob McClure, who escaped early this morning, I'm told, was one of your ghost rustlers."

"What do you mean, Yates?" a small-time rancher asked.

"I heard only today that he was a prisoner, and that he claimed to have had a meeting with McClure. He'd been posing as a cattle buyer. No doubt to size up herds for rustling. Bob obviously recognized him, and that was why he was killed. Now, I'm fightin' mad over this. I am offering a reward of a thousand dollars on this Slocum's head. Dead or alive."

A ragged cheer rose. Harkness raised his hands again to silence the crowd. "The money will be on deposit at the Farmers' and Drovers' Bank. A lot of you have good reason to get hands on this one. You might give that some thought, then gather your men and fan out across the country to find him."

"The sheriff's already sent out a posse," a town loafer commented.

"Yes, I know. And when I talked with him a moment ago, he agreed to organize and lead another one. Volunteers can step inside and be sworn. Five dollars a day, one meal and found for your horse."

With a shout, seven out-of-work cowboys rushed to join up. Smiling, Harkness refused any more questions and turned back inside the sheriff's office.

10

A hard fist slammed savagely into already bloodied lips. "You helped him, didn't you? That's not a question, it's a statement," Harlan Butcher growled as he readied to strike Everet Denny again.

"No, Sheriff, he did it on his own," Denny answered anyway.

Butcher dragged Denny up off his knees and sunk a hard blow to the stomach. Denny retched and gagged. "Ralph already told me about the snakes."

"I—I was seeing strange things, Sheriff. You know how I get sometimes. I was frothing at the mouth."

"Soap, you lying old booze bag." Butcher cocked a fist to hit him again.

Yates Harkness appeared in the doorway at the end of the corridor. "I want to see you a minute, Sheriff. Leave the old man alone."

"Now, dammit, I'm doing the best I can," Butcher protested. "I want to know where Slocum is headed."

Despite his pain, Everet Denny feigned an enlightenment. "Why didn't you say so, Sheriff? He . . . he said something about Amarillo."

"That checks out, Butcher," Harkness stated. "Randall is back with a message from the posse. He says they lost Slocum's trail on the road north to Amarillo."

"Are they going on?"

"Yes. That's why he came back, to let you know. Now, come out here, we have to talk."

Grumbling, Sheriff Butcher slammed Everet Denny back into the corner formed by bars and the outer wall. He relocked the cell and walked heavily toward his office. Something told him this would not be pleasant.

Thirty minutes later, he addressed the men of his second posse. "I'm not convinced Slocum is headed to Amarillo. He's too clever. There's no way he would leave such a clear trail, then suddenly disappear. We're going to fan out like those fellers lookin' to get Mr. Harkness's reward. We'll search everywhere but the road to Amarillo. And we'll do it carefully."

Slocum caught sight of the posse led by Sheriff Butcher in late afternoon of his first trip into the canyon. He had found nothing of significance. Only tracks. Evidently, he figured, cattle were being moved in and out of the Palo Duro on a regular, tight schedule. Given time enough, he could discover where and with whom the cattle took the next part of their journey. That should answer a lot of questions about the shadowy figures behind this large-scale operation.

He pursued those thoughts until he saw the fog of dust rising from the hooves of the posse. He cut south and rode far around the large band of men. At once his mind went to work on how he could discourage their interest in him.

Several possibilities presented themselves. He decided to wait until he got a better gauge of the men involved. An hour before sundown, the posse stopped and went into camp for the night outside the upper entrance to Palo Duro Canyon.

Careful study assured Slocum that most of his ideas held weight. Local cowhands and town loafers, he judged them to be. Not dedicated lawmen by any lights. Tonight, he decided, would be a good time for a little ghostly action of his own.

He withdrew to a secure place in a wash and waited until shortly after midnight. Then he rode to within a half mile of the camp. Ten minutes later, Slocum paused behind a creosote bush on the edge of the encampment. His eyes slid from side to side, to take in the layout of the bivouac and the sleeping posse. One point made itself clear. He had not encountered a single picket. Nor did any sentries ride around the camp on lookout. That would all change, he reasoned. Once he did what he had in mind, few, if any, of the men would sleep well for as long as the posse stayed out.

Satisfied that no one showed signs of wakefulness, Slocum eased down on all fours and worked his way at a sharp angle from his concealment to where he had observed the picket line to which the horses had been tethered.

Hairs on the back of his neck rose in response to the tension he felt when two animals whiffled softly and stamped their hooves in acknowledgment of his scent. Slocum sank into the darkness at the ground line. Not a one of the posse called out in response. Slowly, he edged forward, reached up, and stroked a velvet nose.

At once the horse gave a friendly, puppy-like wiggle. Slocum extended his other hand across the stretched lariat and patted another. Then he undid their halter ropes and moved along the line. The heavy aroma of horses filled his nostrils. Conscious of time passing, and with it the chance of discovery, Slocum worked a bit faster. He had to get them all to do the job right.

Finally he reached the end of the line and drew in a deep breath of cool night air in relief. Boots replaced by soft, silent moccasins, Slocum reversed his course and gathered in the trailing ends of the halter strings. With nerve-punishing slowness he began to walk away from the camp. With hardly an audible hoof clop, he guided the posse's mounts off into the prairie surrounding Palo Duro Canyon.

When he had gone the estimated half a mile to where he had left his mount, Slocum let free the first five horses and sent them off in the direction of Canyon with a slap on the rump of the rearmost. He continued on for a distance before releasing five more. Those he let get nearly out of sight before sending another five after them. With the remaining quintet, Slocum proceeded back to where he had left his own animals.

Mounted up, he set off at a slow walk through the wash, tracks of his two horses obliterated by those of the five following. When and if they recovered their mounts, Slocum thought with satisfaction, let them figure this one out.

Sheriff Harlan Butcher looked coldly at the bare picket line less than a minute after the discovery had been made. Slocum had left behind several headstalls, which added to the confusion. Some among the posse speculated on that basis that the animals had gotten free on their own.

"No," Butcher grated in a cold, hollow tone. "It was Slocum.

He's out there, watching us, laughing at us. I want him found, and fast."

"First we have to find our horses," a young cowhand along for the adventure lamented.

To Butcher it sounded like a wise remark. He fixed the offender with a cold stare. "You couldn't find your ass with both hands. I want the best trackers out there to bring in those critters. Men who can walk for a distance."

"*Walk!* I ain't walked anywhere since my poppa put me on a horse at age three," another drover protested.

"Without those horses, how do you propose to get out of here?" Butcher asked coldly. "Now, get to movin'."

It took till nearly noon to locate the first of the missing animals. With them in hand, the rest of the search went a bit easier. By late afternoon, all but two of the horses had been recovered. The disgruntled posse set to feeding them and grooming out cockleburs and thistles.

"What do we do now, Sheriff?" one man asked in a weary tone.

"We wait for Slocum to pull some other smart stunt."

True to Slocum's prediction, Sheriff Butcher assigned lookouts for the night to guard over the camp. They spent their shifts in bored inactivity. Slocum did not strike again. In fact, he came nowhere near the posse. After an unsatisfactory breakfast of coffee, beans, and biscuits, the volunteer lawmen set off in an attempt to locate the wanted man.

Slocum kept tabs on them from a safe distance. He had left hints of trail that had sent parties off in odd directions, reducing the strength of the main force. For the most part, the amature trackers remained baffled. At last he decided to let them get a glimpse of him.

Their reaction proved amazing. Shouting and goading their mounts to a gallop, three of them started out after Slocum while the fourth set off to rally the posse. That wasted more time, for Slocum led his nearest pursuers on a wild chase that ended in the Red River. By the time the riders closed on the bank, Slocum was out of sight inside Palo Duro Canyon.

Laughing softly to himself, he rubbed down Sugarloaf and the roan packhorse. Then he rolled out his blankets and sat cross-legged while he munched on a strip of jerky and a cold biscuit.

"Tonight," he said aloud softly, "will be a good time for another visit."

Once Slocum had decided on it, he couldn't keep the cold grin off his face. Men and horses alike tended to get plugged up after too long on dry food and scant water. In a soft pouch on the packsaddle, Slocum carried a small brown bottle, the contents of which worked equally well on men and their equine companions.

He would slip out of the canyon, wait for the opportune time, then sneak in and administer a dose of the powerful croton oil to the entire posse. First he would make the best of a few hours' sleep. Boots off, and socks over the open tops to keep out scorpions and other uninvited guests, Slocum lay back on his blanket, fingers laced behind his head.

A universe of stars filled the open gap of Palo Duro Canyon. Their distant, frosty light barely reached Slocum in the gorge. Their presence comforted and relaxed him. It did a man good, Slocum believed, frequently to spend a night like this, out under the hoary shimmer of those far-off points of light. Helped give an idea of how insignificant mere man turned out to be. Slowly new thoughts crowded into Slocum's head.

Memory of his marvelous night with Ginny Stuart created vividly arousing images. Her silken alabaster flesh in the moonlight, muscular haunches rippling with well-developed muscles in an attempt to match him thrust for thrust. A shiver of delight ran from the warmth in his crotch up his hard-flat belly.

Echoes of her voice came to him as clear as though she now whispered the words in his ear. "Harder, Slocum! Oh! Yes-s-s-s-s. I've held back too long."

And later, "This is marvelous, Slocum. Oh . . . oh . . . ooooh!" Her slender, full-busted body writhed atop him, erect nipples on her pert, nacreous breasts swaying with the powerful grinding of her pelvis against his.

Slocum's fingers found the valley between those active hillocks and gently traced a line down her agile torso to the small indentation of her navel. Ginny shivered with delight and drove harder into his upthrust. Fired by their mutual pleasure, pyrotechnics of ecstasy burst in Slocum's head.

Try as he might, he could not recall when he had been so driven. He didn't simply desire this lovely, rose-white-skinned young woman. He had longed for her without knowing her. Now he possessed her so utterly that their eager joining produced a euphoric blending of joy and haunting urgency that thirsted for more, rather than slaked need, when they at last joined in stupendous consummation.

He had thanked her, sincerely and effusively. Ginny responded in kind, then laughed, and cried, and they rekindled their passion, and surrendered to their wants . . . Slocum blinked and jerked his mind away. He would have to abandon that line of reflection if he was to get the rest he needed before paying another visit to the posse.

Slocum quickly located the sentries. The bottle of croton oil in his hip pocket, he approached the sleeping camp on his belly. "Think like the wolf and you become the wolf," an old Sioux war leader had told Slocum once. Now he thought like a snake. Head raised ever so slightly, he kept his eyes fixed on his target.

Careful control of his breathing let him make his approach unnoticed. After what seemed an eternity, Slocum lay beside the ring of stones that bordered the main cook fire. A large granite coffeepot rested on a cast-iron trivet. Tense and watchful, Slocum raised one hand to the lid. By calculated increments, he lifted the hinged cover and let it rest against the high, curved handle.

Slowly he brought forward the other hand. His strong, thick fingers released the lid and twisted the cork in the little brown bottle. It came free without a betraying squeak. Slocum's grin came back. With infinite care, he poured the entire contents of the bottle into the water already measured out for the next morning's coffee.

With the bottle back in his pocket, Slocum eased the coffeepot lid closed. Using all the stealth of his approach, he rose on his hands and knees and worked his way backward into the dark shadows that covered the edge of camp from overhanging paloverde trees, thick sage, and creosote bushes.

His breath carefully guarded, Slocum took half an hour to glide through the night to a safe spot beyond the unaware sentries. He picked a thick screen of scrub to settle in and watch developments. His grin remained pasted in place.

It began with the relieved sentries, who hit the coffeepot first. Slocum watched the process through field glasses, still smiling, the strains of a light tune threading through his mind. Within half an hour, the last night riders began to exhibit discomfort. Shortly followed by the earliest risers. "Time travels in divers paces with divers persons . . . ," Slocum thought, amused, and wished he could remember the source of the quote. Could it be Shakespeare? Probably. He dismissed the thought as he observed the mass exodus of the posse into the surrounding bushes, to relieve the incredibly demanding pressures within them.

When, with a frantic wail and a curse, Sheriff Butcher succumbed to the power of the croton oil, Slocum roused himself. "Bet they'll not drink much coffee for a while," he said to the pale blue sky. Bent double, he trotted off over a low rise and to the paloverde tree where he had tied his stallion.

Slocum knew the odds. Sooner or later, he would make a slip, alert a less-stupid sentry or awaken someone in the posse's camp. Four men left the sheriff's group following the croton oil incident. That helped, yet those who remained became doubly alert. Slocum decided on one last strike. To do so, he waited until well after midnight.

An hour went by with every sense heightened, attuned to the men around him. Slocum crawled into the edge of the camp. After a careful inspection of the changes that his earlier intrusions had inspired, he decided on a change of targets. Where before the men hunting him had spread out, each to a place that might offer comfort and a bit of privacy, now they placed their blankets close together.

Close enough, Slocum suspected, that any approach by him would be detected immediately, with disasterous results. Butcher had wisely added a sentry on the picket line after the horses had been driven off. Slocum eased over to where he could study the man presently on duty.

Fatigue had dropped a velvet hammer on the head of the

gangly cowboy who guarded the picket line. He sat against the trunk of a bristlecone pine which served as a base for the tightly stretched rope to which the horses had been tied. His head had canted backward and rested against the resinous bark. Mouth open, he snored softly, oblivious to everything around.

Perfect, Slocum thought. He eased his way closer. Earlier in the evening, Slocum had used his Barlow pocketknife to fashion a brush from a willow limb. The rabbit he had snared for his supper had provided an ample supply of blood, now in the bottle that had originally held the croton oil. Conscious even of his increased heartbeat, Slocum closed in on his intended victim.

When he reached the right position, to one side, partly hidden by the tree trunk, he took the bottle from his pocket and gave it a gentle shake. Next he slid the brush from his vest, dipped it into the rabbit blood, and applied the swab to the neck of the dozing posseman. With a feather-light touch, Slocum painted in a thin line from up under the man's left ear toward his chin.

"Unn-mumph!" the snoozing guard mumbled in reaction to the vague sensation of tickling.

Slocum waited expectantly. With another grunt, the sentry slipped back into slumber. Slocum painted on. Twice more he had to hold himself rock-still when his application threatened to rouse the sleeping man. At last, satisfied with his handiwork, which included a few downward trickles as a finishing touch, Slocum stoppered the bottle and, as a final gesture of harassment, loosed a dozen horses from the picket line. Then he began his tedious withdrawal.

He removed himself from the camp without incident. Only another quarter mile and he would be in the safety of an arroyo. Sheriff Butcher had kept the posse on the move each day after recovering their horses, and had picked this spot for their overnight stop. One Slocum viewed as highly advantageous. He had only the sentries riding around the camp to elude and all would be well. That's when Fate turned her face away from John Slocum.

"Hey, what the hell are you doing prowlin' around out here?" a gruff voice demanded from Slocum's left.

Slocum had no choice. He filled his hand with the Colt in a smooth draw and settled the sights high for a deliberate miss. Bright white filled his range of vision, swiftly fading to yellow-orange as the muzzle blast dwindled. The slug traveled the intended path, yet still managed to clip the tall peak hat from the camp guard's head.

"Jesus, I'm dead," he blurted in disorganized shock.

Slocum had expected the shot to startle the freed animals, which it did. It also awakened the drowsing sentry, who felt a wetness on his throat and reached up and touched it while he came to his feet. His fingers came away darkly stained, and believing his throat to have been cut, he began to scream hysterically.

Pandemonium broke out in the encampment. Horses bolted and thundered in every direction. Men shouted and fired blindly into the night. Slocum ran forward, yanked the benumbed sentry from his saddle, and slammed a fist into the vulnerable spot at the hinge of his jaw. The man went slack.

Keeping low, Slocum sped off into the night on foot. Behind him, he heard the bull bellow of Sheriff Harlan Butcher.

"Gawdammit! Gawdammit! That's enough."

11

Shortly after daylight, five men left the encampment. An hour later, the entire remaining posse pulled out. Slocum watched them from a small knoll three miles away. When his observations satisfied him that they would continue on to Canyon, he set off on his own affairs.

Slocum had been given the name of a reliable man in the Canyon area by Captain Jack Arnold of the Cattlemen's Association. He took his bearings and headed southwest toward the Bar-C ranch of Carl Hartson.

Hartson himself greeted Slocum when the lanky, dark-haired loner rode up to the main house. "Good to make your acquaintance, Slocum," Hartson stated sincerely after the introductions. "May I ask what brings you to the Bar-C?"

The time for dissembling had come to an end, Slocum decided. He produced the small leather folder and showed Hartson his badge. "I'm the man sent by the Association to look into these rustlings."

"Hummm," Hartson returned. "You are also a man with a price on your head."

"You knew that when I gave my name?"

"Yes, I did. As it happens, I take anything Harlan Butcher puts around with a large hunk of salt." Hartson chuckled softly.

"How about Yates Harkness?" Slocum probed.

"He's a solid Association man, or so it seems. Of late, I've been more than curious about his involvement with Butcher."

"He was supposed to meet with me and Bob McClure in Canyon when I took on this assignment," Slocum revealed.

"I . . . see. And now he's put a price on your head, knowing who you are?"

"So it would seem."

"Tell me about Bob McClure," Hartson challenged.

Slocum told all he knew of the murder of Bob McClure. He added that he had seen nothing of Harkness. "Of course," he concluded, "I got knocked out the minute I walked into the office, so he might have been there."

"Story I heard was he had been called to a meeting in Amarillo and didn't arrive until the next day."

"Do you have reason to doubt that?" Slocum asked.

"Not . . . particularly. In any case, I'm going to trust you. I'll provide any help you need. I know Cap'n Jack Arnold. He don't make no mistakes."

"I appreciate that," Slocum said with a release of tension. "First off, what I'd like is for you to detail enough hands to keep watch on the roads out of Canyon. Butcher's due to visit the smaller towns, and I want word on which direction he takes when he leaves."

"You've got that, and anything else. You're free to make the Bar-C your headquarters for as long as you need, Slocum."

A day passed during which nothing happened. It did give Slocum time to pick his way through the contradictions and unanswered questions that had plagued him from the start. The earliest ones, concerning the ghost rustlers, Slocum set aside until he stumbled up against a recurring fact.

No matter where his trail led the posse, regardless of any provocation, Sheriff Butcher had never taken his volunteers into Palo Duro Canyon. He had, in fact, kept them well clear of the entrance. Butcher had shown up in the Association office only moments before Slocum had regained consciousness. His fabrication of what the evidence indicated would have been laughed out of even a biased court. At the time, Slocum had considered Butcher stupid, or woefully untrained. Now he began to wonder. What he worked out surprised even him.

If someone were to have asked right then, Slocum would have stated with confidence that the sheriff was involved with the rustlers. And why not? He had known bent lawmen before. Everet Denny's background on Butcher and Yates Harkness lent credence to the theory. Provided the old ex-professor could be believed about Harkness backing Butcher in the election, his information implied some involvement by the rancher in the present scheme.

Slocum gladly abandoned such troublesome speculation when a Bar-C rider ran into the headquarters with word that Sheriff Butcher had left town, headed toward Happy. Slocum heard him out then extended a big hand to his host.

"Thank you for all you've done. I may need help later. There's a lot of these rustlers. More than any one man can handle."

"You can count of us at any time," Carl Hartson assured him. "Hell, they done stole my herd. I'm ithcin' to get hands on them."

With Sugarloaf and the roan packhorse made ready, Slocum left the Bar-C ten minutes later.

Sheriff Harlan Butcher turned the key in the steel-clad lock of the Happy jail. "I'm letting you go, Kelso. I hope your time in jail has convinced you to take it easy out there."

"All it's done is make me antsy."

"You're to make yourself scarce around town. That's an order. The Boss wants you to lay low."

Kelso rubbed his palms together in anticipation. "Least I hear you've got that Slocum locked up in Canyon. I think now's a good time to find that snotty slip of a girl and teach her some manners," he muttered darkly.

"Slocum has escaped from the Canyon jail. We think he's on to something. That's why the Boss wants you to keep clear of town. Slocum's likely to come back here."

"I'll take care of that problem, too," Kelso said with a sneer.

"Enough of that. Your mouth is too loose and it could be shut permanently."

"To hell with that, an' to hell with you. Me an' a couple of the boys can fix Slocum's hash. You wait and see." Still grumbling, Kelso left the jail.

Sheriff Butcher gazed after Kelso and scratched his head. He'd had a similar thought and could not pin Slocum down with over fifty bounty-hungry men hunting for him.

Late that night, Ginny Stuart walked home alone from the Virginia House as usual. She had only entered and removed her bonnet and gloves when a soft rap came at the back door. At once uneasy, she went to the drawer of a small side table and opened it. From it she removed a small Smith and Wesson .32 revolver. The little tilt-top, five-shot weapon held tightly in her right hand, she went to the door.

"Who is it?" she asked cautiously.

"John."

At first she didn't make the connection. Then, face alight, she threw open the door and flung her arms wide. "Slocum! Come here," she invited.

After a long embrace, Ginny caught her breath to say, "I was so worried. Everyone's heard about the killing in Canyon and that you were arrested."

"Let me close this door and I'll tell you what happened," Slocum offered.

That accomplished, they walked arm in arm into the darkened parlor. Ginny directed them to a plushly upholstered Queen Ann love seat and settled on one cushion. She made no offer to light a lamp, much to Slocum's relief. He sat beside her and pulled the leather folder from his pocket.

"I'm sure you realize I am not a cattle buyer." At Ginny's silent nod, he opened the cover and revealed his badge, then went on. "Actually, I am a range detective for the Cattlemen's Association."

Ginny's eyes widened. "That's a Ranger badge."

"Yes, it is."

"Slocum, if you have the authority of a Texas Ranger, why didn't you show the sheriff your badge when he arrested you for killing that poor man?"

"Good question, Ginny. I didn't because I have good reason to suspect that Sheriff Butcher is involved with the rustlers." Quickly, sparing no detail, Slocum explained the events since he left Happy and tied them in as best he could to what had gone on before.

"What do you do now?" Ginny pressed, excitement lighting her face.

"I would like to stay out of sight here, in your house. I want time to find out if what else I suspect is correct."

"Of course. You are welcome as long as you want to stay."

A pout formed on her pretty lower lip. "Only . . . that hug was nice, but I think I deserve a kiss."

"You do," Slocum said with a grin. "And you'll get one, too, once you put that gun away."

A stricken expression crossed Ginny's face in the twilight of the room. In a rustle of cooking-odor-scented skirts, she roused herself and returned the .32 Smith to its drawer. Then, with a pirouette, she rushed to Slocum's arms.

Their kiss began firmly, if a bit distantly, then rapidly grew in fervor. The second left Ginny gasping. She felt Slocum's big, hard hand on her buttocks and the insistent probing of his tongue during the third.

"I want you, Slocum. Oh, how badly I want you," Ginny panted when it ended.

"Do you? I was afraid it was only my imagination, reading my own feelings into how I remembered you."

Effortlessly he lifted her off her feet and, at her direction, carried her to the bedroom. Ginny moaned softly as Slocum bared her shoulders and planted quick, light kisses on her exposed flesh. She shivered with anticipation as he worked the dress further off her supple body.

Slocum vibrated with desire, fully tumescent and ready for the amorous contest. He left Ginny to the finer details of removing her undergarments while he shucked his vest and laid it aside. His shirt came next, pulled off over his head. Ginny paused, sighed contentedly, and laid her cheek against his bare chest. Her soft, sweet breath stirred the patch of hair between his nipples.

Nimbly, Slocum undid his cartridge belt and laid it beside the kerosene lamp on the nightstand. He sat on the bed, which creaked alarmingly, and removed his boots. He stood to remove his trousers, and Ginny came into his arms again. Her bare, erect nipples, surrounded by large, dark areolas, pressed into him and set off tendrils of delightful sensation.

"Oh, hurry, Slocum," she pleaded as she found him firm and aroused. "The last time, you awakened something in me that I thought dead and forgotten. Now I can't stand to be without you."

She directed him to the warm, wet patch at the juncture of her thighs. With a determined thrust, he entered her. Together, they fell laughing onto the bed. Slow waves of euphoria washed over them as they adjusted their movements to mirror each other. Slocum's spirit quickened as he thrust in gentle yet urgent penetration. Ginny sighed and wrapped her arms around him.

With the inevitable conclusion in mind, the ecstatic pair toiled away in fiery pursuit of oblivion. Each gave with total abandon. In their joyful surrender they found the ultimate pleasure. Friction became thrilling caress.

"Oh, my, yes," Ginny sighed. "Now's the time, now. Give me all of you."

Gently Slocum rolled Ginny onto her back and increased the angle of his lunges, lengthening and exerting more power. Ginny squealed softly in response. The wallpaper behind the bed seemed to blur and swim in Slocum's eyes. With careful control, he stayed the course, pulled Ginny along from one rapturous peak to another, and at last crashed through the barrier of mortality into the warm fulfillment of a perfect joining.

Slocum panted and swallowed hard, then lay beside Ginny in her bed. Each encased in private thoughts, they studied the ceiling in silence. At last, Ginny spoke, in a tiny, dreamy voice.

"You know something? I think I could go for that again."

"Tell you what," Slocum responded softly. "I *know* I could."

Ginny left him long before dawn, and Slocum awakened to pleasant, warm memories of their night. After ten minutes of contemplating the ceiling, he roused himself, shaved, and dressed. Anger flared in Slocum for a moment when he thought of why he had been unable to escort Ginny to the Virginia House or even to eat breakfast there. Then he saw a note on her pillow.

"Love you," it read. "Breakfast is in the warming oven. Just slide it in and the coals should do the rest. Ginny."

Smiling, Slocum went back to the kitchen. In the overhead warmer of the Acme cooking range, he found a stoneware plate on which were a thick slab of ham, a puddle of grits, potatoes, and three biscuits. A note propped beside it read, "You'll have to fry your own eggs."

Slocum filled up on the ample meal and then fretted through the morning. He wanted to be out, doing something. He needed to make some positive link between Sheriff Butcher and the rustlers. He had a score of wants and needs. Ginny came home in mid-afternoon.

"The pies are baking," she announced first off. "I'll bring you some when I close."

"How do you know there will be any left?" Slocum teased.

Ginny's eyes sparkled. "I'll set some aside." Then her brow clouded. "Another herd was stolen last night. I wasn't going to say anything, but I suppose you need to know these things."

"Yes. Everything has some meaning. The trouble comes in figuring out what."

"Did you expect the rustling to begin again?"

It was Slocum's turn to frown. "Yes. The sheriff no sooner settles in than the ghost rustlers hit another herd close by. It's my guess it works that way so he can conveniently misdirect any search for the cattle thieves."

"What do you do know?"

"I think that rather than trailing another stolen herd, I should work the other way around. They seem to move the stock in and out of Palo Duro Canyon rather quickly. That means they have to be present from time to time, and I can follow them to their hideout. Maybe learn who is running the show."

"That sounds dangerous," Ginny suggested.

"It can be. I'll look out for myself, be sure of that. But I'm afraid I'll miss out on that pie. I need to leave right after sundown."

"You're no fun," Ginny said and pouted. Then tears sprang to her eyes. "Be careful, Slocum."

"I will."

Fifteen men, led by Butch Kelso, rode through the saddle between two truncated sandstone buttes, called mesas throughout the Spanish-Mexican Southwest. Ahead lay the vast, unfenced acres of the upper range of Chance Darlington's Rocking D ranch. Darlington was well known to his fellow Texas ranchers.

A big, bluff man, with a firm handshake and a broad smile

for everyone who treated him square, as he treated others, Chance Darlington had built an empire. He had so many grazing pastures and so large a crew that no one believed he stood any chance of being hit by the ghost rustlers. In actuality, it took less than half an hour for Kelso and his gang to strip Darlington of seven hundred prime head.

At Kelso's direction, the rustlers spread out wide and closed in on the herd from three directions. That left only one way for the alarmed cattle to go. Most of Darlington's cowhands were roped from behind or knocked off their horses with blows from rifle butts. Inevitably, some of the others realized what was happening.

Butch Kelso killed the first one as he drew his weapon. Two more, severely wounded, fell from their horses before the cows began to run. Driven by the shocking noise of firearms discharging, the stream of cattle soon exploded into a stampede. Shrieking, a rustler's horse went down in front of the panicked animals, and better than a thousand hooves turned man and mount into a muddy pulp. Bellowing steers covered their death cries. Bolting about frantically, the desperate stock ground the turf into powder and sent clouds of dust into the sky. All the while, Kelso's gang worked desperately to contain the undirected flight.

One of the rustlers lost his race with death when a nine-hundred-pound steer crashed sideways into the legs of the hooded rider's horse and the pain-crazed mount crashed to the ground on top of its passenger. Kelso spotted this and turned back.

Desperately he tried to extricate the dead man from under his horse. Horns and hooves flashed dangerously close to him, but Kelso knew he daren't leave the man behind to be identified. Slowly the body began to slide on the pebbly ground. Kelso swallowed hard, glanced nervously at the slash of horns, and yanked again.

Legs flexed, he gave another heave and pulled his man free. Kelso slung the bleeding body over the rump of his own mount and stepped into the saddle. Quickly he trotted away from the threat of the maddened herd. Two men dead, he thought in anger. In less than five minutes, he noticed that they had ridden to the east of the twin mesas.

"Time to calm 'em down," he yelled at a rope-swinging outlaw who cantered past.

"Right, Boss."

Word passed quickly, and those at the head of the bovine river slackened the pace. Confused in the darkness, the rearmost animals continued to run full tilt. They rammed into the hindquarters of those ahead and stumbled to a gentler gait. Gradually the terror subsided in the dim brains of the cattle, and they forgot why they had started to run in the first place. Content to be carried along with the rest of the herd, some on the fringes began to dip their heads and snatch up tufts of grass with their tombstone-size teeth. Kelso called a strategy meeting with Ollie Utting and Yancy Hake.

"We have to divide the herd into three parts. Each of us will take one, and the first one in drives on to the furthest side canyon. This time I want some effort made to hide the tracks of the herd."

"Are you kidding? Six–seven hundred woolly-faces and we're going to hide their trail?" Utting brayed. "With what? A road maintainer?"

Kelso bristled, and snapped back, "If you need to. They're going out of the canyon tomorrow night. So do what you have to. We don't want Rocking D hands camping out at the mouth of the canyon waiting for us."

"What are you gonna be doing, Butch?" Hake asked.

"Me? I've got me a little entertainment planned. Once you two get those critters bedded down, come on down to Happy and join me. But first give me time to fix that Ginny Stuart."

12

Slick Bennett set aside the beer schooner he was wiping dry and sighed heavily. A frown clouded his wide, generous features, and his fat walrus mustache wobbled in agitation. He had heard, as had everyone in town, that the sheriff had released Kelso from the jail, on condition he was barred from town. Now here he was, big as life, walking into the Prairie Queen.

"Gimme a bottle, Slick," Kelso grunted.

"You're barred from Happy, Kelso," the big, usually jolly proprietor of the saloon declared flatly. Sweat had sprung into existence over the large bald spot on the top of his head.

Kelso's icy-gray eyes narrowed and he rolled his thick shoulders. "That ain't none of your business, Slick. You're here to sell whiskey an' that's what I want. I got the money to pay for it. So hop to it." The menace radiated in his voice.

Slick Bennett thought of pointing out the sign behind the bar that announced, "We reserve the right to refuse service to anyone." But he had seen Kelso on the prod often enough to decide against that. Sighing—he seemed to be sighing more than usual during the nearly four months Butch Kelso had been in town—Slick Bennett turned to the backbar and selected a lable-less bottle of cheap bourbon and a fish-eye shot glass.

"Lucy workin' tonight?" Kelso asked when Bennett set down the liquor.

"Maybe later," Slick informed him. "She's got moon problems," he elaborated.

Kelso made a face. "It seems like that girl has her curse every time I come in here. A feller would figger that often an' she'd bleed to death."

Bennett's mustache worked sinuously. "I wouldn't know. That'll be eight dollars."

Kelso dropped a five and a three-dollar gold piece on the table. They rang musically. The hard money made a slight difference in Bennett's attitude. "You expectin' company, Mr. Kelso?"

"Might be. If not tonight, tomorrow maybe."

"You got in sorta late tonight. What say I rustle you up a bowl of stew?"

Kelso eyed Bennett. "Antelope or buff?"

Bennett smiled. "Neither. It's that Mex pork stew with the green chilis."

For the first time since he had left the stolen cattle, Kelso smiled. "Sounds tasty. Why don't you do that? An' bring a stack of them tortillas." Kelso mispronounced the word *tore-till-ahs*. "Some o' that red sauce, too."

Nodding, Bennett backed away from the table. In the small kitchen behind the partition that divided the saloon from the storage area and office, Bennett stoked up a small cookstove and ladled stew into a serving-size pot. From a stack covered by a thick, damp cloth, he selected six flour tortillas and tossed them two-deep on stove lids. Every morning, a Mexican lady from town prepared the daily free lunch buffet here.

It consisted of cold roast beef, ham, pickled pig's feet, cheeses, onion slices, pickles, and hardboiled eggs. Homemade bread, fresh every other day, and a pot of special-recipe mustard completed the spread, with, of course, beans. The Prairie Queen attracted the largest drinking lunch crowd of any of the three saloons, and on paydays rivaled the Virginia House.

Slick Bennett took particular pride in that. Which heightened his sense of uneasiness whenever Butch Kelso entered the saloon. He remembered the night Kelso had beaten hell out of French Jack Beaumont. That had claimed three tables and four chairs, not to mention the large, paint-edged window on the left side of the door. Perhaps, considering the sheriff's orders, Bennett thought hopefully, nothing unfortunate would happen this visit.

On Slocum's third night in Palo Duro Canyon, he finally made contact with a stolen herd heading out of the canyon. The full moon had been waning over the past week and now showed only half of its face. Long, dark shadows put bars across the wide, well-traveled trail along the south bank of the Red River. The cattle moved along peacefully through tranquil surroundings. Slocum heard them before he saw the animals ambling along under the direction of three herders.

The point men wore flour-sack hoods over their faces, Slocum noted when they drew nearer. Slocum crouched low over the neck of his horse, screened by a stand of paloverde trees. His keen hearing picked up a muffled thud from the rustlers' animals as they moved. Peering into the darkness, Slocum made out misshapen blobs where usually slender hocks and smooth hornlike hooves could be seen.

Sacking. That's how they did it, Slocum realized instantly. No tracks, little sound. A steady stream of mixed longhorns and brindle Herefords moved past Slocum's hidden position. Unable to move without revealing himself, he made a careful count. He had tallied seventy-five head when he discovered how the rustlers kept their activities hidden from Charlie Goodnight's riders.

A four-span team pulled a large, chisel-toothed harrow along in the wake of the cattle. It ripped and tore away any sign of tracks. Behind it came half a dozen riders. Large clumps of brush had been dallied to their saddle horns by lariats. That wiped out the regular lines of the harrow.

Someone had put a lot of thought into this, Slocum speculated, with grudging admiration for the genius it represented. He would trail along and see where the livestock were taken for sale. He might even get lucky and identify the buyer. That could bring an end to the entire fantastic scheme.

Resigned to a long wait and a longer night, Slocum dismounted and hunkered down to give the herd time to get safely out of sight. After an estimated twenty minutes, he stepped into the saddle and edged Sugarloaf out onto the trail. At a slow walk, he headed his mount toward the upper mouth of Palo Duro Canyon.

When Slocum rounded the last curve, he came face-to-face with a herd of cattle coming *into* the canyon. Surprise registered on his face a moment before one of the point riders spotted him.

"What the hell!" the masked man blurted. "Who's that?"

"Don't know, but he don't belong here. Get him!" a second rustler declared.

Neither man wanted to fire a shot; the cattle behind them would easily stampede. They came at Slocum silently, one shaking out a loop in the lariat he held in his right hand. Slocum had little choice but to turn and run. Back in the canyon eight or ten miles was the Goodnight ranch. He reasoned that the rustlers would not pursue him that far.

His brindle mount had made a single great jump and lined out in a fast trot when Slocum's ears picked out the swish of a rope and the loop settled over his shoulders. Snapped tight around his upper arms, the lariat yanked him from the saddle.

He hit hard and rolled. The rustlers closed in on him with grim determination. He had no choice but his Colt. Arms free from the elbow down, Slocum moved his hand to the grips of the Peacemaker at his hip. The long barrel of the .45 came free with a smooth pull, and he shoved the muzzle toward the nearest night rider.

The rope jerked violently and threw off his aim. The slug went high and wide. Fighting for his life, Slocum switched targets and put a round low in the belly of the man who had roped him. A banshee scream came from the wounded rustler, and his horse set off without direction.

Slocum found himself stretched out full length on the trail, dragged along by the slowly trotting horse. In a desperate situation, Slocum had to do something and had to decide fast. He could shoot the horse, but had little chance of killing it with a single bullet. Any more speed would make it impossible for Slocum to save himself.

With both hands usable, Slocum chose another course. He groped for his big sheath knife with his left hand, while his right still tightly clutched the Colt. It took more of his rapidly waining strength than he expected to pull the blade free. Quickly he brought his arm forward and slashed at the braided strands of the lariat.

They parted with agonizing slowness. First one, then a second, third, fourth cut through. The fifth and last kept him bounding painfully over the ground. Small stones bruised and gouged at Slocum's body. He bit back a sharp cry when an upturned snag ripped the hide along the right side of his rib cage.

Then the keen edge of his Bowie severed the final twist of hemp. Bounding heels over head, Slocum rolled off the trail and into the brush. Gasping, he sheathed the knife and holstered his .45. Then he heard an ominous rumble, that grew louder with each second.

Behind him, the two shots in rapid succession had spooked the herd. In a swirling instant they broke into a frightened, bawling run. While Slocum blinked to steady his whirling head, the stampede thundered toward him. His eyes focused at last—on the flashing horns of the maddened cattle, headed directly toward him.

Butch Kelso sat drinking in the Prairie Queen with Yancy Hake and Johnny Tulip. They had been drinking since they entered to partake of the free lunch at noon. Darkness filled the streets of Happy, Texas. Small pools of yellow light splashed the intersections indifferently. The boys would be moving that last gather from the Rocking D. Within three days they would be on their way to the stockyards at Chicago.

What a place that must be, Kelso thought with longing. Fancy food, fancy liquor, fancy women. Yeah, that's what he needed. A fancy woman. A whole passel of fancy women. He'd roll his face between big, creamy breasts, smell the sweet scent of a woman in heat, wallow in their sweaty arms, their legs clamped around his hips.

"By god, I gotta get me a fancy woman," Kelso announced to the table.

Hake peered at him with bloodshot eyes. "Ain't much to pick from around here," he observed.

"That's for sure," Johnny Tulip agreed, leaned back in his chair to ease the pain in his healing side. His beady eyes, red-rimmed and of indeterminate color, wavered as they tracked a rising smoke ring from the quirley in Hake's full lips.

"Sure there is," Kelso contradicted. "We've got us a real prime specimen right here in town."

"Oh? Who?" Hake asked, sucked on the hand-rolled cigarette, and blew another ring.

"That Ginny Stuart, that's who," Kelso stated in a challenge.

"Yer crazy, Butch," Johnny Tulip blurted. "She'll take that Greener to you sure's I'm sittin' right here."

Butch Kelso produced a sly expression. "Not with what I've got in mind."

"You'd best get shut of that idea, Butch," Tulip went on. "We've got the sheriff hot at us as it is. He might take a serious look at doin' what he said."

Scorn curled Kelso's thick lips. His ice-gray eyes burned with a special light. "That shotgun don't walk her home," he brayed. "But I figger I just might do so tonight. What time is it?"

Hake looked at the octagonal face of the Monitor clock behind Kelso. "Comin' on eight-thirty."

"Hummm. Another half hour." Kelso poured another shot of whiskey. "What you think, boys? You think ol' Butch ain't got enough charm for a right proper lady like our Ginny?"

You've got as much charm as the north end of a southbound buffalo, Yancy Hake wanted to tell Butch Kelso. Wisely, he refrained. "You've got charm, right enough, Butch. You could charm the birds down outta the trees."

"Go on, Yancy!" Butch barked. "I let you boys rag me because I like you. No call to heap the table high with cow plop." He grinned, revealing large, crooked, yellowed teeth. He reached for the bottle again.

"You drink much more of that panther piss an' you won't be able to get it up," Johnny Tulip observed.

Kelso scowled at him. "Speak for yourself, pencil prick. Ain't been a jug uncorked that kept me from ridin' tall in the saddle. I remember the time when I was ridin' with the Doolins. We come up on this whole stagecoach full of soiled doves. Real special gals they was. On their way to Denver. Well, we didn't make much outta the strongbox, but we sure took it out in trade."

"What's that got to do with drinkin' too much?" Yancy Hake asked, eyes squinted against the tendril of smoke from his quirley.

"There was a whiskey drummer on board, too. He had ten cases of first-class likker on top of the coach. We drunk 'em dry and kept takin' turns on the drabs."

Johnny Tulip nodded knowingly. "An' the more you drank the better they looked, right?"

Kelso shot him a one-eyed glare. "What d'you know about it? You weren't there."

"No, but I've been through that before. You go into a saloon and some hatchet-faced painted lady, stout as a potbellied stove, hangs on your arm and asks if you want to go upstairs. Take a shot and she looks a little better than your momma's milk cow. Take a couple more and she's right attractive." By then, Kelso and Hake were laughing loudly, holding their sides as they rocked to and fro. "After a couple more she's the most beautiful woman in the world. Until—until you wake up the next morning and get a good look at her."

"I take it back, Johnny. I take it all back. You've got the right of it, boy," Butch Kelso said and chortled. "Hoo-wee, I ain't laughed this much in three months."

Kelso poured drinks around, and they settled into spinning stories about barroom encounters with the hard-faced working women of Texas, Kansas, and points beyond. Their jawing session lasted far too long for Butch Kelso to carry out his plan for Ginny Stuart, who went home alone, as usual, unharmed and unthreatened.

Slocum drew and fired the moment he recognized his peril. A fourth shot veered the leader of the crazed cattle slightly. The fifth and final round sent them more surely onto the trail. Swiftly, Slocum opened the loading gate and began to shuck empty casings. With each he replaced a fresh .45 cartridge. He had the third in the chamber when the swelling bulge of the animals behind the leaders reached him.

They loomed tall and dark over him. Certain he would die any instant, Slocum spun the cylinder and snapped the hammer to full cock. He fired rapidly, twice. The nearest animals jinked to one side. The last round came under the hammer. The dust-filled air in front of Slocum turned white, and he felt the buck of the Colt a moment before a hoof slammed into his head and blackness swept over him.

Slocum awakened to a world of pain. Also to a brightness that burned through closed eyelids. Any movement of his head exploded new agony behind his forehead and down his neck. His mouth gave the impression that the stampede had run through it. Joltingly he recalled the last desperate minutes before he had lost consciousness.

He had clashed headlong into the herd he had been following. No, that could not be right. His dizzy mind fumbled. *Another* herd, this one headed in. That made sense. The harrow could do double duty, covering tracks both ways. Now that he had that worked out, Slocum urged his reluctant body, he had better do something about his present condition.

Slocum decided to open his eyes. At first it hurt as if slivers of steel rammed into his skull. Slowly the agony subsided, his vision cleared, and he saw the distant, multicolored wall of the Palo Duro. He had been booted into the brush by the cattle. That had saved his life two ways.

It provided a barrier to steer the panicked livestock away from where he lay. Also, the greasewood and sage had hidden him from the rustlers who accompanied the stolen beeves. Groaning, Slocum raised himself to his elbows. The canyon swam around him.

He filled his lungs with a deep breath and discovered a severely bruised back. Only then did he become conscious that he had lost his hat. Thirst taunted him. His head throbbed, and as his strength grew, he freed one hand to explore this source of his most severe discomfort. He felt a crusty patch, like packed sand, and worked gingerly around its edges. His fingers came away smeared with crimson.

A good kick in the head, Slocum evaluated. At least it beat the possibility of taking a foot or more of wicket horn. No chance of trailing the herd that had left the canyon, he thought as he reclined on his elbows and forearms and let a hint of renewed vigor seep back into his tormented body. For that matter, he needed his horse to do anything constructive.

That included getting himself cleaned up and patched. He felt up to taking a more thorough inventory. His vest had been slashed and abraded by the dragging he had endured, as had his shredded shirt. Red welts and scabbed-over scrapes stood out on Slocum's chest and belly. His rib cage heaved and his consciousness threatened to flee when he forced himself upright on his knees.

When he steadied down, he could see over the screen of brush. Sugarloaf grazed calmly on a tuft of grass not far away. The animal held its left hind foot off the ground and stood in a hip-shot manner. Suppressing a groan, Slocum levered himself upright.

Thought of water, to ease the torment of his parched throat, compelled him onward. He limped as he walked. The tattered remnants of his hat came into view on the trail side of the wall of brush. He stooped to retrieve it with a wry expression. Sugarloaf whiffled familiarly as he approached. His clawed, dirty hands closed on the canteen slung on the skirt of the horse's saddle.

Slocum opened the cap and pressed it shakily to his lips. He gulped greedily, and the constrictions of his throat matched the awful throbbing in his head. His gnawing dryness assuaged for the moment, he turned his attention to the animal's upraised hoof.

A thorough, gentle examination soon gave Slocum the worst news. His mount had pulled a tendon. He now faced the possibility of being discovered by the rustlers with a crippled horse. His chances of getting safely away from the canyon had been severely reduced.

13

"We have to run them back and get every head in that canyon," Ollie Utting said with a curse.

"Hell of it is we haven't a lot of time. It's already daylight. We might be seen by some of Goodnight's crew," Griffin Quinn replied in a low voice, leery of rekindling the panic among the steers they had rounded up.

"It's a chance we have to take," Utting persisted. "If we get spotted by any of Goodnight's hands, we just have to take them out."

"Oh, no," Quinn protested. "You get Charlie Goodnight riled up, you've got trouble. He has forty hands. Most of them good with a gun."

Utting considered by how much they would be outnumbered and nodded with a grim expression in place. "All right. Keep the boys pushing these critters along. The closer we come to the canyon, the less chance, there'll be of being caught out."

Two more of the rustling gang rumbled in, a dozen more head pushed before them. Utting nodded, and his frown smoothed into a bright sun squint. Given another half hour, they should have all of the stock back. Another problem tugged at his mind.

Who was the man in the canyon? What had he been doing there? One of his crew shot and no trace of the one who had done it. None of it added up. Then he recalled talk about the cattle buyer, Slocum, who was supposed to have killed McClure and escaped from the Canyon jail.

It might . . . It just might be him. If so, Utting reasoned, he would not be likely to report anything to the law. No, not at all. That left only the riders for Goodnight's spread to worry about. Satisfied, he turned aside to pop some more brush for strays.

• • •

Slocum retrieved his packhorse from a small draw in the canyon. Keeping alert to the possible presence of the rustlers, he proceeded southeast through the canyon, toward the Goodnight ranch. He had bound the game leg, yet Sugarloaf limped along, only gingerly putting weight on it, which compelled Slocum to walk. Progress seemed almost nonexistent. The high, colorful walls, speckled with lone bristlecone pines and struggling cottonwood trees, projected a sameness that defied marking his advance.

Not until he saw long stretches of split-rail fence and man-made rock borders to fields did he realize that he had only a short way to go. Over the years, Charlie Goodnight had prospered. Alone in the canyon, except for a few marginal ranchers and some die-hard prospectors who stubbornly sought that which wasn't there, Goodnight had established a regular little empire. In the distance, Slocum could make out the regular angled shape of a barn roof.

He encountered his first man a mile from the emerging buildings of the ranch headquarters. He rode stiffly over to Slocum from a small gather of longhorns. At a distance of twenty feet, he halted, tipped up the brim of his Montana Peak Stetson, and dropped his right hand to the grips of a use-shiny Colt Peacemaker.

"Howdy. You lookin' for something special, mister?" He was clearly on the prod.

Who wouldn't be? Slocum thought, considering the ghost rustlers. "I am. Do you mind if I reach in a pocket? I have something to show you."

"Do it slow," came the cowhand's growl.

Slocum pulled his leather folder from his hip pocket and opened it to reveal his badge. The cowhand's eyes widened, and then he peered closely at Slocum's damaged condition.

"You look like you was rode hard and put up wet, Ranger."

"Might say that," Slocum allowed. "I ran into the famous ghost rustlers."

The Goodnight rider uttered a muffled oath, then introduced himself. "Name's Parker. You're lucky to have come out on the other side, from what I hear."

"Slocum. I've come to see Mr. Charles Goodnight."

"Well, Ranger Slocum, you took a bad tumble for nothin'. Ol' Charlie's not here."

"Oh? When will he be back?" Slocum asked.

"I'd best let his son, George, explain that to you, Ranger. I'll ride on in with you. Those snuffies have their heads down; they can look out for themselves for a while." The yearlings continued to graze, oblivious to the men, underlining Parker's observation.

Twenty minutes later, Slocum and Parker stopped outside the main house, a sprawling edifice of stone on the lower floor, with windows designed like firing ports—narrow, vertical slits with outward-slanted casements. A robust man in his mid-thirties stepped out on the shaded veranda and mopped at his balding head with a paisley neckerchief.

He greeted in the form of a question. "Howdy?"

"Boss, this is Ranger Slocum. He's come to see your paw," Parker said by way of introduction.

"Come on up and set a spell, Ranger. I'm George Goodnight. Paw's not here; he's off in Austin politickin'. You're right welcome to stay a piece."

"Thank you," Slocum answered and tied off his animals to the long rail that divided the yard. "Actually I'm a Ranger by courtesy. I'm a range detective from the Cattlemen's Association."

George Goodnight nodded as though he had expected that. When Slocum had seated himself on a wicker chair, George nodded to him. "It looks like you could stand some refreshing." He raised his voice to call out, "Lupe!"

A small, rotund Mexican woman, barefoot and dressed in a long earth-colored dress, appeared around the corner of the veranda. "*Sí, Señor Jorge?*"

George Goodnight responded in Spanish. "Bring us coffee and a pot of warm cream. Some sweet bread, too."

"*Immediatamente, señor.*"

When she had departed soundlessly, George turned to Slocum. "Now, then, what brings you way up here? As if I didn't know."

"The so-called ghost rustlers, of course," Slocum began, then gave Goodnight a rundown on what he had discovered and suspected so far.

He had reached the halfway point when Lupe returned with a large tray, on which sat a terra-cotta pot of steaming coffee, glazed on the inside only, another of cream, and a large stack of sugarcoated sweet rolls. Slocum's stomach lurched. He had been getting along on jerky and old, stale biscuits for three days—no, four now. He accepted the snack gratefully.

Munching on a raisin-studded *pan dulce*, he completed outlining his scanty accumulation of facts and ample speculation. George Goodnight nodded as he listened. When the narrative ended, the rancher screwed his mouth into an oval. The pencil line of mustache on his upper lip wriggled like a snake.

"We've had our doubts about Harlan Butcher since before he was elected. Yates Harkness, too, for that matter. He came to Texas from somewhere back east. And he's been entirely too successful for a greenhorn. Butch Kelso is, in my estimation, a saddle tramp turned rustler. Or more accurately, a rustling back-shooter."

Slocum flashed a smile. "I did sense a yellow streak on the occasions when we met."

Goodnight cocked his head. "Oh? How's that?"

"It was never alone. He talked a good fight, but when he drew on me, he had two other guns siding him."

"And you let him live?"

Slocum's smile turned rueful. "At the time I didn't know all the players. Not too late to correct that mistake if it comes to it."

"From what I know of Kelso, it will," Goodnight said grimly. "Now then, what can we do for you here?"

"The grub's helped a lot. I'd like a chance to clean up, rest some. Also I need a fresh horse. I'll gladly pay for use of one of yours, while my mount heals up. I can come back for him later."

"All done and no charge," Goodnight promised. "Anything else?"

"You might have your hands check to the north in the canyon for any sign of the rustlers. They're not ghosts. I put a slug in one, and ghosts don't bleed. Tell your men to be careful. This bunch shoots fast."

George Goodnight nodded in agreement. "We'll have every hand on the alert for strangers and strange cattle from now on.

Find a spot in the bunkhouse and take your time refreshing. We'll pick you a horse later. Supper bell is at seven o'clock. Cookie's doing brazed short ribs for the hands, but you'd honor me if you took supper with the family."

"Obliged," Slocum stated shortly. He took another roll and nibbled at it as he rose from the chair and started for his horses.

Still defying Sheriff Butcher, Butch Kelso gathered with Yancy Hake and Johnny Tulip in the Prairie Queen yet another night. Tulip found himself an alluring bawd early in the evening and departed for upstairs. Kelso and Hake played a desultory game of pitch for a quarter a game, ten cents a set. Kelso put away whiskey at a slow, but steady, pace.

Tulip showed up an hour later, with a silly grin on his face. He came down the stairs noodle-legged and absently poured a shot of bourbon. "Boys, that's one fine woman," he declared.

"Got your ashes hauled right proper, did you?" Kelso prodded.

"Sure thing. We went at it twict. What you been doin'?" Then Tulip saw the cards. "Playin' cards! Hoo-boy! While I had fun, you was playin' a silly game."

"Shut your face or I'll fill it with knuckles," Kelso growled.

Tulip backed down. "Yeah, sure, whatever you say, Butch."

"I was just waitin' for nine o'clock."

"Why?" Tulip pressed.

"You know why. Tonight I'm gonna do it. Tonight I'm gonna find out what it's like to ride a thoroughbred."

Hake and Tulip shot glances at the clock. Five minutes of nine. "You don't want to do nothin' that'll cause trouble," Tulip cautioned. "The sheriff done ordered us to stay outta town."

"The sheriff takes his orders just like we do. He ain't got no call to push me around," Butch snarled and shoved up out of his chair. "This is gonna take a while, fellers. Don't wait up for me."

"Now, dang it, Butch," Yancy Hake protested at last, but Butch Kelso was gone out through the door.

• • •

Ginny Stuart closed up as usual at nine. She spent a half hour tending to final details in the kitchen, then picked up the bag that contained the day's receipts and let herself out the front door. The night had turned out nice, one of those soft spring evenings that held the promise that winter would be gone for a long while. She breathed deeply of it and stepped off with a purposeful stride.

She did not see the dark figure that ghosted along through the shadows across the street. Her auburn hair seemed to take fire in the lamplight at the corner. It glowed tauntingly long after the rest of her had melted into darkness. At the next intersection, she turned right and headed the short block to the one on which her small house rested. Her thoughts strayed to Slocum.

He had been gone a lot longer than she had expected. Had the worst happened? Did Sheriff Butcher have Slocum locked away in the jail again? No, the sheriff remained in Happy, fat and slothful behind his desk. Had Slocum stumbled upon the rustlers? Had there been a shooting? Did Slocum lie dead in some awful place, unknown to anyone but his murderers? Ginny shuddered as a chill of mild horror ran up her spine. The next moment, she froze in mid-stride.

Had she heard something? Did someone lurk over there, behind the bushes in the Mitchells' yard? Not daring even to swallow, Ginny listened with nervous intensity. No, she chided herself, only her own dark imaginings. She continued on around the corner. Only half a block.

Her breath came easier as she stepped up onto the porch. Home again. She opened the stained cotton screen, which flopped listlessly in its wooden frame while the unoiled hinges shrieked in protest. Ginny had her hand on the doorknob when she stiffened at the thud of running bootheels behind her.

A big, muscular arm snaked around her, and a hard ham hand clasped tightly on one firm breast. Another arm circled her neck and choked off the scream that bubbled up in her throat. Outrage warred with terror within her, and Ginny flailed ineffectively with her free hand. Her strong, sharp nails gouged scarlet furrows across the bare forearm that closed her painfully burning airway.

"Don't scratch me, you bitch-kitty," a low voice purred in her ear. Whiskey fumes enveloped her face in a brief moment when the pressure relaxed enough for her to suck in a deep, hurried breath. "We're gonna have us a little fun."

Ginny wanted to scream, to cry for help, but no words, not a sound, would come. She kicked backward, struck nothing. Suddenly she felt herself lifted off the porch. She swung her legs again. Harder, higher, she urged herself in desperation. A shock ran from ankle to knee when she made contact.

A soft grunt came from the man holding her. Then he increased his grip on her pain-radiating breast and across her throat.

"Open it. Turn the knob an' open the door," a harsh whisper commanded.

Stark fright washed over Ginny as she recognized the voice. Butch Kelso! A sob of resignation came from her chest. Her nails raked his arm again. Then Kelso shifted his stance and rammed her painfully against the closed door.

"Open up, damn you," he hissed.

Revulsion rose in Ginny as she felt him jammed against her, his rigid member thrust boldly into the parting of her buttocks. All at once she wanted to vomit. Kelso pushed her harder. Desperate to be rid of the pain, Ginny turned the knob, and the door flew inward.

Kelso staggered inside, Ginny still tightly in his grip. A small table clattered noisily and tipped over when his hip struck it. Glass shattered with a pop-tinkle sound as a vase of early roses burst on the bare floorboards. Kelso groped blindly toward his goal.

Out of the darkness swam the white-painted molding of the bedroom door. In a last, desperate effort, Ginny flung wide her arms and legs to bar their progress. Kelso grunted and slobbered with the urgency of his lust. One arm at a time, he yanked her free of the door casing. Ginny heard a muted whimpering and realized with a start that it was she doing it.

One by one, Kelso wrenched her arms free of the doorjamb and waddled into the bedroom. Ginny kicked and fought with all her ability. Laughing, Butch Kelso hurled her violently onto the bed. She struck and bounced. Then he was upon her, knees pinning her open thighs to the mattress. Ginny clawed at his face. Bright light exploded in her head as he struck her with a balled fist.

Pain brought her out of a momentary blackout. Kelso held the front of her blouse now. With a powerful yank, he ripped it to her waist. Her breasts, covered by a cotton chemise, swelled outward, and Ginny sobbed in humiliation. Kelso snatched away the cloth covering and buried his face between her alabaster spheres. His wet lips slobbered over the tender nipples. She struck at him with a free hand.

He snarled something at her and began to rip away her clothing below the belt line. When he had bared her every secret, he clawed at the fly to his trousers. His reddened, engorged member came into view. Sickened at the sight, Ginny turned her head away. His thick fingers dug into her auburn tresses and yanked her face back around.

"Look at it. Take a good look, Miss High and Mighty."

Ginny found her voice now and screamed. The sound came out a pitiful squeak. Butch Kelso looked down on her, his hand holding his rigid manhood, and laughed. "No," he crooned. "Don't just look at it. Take it. Make it your own. Take it in your mouth."

Shortly after sunup, Slocum sat down to a generous breakfast. Never one to eat to excess, he stared in astonishment at large platters of fried pork chops and eggs, bowls heaping with fried potatoes, pinto beans, and hominy grits. A mountain of fresh biscuits sat in the center of the table. All of the off-duty hands gathered around. In strict accordance with the rules of Charlie Goodnight, the cook said grace before the hungry cowboys sat down and dug in.

All of that food disappeared within an amazingly short time. Slocum had to admit he had done his share. He sat back highly satisfied and unaccountably at peace. No wonder the story went around that once a man signed on for Charlie Goodnight, and he worked out, he never left. A man could get used to a life like this.

Slocum twirled a quirley and snapped a sulfurous lucifer to life with a thumbnail. The tobacco smoke from the Bull Durham clawed at his windpipe. He finished off the last of his fourth cup of coffee and stood to take his leave. The cook came to him, with a cinched-up flour sack.

"I put up some biscuits, fried fatback, and some of Lupe's beans," he told Slocum, offering the bag.

"I'm grateful. I'll enjoy it, that's for sure. Thank you, old-timer."

"I ain't so dang old," the grizzled elder protested. "I've only knowed Charlie since he was nigh onto ten years young." That made the old boy at least seventy, Slocum calculated.

At the main house, Slocum said his good-byes to George Goodnight, thanked him again for the borrow of a horse, and swung into the saddle. Before he departed, he reminded George about the men keeping a lookout for the rustlers.

"I've got a feeling they'll be seeing them sooner than they might expect," he added in farewell.

14

Slocum found it not at all surprising when he topped a low swell and saw some twenty men gathered around a large cottonwood. He reversed direction quickly and disappeared without discovery. On the back side of the crest, he dismounted and pulled an old, battered pair of field glasses from his saddlebag.

He wormed his way to the top and rested his elbows on the uneven turf. Slocum saw the horses brought into sharp relief. They were ground-reined, saddles removed, while the men went about fixing coffee and preparing a meal. He knew that Butcher had given up on the search, yet this was clearly a posse. Half a dozen wore white collarless shirts and tailored suits, heavily stained with trail dust. He studied them for five minutes and decided he needed to know more about the nature of the hunt.

Slocum studied what he could see of a deep draw beyond the tree and the relaxed posse. It would serve, he allowed. Only hard part would be reaching it without being seen. With a map of the terrain clear in his mind, he returned to the horses and set off on a wide swing to skirt the gathered men.

A soft breeze sighed across the rolling ground as Slocum rode along to a point where he could cross over the rise to his left and cut directly to the brushy draw. Into his plan he weighed the fact that he would have to walk, or crawl, the better part of a mile. Time—never enough of it. They could be gone, he realized. Which would gain him nothing.

When he crested the rise, he was out of sight of the men around the cottonwood, and downwind. Slocum could smell the tantalizing aroma of frying meat and, fainter, the beckoning scent of boiling coffee. To his right now, he could see the uppermost pale green leaves of the huge old tree. He revised his estimate of the ground to be covered—not quite a mile.

Slocum entered the draw, dismounted, and tied off his horses to greasewood bushes. For the time being, at least, he could walk. The thought occurred to him as he strode along the bottom of the brush-choked arroyo that this could be a risky thing to do, even foolhardy. The nagging need to know how the posse felt about the chase drew him onward.

He had covered close to half a mile when he bent double and advanced with greater caution, careful of each footfall. The food odors had grown steadily stronger, and then began to diminish. They would be eating now, he reckoned. When the low, indecipherable murmur of voices reached Slocum's keen ears, he dropped to all fours. His advance slowed literally to a crawl.

At last he could make out the words exchanged by the lounging posse. He eased up the side of the draw until he could see down the slight rise to the base of the cottonwood. Several men scraped scraps from tin plates into their mouths. A few hunkered around the fire, sipping coffee.

"I say we might as well stop here for the night," one of the townsmen suggested.

"The sheriff's damned anxious to have us catch up with this Slocum," a burly man with the big red hands of a butcher responded.

"Then why ain't he with us?" the first, some sort of clerk, Slocum surmised, complained.

A guffaw came from a lanky cowhand. "I hear him an' the posse he took out wound up with the running trots."

"Coulda been bad water," the meat cutter suggested.

"Around here?" the cowboy challenged. "You show me where."

"I'll tell you one thing. I would a lot better be out like this, instead of with the sheriff," a third man added. "At least this way we get a chance at that reward."

"Yeah," the cowhand replied. "An' ol' Harkness put another thousand dollars on Slocum."

"That's dead or alive, too," the butcher reminded them. "So we don't have to worry about any risk in capturing Slocum."

"*If* we find him," the store clerk added gloomily.

"Are we going to camp here or ride on to Happy?" a mustached townie said to revive the discussion.

"I'd as leave head for home," the clerk lamented.

"That'd be dumb," the butcher snapped. "What with three thousand dollars reward to collect."

Slocum had heard enough. He eased his way back into the arroyo and retraced his steps to his horses. On the way, he mused over the reluctance of this posse to press the search. Unless he did something incredibly stupid, like walking into their camp, he doubted he had much to fear from them. He estimated he could reach Happy by nightfall, if he pushed it.

That would be fine by his lights. He could be waiting for Ginny when she closed the cafe, and learn what had happened in town during his absence.

Slocum eased open the large rear door to the modest-size stable behind Ginny's house. A single, frail light showed against the drawn blinds of the living room. Good, Slocum thought. She had taken his advice about that. With the borrowed mount and his packhorse in stalls, noses down in rations of oats, Slocum slipped saddlebags over his left shoulder and started for the back door.

He let himself in quietly and froze after two steps. The soft, distinct sound of sobs came from the yellow-lighted living room. He listened a moment longer, concern growing, and then hung the saddlebags over the back of a chair and strode quickly into the light.

Ginny Stuart stood in the middle of the floor, her face bleak, stricken. Tears coursed down her pale cheeks. The blank gaze of a frightened animal filled her eyes. She wore a dressing gown, belted tightly, her bare toes peeping out from under the hem.

"Ginny? What's the matter? What happened?" Slocum's voice came out a croak.

Ginny started, and a tiny yelp of alarm tore from her throat. Then her big, blue orbs took on conscious focus. Her chin quivered and her lips trembled as she spoke. "Slocum . . . Oh, thank god, you've come, Slocum."

Slocum judged her shock at seeing him as genuine, but didn't know the cause. "Tell me, Ginny. Tell me what's made you like this?" he pleaded.

"I . . . I th-thought you were dead. The whole town has been buzzing about how the man who fixed Butch Kelso's clock murdered an Association agent in Canyon and then was killed in a stampede of cattle he had rustled. That's *you*, Slocum," she concluded.

"Ginny, I didn't kill any Cattle Association agent. And I didn't rustle any cattle."

"I know that. I never believed it. Only, they said you were dead."

"I'm here, aren't I?" Slocum said soothingly. "I have something to show you that will explain a lot."

"Please, not now. There's something else I have to tell you. Sheriff Butcher has released Kelso and his henchmen from the jail."

"Yes, I know," Slocum informed her.

"Well, he . . . he heard about you being . . . uh . . . supposed to have been killed. It made him feel safe. He . . ." Ginny lowered her eyes, unwilling to reveal everything that had happened in the past few days. "He smashed up the Virginia House. Broke every dish, threw chairs through the windows, overturned the stove."

"Did you tell the sheriff?" Slocum asked, knowing she had.

"Of course I did. It didn't do any good. He said that since it happened at night and no one had seen Kelso doing it, I had no proof and he could do nothing."

"Butcher's crooked," Slocum announced bluntly. "I suspect he is connected to the rustlers. And I think now is the time to tell you what I need to say."

Ginny appealed to him, "Please, please, just hold me and keep me safe."

Slocum took her in his arms and held her close. She hadn't told it all, he knew. "There's something more," he pressed.

"Y-yes." Her voice quavered. "Th-the same night, before he tore up the cafe, he . . . he . . . Ooh, Slocum . . . He h-had his way with me." Trembling uncontrollably, Ginny dissolved into great, heaving, throat-aching sobs.

•   •   •

Slocum fixed coffee. He grew steadily angrier, though he managed to conceal it well. Ginny said nothing more about her ordeal. By sparing him the details, she spared herself. After the warm brew had calmed her, Ginny looked up at Slocum and rearranged her features into a mask of calm. Slocum had made up his mind what needed doing next.

"Where is Kelso?" he asked hollowly.

"I suppose at the Prairie Queen, soaking up whiskey." Ginny's expression changed to one of alarm. "You're not thinking of . . . of going after him?"

"I am."

"But you can't. There's a price on your head. People are looking for you everywhere."

"You forget, I have the same authority as a Texas Ranger," Slocum told her, his voice cold, direct. "No one is going to arrest me, or put me in jail."

"You're wanted dead or alive," Ginny continued to protest.

Tight little lines around Slocum's mouth gave his attempt at a smile a grim appearance. "There's no one in Happy I have to worry about."

"Unless . . . they shoot you . . . in the back," Ginny stammered.

"I'll be *facing* Kelso, and he's the only one I can think of yellow enough to do that."

"Slocum . . . Slocum, it's too dangerous," Ginny cried. "It's not like he killed me, or scarred my face."

"The hell it isn't!" For a second, Slocum's anger and outrage seeped through. "He's hurt you, scarred you in a far worse way than any man could do with a knife, or a club, or a gun. Only animals take their partners by force. And this animal I intend to shoot down like a mad dog."

Ginny's eyes went wide. Her hand flew, tremblingly, to her mouth. She swallowed and her throat convulsed painfully. "No. Please, no, Slocum. If something happened to you, my . . . my life would be utterly destroyed."

"The way I see it, if something doesn't happen to Kelso, both our lives will be worthless," Slocum responded with more harshness than he had expected. He levered upward from the chair he had been sitting on backward.

"Oh my god, I should have never, never told you."

"I'm glad you did. This whole thing is coming to a head. I have trustworthy cowboys watching for the next stolen herd to enter the Palo Duro. The rustlers have already made mistakes. Killing those drovers and letting me get away among them. They'll make more and bigger, before long. Kelso and Butcher seem to be in this together. I'm betting Kelso runs the gang. So taking care of him now is only insurance that the whole plot falls apart sooner."

Ginny blinked. "You've learned a lot in the last few days," she brought herself to say. "Even so, I fear for you, Slocum. You're only one man."

Slocum forced a grin and responded, for her sake, with an uncharacteristic boast. "Yes. But I'm the meanest son in the valley."

Then he was gone. Ginny covered her face with both hands and wept softly, purged for the moment of her stronger passions.

A recurring chord rang falsely in the merry tinkle of the piano inside the Prairie Queen. Slocum noted it as he approached. A dozen horses had spread out between the three tie rails outside the corner establishment. Braying laughter followed tobacco smoke out over the batwings. The shadows of the occupants moved across the painted windows. Slocum paused momentarily in the intersection and slipped the retaining thong off the hammer of his .45 Colt.

Hatless since the incident in the canyon, he felt almost naked as he stepped up the two risers to the boardwalk. He paused again and slid the Peacemaker from leather, opened the loading gate and thumbed in a sixth cartridge, then reholstered. He'd be needing that within the next minute or two, he reasoned.

His big hands reached for the batwings, and he pushed them inward ahead of his tall, hard frame. Heads turned at the bar, and the tune the piano player banged out halted in mid-phrase. Slocum took three steps beyond the swinging doors and let them fly free behind him. Red-eyed from a long day of drinking, Butch Kelso looked up from the table where he sat with three companions and pulled a scowling sneer.

"You picked the wrong place to come, Slocum. Now you're gonna die for it."

"Not by your hand," Slocum told him coldly. "You haven't got the guts."

"By god, no two-bit saddle tramp talks to Butch Kelso like that," Kelso snarled.

"I thought you would have learned by now that I'm not a saddle tramp."

"Then who the hell are you?" Kelso roared.

Slocum's left hand slid to his hip pocket. He came out with the badge folder. Gaslight, from the carbide-generating plant in the basement, twinkled off the star. "Texas Ranger, Kelso. You and these scum sacks with you are under arrest."

Butch Kelso could not believe what he saw and heard. "You got nothin' on us. I've got a good mind to kill you and dump you down an old well."

"If you had any mind at all, you would have lit a shuck out of this country after the first time I put you in jail. As to charges, let's start with vandalism and destruction of property."

"Wasn't us tore up that high-toned bitch's place," Pete Lang blurted stupidly.

"Did I say whose property you destroyed? Drop your guns on the table and come with me."

Butch Kelso rammed his captain's chair back with enough force to make a loud shriek. "Like hell we will! Take him, boys. Only gut-shoot him. I want it to take a long time for Slocum to die."

Time compressed for Slocum and slowed down dramatically. He saw the foolish Pete Lang snag the grips of his Smith American and begin to haul it clear of the leather. The front sight had barely come into view when Slocum's bullet smacked into his sternum. Pete went over backward in the chair, and his head hit the sawdust-coated floor with a loud thump.

His Smith and Wesson discharged reflexively and added insult to fatal injury by blasting a slug into his leg. Three chairs went flying. Yancy Hake dove for cover behind the edge of the small stage where the piano player sat cowering. He snapped off a shot in haste on the way. The glass globe of an overhead gaslight shattered and rained down sparkling shards.

Two of them stuck in the green baize of the table, which Johnny Tulip had overturned and taken refuge behind. Slocum had moved, too, a jink to his left, toward the bar, and a half turn, which put him in line with a punk gunhawk named Lefty Jarvis. Jarvis, with more flash than substance, had yanked his brace of Colts and blazed away wildly at the balloon of powder smoke that marked the spot where Slocum had been.

Slocum experienced the kick of high elation and offered aid to the tyro. "Over here," he said simply.

Jarvis turned his way and raised his right-hand six-gun. Slocum put a round in the punk's thigh. Howling, Jarvis went down, but not out of the game. His left-hand revolver spat fire, and he chewed a chunk from the front of the bar. Slick Bennett dove behind the mahogany and gazed upward with a pitiful expression at his stock in trade.

Elsewhere in the crowded saloon, men and painted doves scrambled for safety. One cowhand opted for the second floor. His boots thudded on the carpeted treads, and Butch Kelso jerked that way. His hammer fell before he realized this was not Slocum.

Kelso's bullet took the hapless cowboy under the right armpit and spilled him lifeless on the staircase. Slocum cut a strip from Kelso's back, across both shoulder blades. With a bellow of anguish, Kelso turned on Slocum. His eyes went wide at the deadly still muzzle of the .45 in Slocum's hand. Hastily, Kelso holstered his smoking six-gun and showed empty hands.

"No. I ain't gonna go against you this time, Slocum," he whined.

Yancy Hake had different ideas. With Slocum partially distracted by Kelso, he showed himself and tried a shot. His slug sizzled past Slocum's head and smashed two bottles of rye on the backbar. With an angry snarl, Hake eared back the hammer for another try. Slocum shot him between the eyes.

An expression of stupefaction crossed Yancy Hake's face. His eyes crossed and rolled upward, as though inspecting the new addition to his forehead. Then he pitched face-first into the sawdust. Slocum turned back to Kelso.

With the distractions presented by his underlings, Butch Kelso had recovered himself enough to ease the small Herington and Richards .32 belly gun from its hiding place inside his vest. He whipped it outward only ten feet from Slocum's chest.

"I count five. That thing's dry, Slocum."

"Is it? Are you sure?" Slocum taunted.

"I've got the gun now, you bastard. And you're gonna crawl, Slocum, crawl on your belly like a snake." Kelso began to wave the small weapon wildly, menacing the entire room.

"You're sure of that?" Slocum asked. "Do you feel lucky, Kelso?"

"Damn right I do."

"Sorry," Slocum told him, and taking careful aim, he shot the revolver from Kelso's hand, the hot lead smashing against the cylinder.

Kelso bent double and wailed in agony. Tears formed in his eyes and blurred his vision as he looked up. What he saw he didn't believe. Slocum slid the big Colt back into the holster. Then he pulled out a thin pair of leather gloves that had been folded over his cartridge belt and slipped them on.

"Oh, goddamn you, Slocum," Kelso moaned. "You broke my hand. It's over, you hear? Over."

"No," Slocum said in contradiction, advancing on the miserable figure of Kelso. "It's only beginning."

15

Slocum's first punch drove Kelso back with enough force to lift him off the floor and slam the rustler onto the top of the table behind him. The legs gave way, and the circle of green baize collapsed in a cloud of sawdust. Kelso wasted not a second in springing to his feet.

His jaw ached. Vision blurred, he clumsily blocked Slocum's second and third blows, then lashed out with a vicious right. Slocum shrugged it off the point of his shoulder. He came back with a right of his own, driven deep an inch above Kelso's belt buckle. It doubled the six-footer over, air whooshing out of puckered lips. Slocum slammed a sharp left to the side of Kelso's head.

Even with the protection of the gloves, his knuckles stung from the impact. Thoroughly enjoying himself, Slocum brought up his knee and smashed Kelso's nose. Blood smeared the gunman's face in an oily mask. In desperation he sidestepped. The effort to force himself upright left Kelso dizzy and gasping.

Before he could set himself, Kelso caught a left-right-left combination that punished his ribs and drove the last of the air from his lungs. Face purple behind its wash of crimson, Kelso struggled to suck in a fresh breath. Slocum didn't give him time.

A gloved fist appeared in the center of Kelso's vision and blocked out his left eye a split-second before the thin leather tore a long rip in the skin over Kelso's left cheekbone. Fiery pain exploded in Kelso's head. Slocum's other hand connected with the opposite side of his face, and Kelso heard the warning creak of his jaw hinge.

Desperately Kelso tried to counteract the damage. He lashed out with a boot toe, directed at Slocum's crotch. Slocum pivoted to the side and took it on the outside of his thigh. Misery came to life in Slocum's leg. He swung his left backhand, and the knuckles cracked off Kelso's temple.

Rubber-legged, Kelso went to one knee. His mind numbed by the ceaseless castigation, he clawed for the handle of the sheath knife at the small of his back. Slocum saw the flash of steel and stepped into it. His hands grasped Kelso by the wrist, and he slammed the rustler's forearm downward, while he thrust his knee upward.

Kelso's arm bones broke with a loud crack. A thin, high-pitched scream came from his bruised, bloody lips. His right arm jerked spasmodically in sympathy with the ruined one. The knife fell from useless fingers. At once, Slocum pumped his arms back and forth as he pounded Kelso's face.

Droplets of blood formed a halo around the rustler's battered head. With a final, whistling left, Slocum caught Kelso in the nerve cluster behind his jaw hinge. Kelso straightened up, shuddered, and fell in a pool of spilled liquor.

"Jesus, Ranger," Slick Bennett blurted from his vantage point behind the bar, "I ain't never seen a man give another such a beating."

"He got off easy," Slocum grunted. He breathed deeply, but slowly.

"That one's still alive," Bennett declared, a shaking finger aimed at Yancy Hake.

"Get a doctor for him. I'm taking Kelso to jail."

Sheriff Harlan Butcher looked up from a two-day-old Amarillo newspaper when the door banged open and Slocum, blood running from a cut under one eye, entered with Butch Kelso. He had dragged Kelso by his shirt collar and accumulated bits of the street shed onto the floor from the flannel cloth.

Butcher's eyes bugged, and his hand dropped to the grips of his Colt. The .45 flashed into sight from the holster, pointed at Slocum's middle. "Stand right there, Slocum, and get your hands in the air."

"I have something for you, first, Sheriff. I'm going to reach to my back pocket. Don't get trigger happy."

"By god, I can't believe you walked in here to give yourself up," Butcher blustered.

"I didn't. Here, take a look at this." He showed the badge, and Butcher's eyebrows climbed his over-wide forehead.

"What the hell's this mean?" the lawman growled.

"Exactly what it has always meant. I am a duly authorized range detective for the Texas Cattlemen's Association. This is a Texas Ranger's badge. To make it easier to understand—I could not, would not, and did not kill Bob McClure. He is the one who came to Fort Worth to outline the difficulties to me when I accepted the assignment. That was the first and only time I ever met him. When I entered his office, he was already dead." Slocum's eyes narrowed as Butcher's face paled. "But I strongly suspect that you knew that, Sheriff."

"Are you accusing me?" Butcher snarled, his voice low and menacing.

"Not . . . yet. I haven't all the evidence. I brought Kelso here to be locked up. And this time I don't want to see him out on the streets five minutes after I turn the key on him."

"Kelso's done nothing wrong," Butcher challenged.

"Hasn't he? Try vandalism and destruction of property for starts. Also a charge of assault on and attempted murder of a law officer. I expect to see him held for trial without bail. There won't be any trouble making those charges stick."

"Petty offenses," Butcher said dismissively. "Any lawman worth his salt expects to get thumped on from time to time."

"I left two dead men and one dying, who had been ordered by Kelso to gun me down."

"You're wanted dead or alive," Butcher continued to bluster.

"Bullshit!" Slocum's hot retort echoed off the brick walls of the small office. "There's also a complaint to be filed for rape. I anticipate watching Kelso hang for that."

Butcher's mouth sagged. Once more he pointed out that Slocum was wanted for murder and rustling. Slocum laughed and handed Butcher a letter-form warrant, commissioning him as a special agent of the Texas Rangers. When Butcher had worked his way through it, lips moving to form the words he read, Slocum plucked it back from his numb hands.

"As you read, Sheriff, I was to work undercover. I chose the pretense of being a cattle buyer. I'm no more a buyer than I am a rustler. I did find out the rustlers are flesh and blood."

Slocum went on to give an account of what happened in Palo Duro Canyon and his description of the way the rustlers handled the stolen herds. When he concluded, he raised the letter to Butcher's eye level.

"If there is still any doubt or confusion as to my part in this, wire the Association headquarters for my bona fides."

Hatred glittered in Harlan Butcher's eyes. "If if that badge is genuine, it doesn't make you innocent of anything. There's been crooked lawmen before."

Slocum struggled to maintain his patience, eyelids slitted nearly closed. "Yes," he grated dryly, "I'm well aware of that."

Butcher started to give Slocum more lip. Slocum's resolve snapped. His big hand lashed out and bunched the front of Butcher's shirt. He gave no sign of effort when he lifted the spluttering lawman off his feet. With two long, swift strides, he shoved Butcher up against the brick wall.

"It wouldn't take much for me to change my mind about connecting you to the ghost rustlers, Sheriff. Considering the number of murders that have happened, you'd hang for certain. Think about that."

His wind cut off by Slocum's huge knuckles, Butcher could only squawk ineffectually. The wrath left Slocum, and he released the sheriff. Butcher's boots thudded hollowly on the floor.

"Goddamn you, Slocum!" Butcher choked out when he caught his breath.

Slocum ignored the outburst. "Help me get Kelso into a cell, Sheriff. He has a broken arm, so go easy."

Grudgingly, Harlan Butcher opened the door to the cellblock and lifted Butch Kelso by the shoulders. He duck-walked backward down the aisle. All the cells gaped empty; there wasn't a lot of enforcement going on in Happy. Slocum swung Kelso's legs through the door, and they laid him on the bunk. Butcher turned the key in the lock.

On the silent walk back to the office, Butcher considered the rage he had read in the face of Slocum, and the fury in his green eyes. He decided to swallow his own pique and try what he could to restore his protective coloration.

"I will allow as how, considering who you claim to be,"

Butcher began hesitantly as he seated himself behind his desk, "your story of what happened in Canyon and in the Palo Duro are probably true. That being the case, the charges will probably be dropped."

Slocum eyed him, his smoldering ire close to the surface again. "They had damned well better be dropped," he growled and strode stiffly from the office.

"What about a doctor for Kelso?" Butcher shouted after him.

"Send for him yourself. Kelso's in your jail," Slocum flung over his shoulder.

With far from a gentle touch, Sheriff Harlan Butcher wiped the dried and fresh blood from the face of Butch Kelso. He loomed over the bunk where the unconscious Kelso lay, a sponge in one big hand. Water trickled down Kelso's cheeks as Butcher dabbed at the cut under the rustler's left eye. He returned the swab to the bucket, and it made a musical tinkle as he rinsed it. Silently he cursed Kelso for his stupidity.

Kelso groaned and stirred. Butcher plopped the sodden sponge on his face. Spluttering, Kelso came around. "Gawdamn, you don't have to drown me," he growled huskily.

"You don't have a brain in that head of yours, Kelso," the sheriff snapped when Kelso opened his eyes. "You fool. You miserable fool. I told you to get out of town and stay out. But, oh, no, you had to show everyone that no one gave Butch Kelso orders. It's bad enough you smashed up the Stuart woman's eatin' house. *That* I could cover up. Nobody saw you. But you had to have your way with her."

"Who said?" Kelso challenged in a gravelly croak.

"Slocum. After he killed two of your boys and beat hell out of you. From what he said, I gather he went directly to the Prairie Queen after seeing her. She told him everything that had happened." Butcher's face purpled. "Goddamn you, if you couldn't keep that thing in your pants, why didn't you pay for it like any other saddle tramp?" he raged.

"She had it comin'" was Kelso's surly reply.

Butcher wanted to hit him, but considered the damage already done and refrained. "No respectable woman has that coming," he snarled. "I gather from Slocum that she will sign a complaint. If she does, and you're convicted, you could hang."

"I'll see that she doesn't say anything," Kelso muttered.

"You stay away from her," Butcher ordered.

Kelso brightened, raised himself on his elbows, and winced at the pain. Although the doctor had been there, set and splinted his arm, it hadn't eased his misery by much. "Does that mean you're lettin' me out?"

"Yes," Butcher replied with a surly hiss. "Much against my better judgment. I want you to round up the boys and go after Slocum. He's become too dangerous to allow running free. He's a range detective, got the Ranger badge and everything. And, this time, do it right. There's to be no slip-ups. Mr. Harkness would be terribly disappointed."

Butch Kelso gave Harlan Butcher an odd look, head cocked to one side in surprise. "Jeez. So that's who the boss is?"

"I've said too much. You had better forget that if you want to stay healthy. Just go find Slocum and kill him."

Slocum knocked softly on the kitchen door to Ginny's small house. She answered, again with the .32 Smith and Wesson in hand. She greeted him in silence, with a grim expression, then went into his arms.

When their embrace ended, Ginny looked at him from arm's length. "I heard shooting," she prompted.

"Yes. I found Kelso. He's in jail again. I had to wound one of his henchmen."

"There were more shots than that," Ginny accused.

"Yes, well, I had three of them to deal with. I didn't have time to be choosy. I'm sorry . . . Two of them are dead."

A fierce light glowed in Ginny's blue eyes. "Good. What did you do to get Kelso into jail?"

Slocum rubbed his sore hands. "I tried to break my knuckles on his head," he responded ruefully.

Her smile was genuine. "I hope you hit him a couple of times for me."

"They were . . . all for you," Slocum answered honestly. His gaze darted over his shoulder, toward the stable behind the house.

Correctly sensing his intent, Ginny went to him again,

wrapped arms around his deep chest. "Stay here with me, Slocum. I need you. I want to have you close to me tonight." She almost said, *Every night.*

Slocum rested his chin on the top of her head. "I'm sorry, Ginny. I can't. At least not now."

"Why?" Ginny recoiled from him in alarm.

"I've . . . started something in motion. There's a nagging little something inside me that keeps telling me that Kelso won't stay in jail much longer than it takes to set his arm and bring him around."

"What makes you think that?" Ginny asked, worry coloring her words.

"I told you before I went after Kelso that I suspected Sheriff Butcher to be involved in the rustling activity. I showed him my badge—had to, to keep him from trying to lock me in the same cell Kelso now occupies. The sheriff gave in too easily. I got the impression he knew that a range detective had been sent from Fort Worth."

Slocum felt Ginny tense under his light touch. "Then there's two of them I have to worry about?"

"I don't think so. The sheriff, maybe, but Kelso will be busy with other things."

"What other things?" Ginny repeated Slocum's phrase.

Slocum didn't want to tell her, had no desire to have her worried for his sake. "If Butcher is involved, he can't afford to have Kelso alive and in jail." He tried to make it sound plausible. "He'll see that Kelso gets out of town this time and stays out. I think I know where he'll be going."

Frown lines made Ginny's forehead even more appealing. "That's worse than going after him here in town. It will be terribly, terribly dangerous."

Slocum forced a mirthful snort. "*Life* seems dangerous around here," he said lightly.

"Slocum, you know what I'm saying," Ginny complained, her purpose frustrated. "I . . . I think I've fallen in love with you," she blurted on the instant.

Slocum's eyes widened, one eyebrow cocked above the other. "That's rather sudden," he chided gently.

"I . . . I've never had anyone beat the tar out of someone over me. At least not since the seventh grade." She sealed her serious intent with a fleeting smile.

Slocum relented in part, took Ginny in his arms, and held her tight. "Lock up, keep a light low in the parlor, and go to bed. You'll be safe enough. When this is over, I'll come back."

"Promise?"

"Y-yes." The word nearly stuck in Slocum's throat. "I promise you, Ginny Stuart, that once this has run its course, I'll come for you."

She kissed him stoutly and explosively on the lips. "You do that, John Slocum. You be sure you don't forget, hear?"

Slocum resisted the urge to pat her on the head. "Now, there's my Texas hardscrabble farm girl."

Ginny took her arms from around Slocum's neck, fisted the hands, and put them on her hips. "Oh, pooh, Slocum!" Accepting it now, she leaned forward again for another kiss. "Be careful, Slocum. For your own sake, be very careful."

"I will," he promised.

Their kiss had less ferocity this time, but was a lot sweeter. Ginny twined her arms around the thick stump of Slocum's neck and held him tightly. Their lips moved in lively contact and parted, the eager tip of her tongue probing past his teeth, exploring his mouth hungrily. Every nerve in Slocum's body screamed for him to stay the night, to lose himself in this delightful, passionate young woman.

Yet he sensed the end drawing near. He had taken on this job; now it was time to complete it. A good man, Bob McClure, had died—hell, a lot of good men had died, because of these rustling scum, and Slocum knew confidently that he had the answer. It would be a matter of the right place and time. And he had the eyes watching, watching.

Their embrace ended. "You make it difficult for a man to say no, Ginny," Slocum admitted, somewhat breathless.

"Then . . ." She paused, gasped. "I won't say it. Be careful, Slocum. I want you back all in one piece."

16

Slocum worked silently and in the dark to saddle his mount and packhorse, then load his pack frame. With that accomplished, he went to the borrowed Goodnight horse and raised his knee in a swift jab to the animal's ribs, to boot out enough air to draw tight the cinch strap. He gave a backward look at the house, filled with real regret, and led the animals from the low stable.

Without hesitation, Slocum walked his horses the two blocks to the open prairie before mounting. Behind him, a hard-faced man raised his Winchester to his shoulder and sighted in on Slocum's back. A gloved hand reached across in front of him and covered the rear sight.

"Not here, not in town," Butch Kelso whispered roughly. "We might get seen and recognized. He's packin' a Ranger badge, an' all hell would bust loose if we done it in the open."

"Then just how do you suppose to do this?" the back-shooter asked in a snotty tone.

"Way I see it, we have to figger out a way to make him disappear. We'll follow, see where he leads us, then pick our spot."

By then, Slocum had gone the full two-block distance. A darker silhouette in the night, he swung into the saddle and set off at a gentle lope, headed north out of Happy. Kelso, Ollie Utting, and five others gave him half a mile, then trailed along behind.

Slocum stretched out the powerful horse he had obtained from George Goodnight. He stuck to the road to Canyon. The moon rose in a slim crescent above the higher, rolling country to the east. He kept up the pace for five miles, until he came to a dry creek bed. There, he pulled aside and took field glasses from his saddlebag to check his backtrail.

His suspicions proved correct when he made out a dark, rapidly moving mass that could only be a number of men. He had plenty of time, Slocum decided. He debated for a moment setting up one of his nasty surprises, then decided against it. He wanted them to follow him, or lead him to where he suspected this bizarre situation would end. Slocum replaced the field glasses and rode up the far bank of the empty stream.

He had a long way to go and little time to plan as he pushed the gait up to a brisk lope. He had the means to make life miserable for those following him. He could make enough noise to lead the watchers to where he chose to put an end to the rustling gang. All that mattered to Slocum was that they end up in the same place.

Five miles south of Canyon, Slocum left the road and cut northeast toward the upper mouth of the Palo Duro. He made no effort to hide his trail.

Nate Hoople made his disagreement known to Butch Kelso. "I still say he's headin' into Canyon."

"Not likely. Slocum's headed to the Palo Duro. You can count on that," Butch stated forcefully.

"You think he knows we're behind him?" Grant Stark asked.

"What difference does it make?" Kelso snapped. "Once we get him in the canyon, he's dead meat. Us and the other boys will swarm over him."

"He's got away before," Hoople pointed out.

"Not this time. Slocum will be caught between us. I sent Putnam ahead to pass the word to the boys watchin' herds. They'll cut him off or run him to ground. Then Slocum is mine," Butch vowed, a weird light in his eyes.

Not a one of the hardcases with him doubted the source of that unholy glow. A numb ache had to fill their boss from his broken arm. Every step taken by his horse seemed to jolt Kelso harder. Every mile they had covered had to have been an unending misery for him.

Kelso hadn't an easy way out. Sheriff Butcher had ridden with them to the edge of town and seen to it that every one of Kelso's men in Happy left ahead of or with him. He could not sit in the Prairie Queen and numb his agony with whiskey while his minions did the work. Truth was he didn't want to.

He longed to get his hands on Slocum's throat. To squeeze and twist until the life slowly left the miserable Ranger bastard. A new twinge of pain reminded Kelso that he had only one good hand with which to do that. And that one still throbbing from the gunshot wound.

"Gawdamn that Slocum!" Kelso blurted to release some of the fiery hurt inside him. At the startled looks of his followers, he explained. "I've run up against some tough hombres in the past. But never have I seen anyone so piss-ant lucky as this Slocum. Look," he emphasized, determined to iron out his powerful misgivings, "Butcher had him in jail in Canyon, right? He could have done what the Boss wanted and killed him right there. You know, made it look like he done himself in, hung himself with his pants leg, right?"

No one responded to Kelso's rhetorical questions. "Sure he could," Butch went on. "Or he could have shot him the second he came through that door to the jail."

"Draggin' you by the collar," Nate Hoople said with a snicker.

"Put a rein on that or I'll kick your ass up twixt your shoulder blades," Butch growled. "Butcher told me Slocum drove his posse nuts. Made fools of them, and laughed. They never once got a clear shot at him."

"Maybe *he's* a ghost," Hoople suggested tauntingly.

Kelso scowled in the weak moonlight. "You've got a bad case of running off at the mouth, Nate. I'd sure hate to see that become a permanent thing."

"No trouble, Boss. But it did seem kind of funny, scary funny I mean, that he done in three of the boys, beat hell out of you, an' took you off to jail and not a one of the rest of us knew a thing about it."

"You all had your noses in the bottom of a bottle, or a split fur piece, if I know you," Kelso grumbled.

"Hey, Boss, that ain't fair," Grant Stark protested. "Nobody told us Slocum was gonna be in town."

"You've got eyes, don't you?" Kelso snarled.

"Ears, too," Grant agreed. "We heard the shots. But we thought that was you, raggin' some local sissy or such."

"Shit!" Kelso exploded. "Not a one of you got curious enough to come take a look? I say again," Kelso changed the subject, "Slocum's headed for the canyon. We'd best keep after him."

Sheriff Harlan Butcher sat in his office, gulped bitter, day-old coffee, and thought of what Slocum had revealed. Icy unease slid along his spine. That damned Ranger knew too much. Kelso would have to silence him for good and all this time. His last admonition to Kelso had been that the leader of the gang of rustlers finish off Slocum and then return here to jail, to provide himself with an alibi.

With Slocum missing, and word put about that he had been killed, he felt certain that Miss Ginny Stuart would not have nerve enough to go forward with her complaint for rape. Few women did, his experience as a lawman told him. It was just too . . . humiliating. It degraded them in their own eyes, and those of the other "good" women of a community. Sort of like being captured by Injuns and being pestered by the bucks.

Although, the more he thought of it, the more convinced Sheriff Butcher became that it would not do any harm to exert a little pressure to insure that the hot-tempered young Stuart girl kept her nose, and her mouth, out of the law business. So decided, Butcher hitched himself out of his oversize chair and started for the door.

He got his first surprise when he noticed a soft yellow glow coming from the parlor of Ginny Stuart's house. He doubted she was up. All the better for what he had in mind. Awakened in the middle of the night, and urged by the sheriff not to press charges, would have to put her off balance. Butcher cleared his throat and wiped his damp palms on the legs of his trousers before he opened the low gate in the picket fence and walked to the porch steps.

At first his knock brought no results. He tried again. Straining his ears, Butcher thought he heard a loud creak, as though of leather bed lacings. A whisper of footsteps followed. He raised his big hand and rapped again.

Still not a response from anyone inside. Though he did detect the soft slide and rattle of a wooden drawer. A moment later, a lamp or candle flared inside and increased the illumination. The curtain over the oval window in the front door twitched, and he heard the pleasant, musical voice of Ginny Stuart.

"Who is it?"

"The sheriff, Miss Stuart. I need a word with you."

"At this hour? Can't it wait until morning?"

"I'm afraid not. It's urgent, you see. There's some important people puttin' pressure on me to grant bail and release Butch Kelso. I need to know for certain you intend to file a complaint of a capital crime."

A skeleton key rattled in the cast-iron lock, and the white ceramic knob turned. The door opened a narrow gap. "Oh, I certainly do, Sheriff. You can assure them on that count. Kelso is a menace. He beat me, misused me, and destroyed my business, while out on bail from your jail. I don't intend to see him get away with something like that again. He's . . . he's an animal."

"In that case, might I come in and we can discuss it?" Butcher urged in his most diplomatic tone.

"I . . . think not, Sheriff."

"May I ask why? It's not a wise thing for a young woman to be alone at times like this. Particularly if word gets around about your misfortune. Someone . . . might seek to take advantage," he suggested bluntly.

"I'm not worried about that. It is a bad time, Sheriff. I . . . I have someone here with me."

"Who is it?" Butcher demanded. "It can't be Slocum," he let slip before he realized that she had no way of knowing he had watched Slocum leave town.

"Well, actually, it's two someones," Ginny responded coyly. "Mr. Smith and Mr. Wesson."

Sheriff Butcher stared bug-eyed at the small muzzle of the .32 revolver that Ginny shoved around the edge of the door. Hastily, he departed from her porch. His face burned with rage, and he fumed inside over her temerity.

Butch Kelso halted at the southern bank of the Prairie Dog Town Fork, extended his usable right arm, and pointed toward the distant smear of greater black. "I told you. Slocum's headed straight for the canyon. We have him now, boys."

"Yeah. Or he's got us," Nate Hoople muttered.

"What was that?" Kelso snapped.

"Nothing. I sure hope Putnam got there ahead of him."

"Slater's chasing shootin' stars, Nate. He don't know any-thing for sure. We get him in the canyon, we've got him cold."

Kelso and his five men rode on in silence. Tension built to a palpable level. The moon had slid to a position behind their backs. Long shadows preceded them. In one, projected by a tall fingerlike rock formation, Slocum waited for them to draw near.

Slocum watched as the men who had been following him approached the entrance to the Palo Duro. He smiled a secret smile as they spread out to cover the entire roadway that followed the bank of the Red River into the towering walls of varicolored splendor. Not long now, he thought to himself.

Suddenly, three of the rustlers left their saddles with cries of alarm. A rope stretched at chest height through the pitch-black shadow of the rock needle had clipped them off without warning. Curses rose from the ground, along with the nervous cavorting of horses, riderless and without control. Chuck-ling softly, Slocum silently walked his mount and the pack animal away into the engulfing silence. There'd be more. Many more.

Shortly after sunup, Kelso and his henchmen lost Slocum's trail. In lieu of hot food and strong coffee, they broke out a couple of bottles of whiskey. While the levels of the bourbon went down, their bravado soared. The favorite topic became what would be done to Slocum when they caught him.

"Y'know what I say we should do?" Grant Stark opined after a gulp of whiskey and a wipe of thick lips by the hairy back of one hand. "I say we oughtta take our time. Skin him alive. That's what."

"That's Injun doin's," Butch Kelso said and sneered dis-dainfully. "Slocum's tough and he's dangerous, but he don't deserve that kind of dirty business. All we need to do is shoot him and put him in a hole where no one will ever find him."

"Does that say we have to do it all at once—plug him through the head and be done with it?" Nate Hoople asked. "What about we put a couple in his legs, then in his shoulders, his belly next. Make him know he should have never messed with us."

"Big talk," Ike Baker grunted. "But I agree with Butch. Slocum's caused us enough grief. We'd be smart to finish him quick and get back to rustlin' cattle."

"I wanna cut off his balls and feed 'em to him," Big Mac Kronk stated forcefully.

Baker gave Kronk a fish-eye. "You're good at dishin' up disgusting cuts of meat, ain't'cha, Mac?"

Big Mac bristled. "What do you mean by that?"

"Nothin'," Baker said, backing down. "I was just thinkin' of that overripe pork you served us in camp last week."

"Ain't my fault it was spoilt when we got it," Kronk said in defense of himself.

"You coulda smelled it clear an' gone to Amarillo," Grant Stark contributed. "Least you coulda done was dressed out one of them calves got dropped in the canyon."

"A lot you know. Butch tol' me they was to be set aside special." Big Mac pouted.

Butch Kelso cut through their banter. "Getting back to Slocum," he said, "first we have to find him. If he's the one who jumped you boys a couple of nights ago, he knows which side canyons we use. We'd better split up and cover all of them fast. Anyone comes on him, hightail it over and get the rest of us."

"There's seven with that last herd," Stark reminded Kelso.

"Good. We'll need them, way I see it. Grant, you, Ike, and Nate take the draws on the south side. We'll cross over and check the north. Whatever you do, don't let Slocum know you've caught sight of him."

Hunkered down in the brush, Slocum watched the search for himself develop. He munched on a strip of jerky, somewhat amused at the antics of the rustlers. By now, he judged, they had enough alcohol fumes in their heads to rob them of caution and, especially, judgment. He waited for them to discover his next nasty surprise.

He learned that they had in the form of a loud, pain-filled scream. Angry shouts followed, then silence. Time to move on, Slocum decided.

Nate Hoople sensed a falter in the stride of his horse. Then he heard the loud swish of wind moving through the leaves. Only it turned out to be the leaves themselves that moved.

When his mount struck the trip line, it released a forearm-thick sapling that Slocum had bent sideways away from the trail, into one of the lesser canyons in the Palo Duro. Freed from its restraint, the sapling whipped outward across the pathway with enough speed to prevent escape by the man who had sprung the trap.

The stout, springy paloverde struck Hoople full in the chest and swept him clear of the saddle. His shriek of agony alerted and alarmed his companions who were riding behind. Hoople hit the ground with punishing force that brought another howl of pain.

"What the hell!" Ike Baker blurted.

"Hoople—where is he? What knocked you off your horse?" Grant Stark demanded.

"Stark—oh, god, Stark . . . It was a tree. It swung out an' hit me." Pink froth formed on Nate Hoople's lips. "Busted all my ribs," he panted. "I think one punched a hole in my lung." A steady flow of crimson added verity to his speculation.

Grant Stark rode forward, eyes set on searching the surrounding terrain. Slocum had to be out there somewhere. Tense, cautious of exposing himself, Stark dismounted and knelt beside the injured Hoople. His lightest touch brought whimpers of misery from Hoople.

"Jeez, who'd do something like that?"

"Slocum, that's who, you idiot," Stark snapped at Baker.

"What do we do now?" Ike Baker asked plaintively.

"We can't move him," Stark reasoned aloud. "He's all busted up inside. Best you go on through the gorge an' get the buckboard from the boys there. Bring a plank, too, or something to lay Hoople on to keep his chest from movin'."

"Me? You want me to go in there alone, with Slocum on the loose?" Ike bleated.

"Why, hell yes," Stark responded irritably. He looked around

at the offending paloverde and the narrow confines of the side
draw they had ridden into. "This ain't the kind of thing a feller
would rig up an' then sit around and wait for somethin' to
happen. Now, get to it. Nate's hurt bad."

On foot, Slocum left his vantage point and skirted three more
unpleasant surprises he had taken time to construct. He wished
that he had time to dig a pit, line it with stakes, and cover it.
Through his voracious reading as a youth, Slocum had learned
how effective those obstacles had been in siege warfare during
the Middle Ages.

A few more run-ins with the snares and traps he had set up
would have the rustlers spooked enough to be shooting at one
another, Slocum surmised. Then they would be ready for the
second phase of his program. That idea pleased him.

17

Slocum observed with growing concern the increase in the number of rustlers involved in the hunt for him. That figure had grown to thirty-five by nightfall, and that didn't include those who'd fallen victim to Slocum's traps. With the search halted by darkness, Slocum slipped away from his vantage point to continue his campaign of disruption.

Two hardcases rode watch together in a north side canyon. They paused to talk and stare at the half-moon-silvered treetops only an hour after they went on sentry duty. They chose to take their ease under the widely-spread limbs of an ancient cottonwood. Abruptly the night turned bad for them when the wide loop of a lariat dropped over their shoulders and snapped closed, which jammed them together face-to-face. Before either could react and call an alarm, the heavy butt of a rifle descended from the overhead branches and knocked consciousness from them with two swift strokes.

Smiling, Slocum slid down from the tree and tied off the bite end to the saddle horn of one horse. Then he slowly backed the animals away, hoisting the trussed pair up into the concealing foliage. That accomplished, he tied the reins of both mounts to the trunk of the cottonwood. Pleased with his handiwork, Slocum slipped silently away into the darkness.

He found a small camp of three searchers in a brushy draw. Two had already rolled into their blankets, while the third poked a stick into dying coals. Slocum eased up on the unsuspecting rustler and silenced the man with a solid blow from the barrel of his Peacemaker. He lowered the unconscious form away from the fire and skirted the ring of stones on quiet, moccasined feet.

Quick, hard smacks on the heads of the sleeping outlaws ended the chance of an alarm being given. Next, he stripped each of them of boots, guns, cartridge belts, and trousers. Without a backward glance, Slocum faded away. Twenty minutes later he found the main camp.

Half a dozen rustlers sat awake, drinking and talking. It would sorely stretch his inventiveness to pull off something here, Slocum admitted. He gave it a long study, and rejected the first few ideas he devised. The risk was simply too great. Any overt attack would immediately raise the alarm. Patiently he observed the camp while first one, then a second drinker gave up on whiskey and stumbled off to his bedroll.

Soft, liquid snores soon assured Slocum that these two would pose no threat. Gradually he formulated a plan. He knew for certain that no more than three or four of these hard-faced men knew him by sight. With the brains of this quartet befuddled by liquor, the chance of any of them identifying him should be slight. He needed to pull off something bold and outrageous before he snuck away to prepare more dirty tricks for the next day.

His best chance would come when the four remaining rustlers consumed the last of the whiskey, and so he waited. A quartet of heavy drinkers, pulling on a single bottle, didn't take long to reduce it to a single swallow. One spoke up to say he had another jug tucked away in his saddle bags.

Slocum used the sound of his movement to change his position. Stealthily he worked around until he came to the picket line for the horses. Then he crept forward in the outer gloom until he could again see the men around the fire. Slocum still held back, until they had each taken two long gulps from the new bottle. Then he rose and walked into the low, flickering orange light.

He headed directly toward the fire, held up a hand in greeting, and spoke softly. "We've got a problem over here with the horses. You want to come help me straighten it out before it wakes everyone in camp?"

Groans of protest answered him, though all four men got unsteadily to their feet. With Slocum in the lead, they made their stumbling way to the edge of the lighted area. There, Slocum hung back while the four rustlers walked into the darkness in the direction of the picket line.

Slocum had the one at the rear laid out on the ground by the time the other three reached the horses. The hardcases looked at the quiet animals, some still munching from canvas feed bags, and turned questioning expressions on Slocum, who approached, smiling through a frown.

"Down there near the far end of the string," he instructed. He pointed to one of the men. "You wait with me, so we can keep these quiet."

Shrugging, the other drunk men wavered along the line of standing horses. Slocum moved closer. When the whiskey-fogged rustler craned to look after his friends, Slocum took the opportunity to chuck a small stone into the brush off to one side.

"Over there," he announced tightly.

When the bleary-eyed outlaw strained to see into the dark, head turned to one side, Slocum caught him with a hard right to the jawline in the knockout zone. A soft grunt turned to a sigh, and the rustler went down in comparative silence. Slocum started after the remaining pair.

He found them near the end of the line, staring, with hands on hips, at a wet, trembling gelding. "Hell, somebody didn't cool out his horse, that's all," the nearer one remarked to Slocum. "I sure ain't gonna do it for him."

"There's a skittery one over there that bothers me," Slocum said, inventing this as he pointed to the far side of the picket line.

Turning to look, the rustler who'd spoken put himself in perfect position for Slocum to clip him behind the left ear with the long, steel barrel of his .45 Colt. He dropped like a stone, and his partner found himself gawking down the round, black hole to eternity.

"Don't make a sound," Slocum cautioned. "It would be a shame to spoil all this good work."

He stepped over the body of the unconscious hardcase and approached the last one. With his eyes drawn to the threatening muzzle of Slocum's gun, the last thing the nervous outlaw had in mind was shouting an alarm. Slocum reached him, raised the six-gun to eyeball level, then higher—and slammed the barrel down on the man's baldpate.

With the Colt back in leather, Slocum went to work draping the unconscious rustlers over the bare backs of four horses. These he released from the lariat tether and led away from camp. The thin sliver of moon remained the only witness.

Slocum spent an hour evading contact with any of the other gang who might be awake or roaming about. At last he brought his dazed, bound, and gagged prisoners to the site he had selected for another unpleasant trap. He had finished cutting, fitting, scraping, and tying off the third in a linked series of snares when they made muffled, urgent protest. Slocum looked up, thought about it, then went back to work.

Two more hours went by while he rigged another deadfall, which would surely brain up to five of the rustlers at the same time. At last he went to his captives. He released the gag from the balding one's mouth.

"You can't get away with this," came the first words out of the bound man's mouth. "Kelso'll find you and fix your wagon good."

Slocum drew his .45 Peacemaker and screwed the muzzle tightly into an upturned ear. He made certain the other three could clearly see. "If you don't want to wear your brains on your shoulder, you'll listen to what I say and do as you are told. When I'm finished with this, I'm going to take you far to the south of here. Then I'll let you upright on those horses. If you are smart, you'll ride off and never look back. If not, and you come back, I'll kill all four of you anyway."

They had no problem in believing him.

It took Slocum until nearly daylight to take his prisoners to the edge of Charlie Goodnight's ranch. He admonished them to keep heading southeast.

"Until the people talk French," he added.

That should keep them thinking about something, Slocum figured, until the Goodnight riders found them and took them captive again. They were killers and rustlers, both still hanging offenses in Texas, so he had little sympathy for the quartet of hardcases.

He would take his own time going back into the upper canyon, Slocum decided. Let Kelso's gang run themselves ragged, and get good and spooked on his hidden traps. From friendly Indians and a crusty old mountain man, he had learned the tricks that allowed one man to hold more than thirty at bay. Never before had he been compelled to use quite so many of them in one encounter.

But then, the ghost rustlers scheme had been a brilliantly conceived strategy, carried out by men with enough courage and intelligence to make it work. Slocum didn't even begrudge giving credit for that. He had met clever enemies in the past. Men like Dobie Welsh, who wanted the whole of a large, lush valley in Dakota Territory all for himself. Including the town of Butternut. Welsh learned the error of his ways the hard way when the town fathers hired a new marshal to tame their town—a man by the name of John Slocum.

Then there had been Captain Godfrey Howard and his band of brigands. Worse had been the men behind Howard: Cyril Anstruther, a man steeped in mystery, Kansas State Senator Victor Dahlgren, Kansas Supreme Court Justice John Duffey, and banker Walter Black. Their goal had been far more ambitious—to take over the entire southeastern quarter of the state of Kansas and make it their own empire. They, too, met up with Slocum, and few lived long to regret it. Slocum had respected all of them, for their talent for evil, while despising the aftermath of their greed.

This would be another time, Slocum vowed to himself, that even though outnumbered, he would be on top of the situation. The surprises he had set for the rustlers would insure that. He set off at a faster lope, eager to find out how successful his planning had been.

Confusion ruled over the rustlers. Two new men had been mistakenly shot and killed by older members of the gang who did not know them. Butch Kelso sat with his back against the bowl of a pine, a tin cup of coffee in hand, and considered the shambles this search had become.

"Damn that Slocum," he burst out in frustration. "Where'd he learn all those tricks?"

"I'd say they's Injun tricks," Ollie Utting opined.

Kelso scowled at him. "Never heard of the Kiowa or Comanche usin' this kind of shit," he said.

"There's Injuns who live in mountains, where there's trees to make traps with," Utting suggested. "Like the Arapaho up Colorado way."

A shrill, prolonged scream, followed by immediate, reflexive gunshots, cut off further speculation on Slocum's nasty traps. Utting went pale. "What the hell?"

Rising, Kelso poured the dregs of his coffee onto the small fire. "We'd better go find out."

In a branch canyon, off the large box draw where they held some of the stolen cattle, Kelso and Utting came upon four men. Three, visibly shaken, sat their mounts and stared nervously at the fourth. He lay draped over a short section of tree trunk, suspended by ropes from an overhead limb. Two large, bloody, wooden spikes protruded from his back. Kelso's lips compressed and thinned into a tight line. Utting turned aside and vomited.

Anger flared in Kelso's chest. "Well, gawdamnit, get him off there."

"We're afraid to touch him," one responded dazedly.

"Don't know what else might fall on us," another added.

"*Nothing* else is going to fall, Jake," Kelso snapped. "Come on, give me a hand." He urged his skittery horse forward.

"We was . . . just ridin' along," the third rustler related in a cowed tone. "An'—an' this . . . thing dropped outta the tree and . . . got Frank."

"He ain't dead yet," the first benumbed hardcase reported. "At least I don't think he is."

Kelso studied the gorey damage. "He won't last long in any case. Least we can do is what's decent for him."

He started to pull at the slack arms. Frank groaned, roused enough to scream again. Kelso looked with helpless anger at the reticent outlaws. "At least hold this thing still," he growled.

Once more Kelso raised Frank by the shoulders and pulled him forward. The wooden stakes made a sucking sound as they slid through ravaged flesh. As though in a waking dream, Kelso saw the images before him of the squatter family he had been ordered to remove from the open range in New Mexico.

One of the infrequent range wars had flared anew when settlers began to erect fence on what the cattlemen considered "open range." Every fast gun and wannabe hired on to "cleanse" the sparsely grassed veld of central New Mexico. Kelso ran a crew of hardcases and cutthroats who soon became notorious for their viciousness. On this particular day, the squatter turned out to have three big, strapping sons. The fight worked down to hand-to-hand. In the end, Kelso had driven a spike-end pry bar through the chest of one of the sons.

When he pulled it out, it had made a noise like that which came from Frank's chest. It unnerved Kelso for a moment. He hesitated, then yanked with greater force.

Frank came free with a lurch and slipped from Kelso's grasp. At once, Kelso heard a whirring sound like rope running through a pulley block. The thigh-thick trunk shot upward and a bent sappling whipped toward him. Kelso's arms went up defensively, and he recoiled from the threat with enough force and speed to throw himself out of the saddle. He landed with a painful thump beside the body of Frank.

Jake parroted Kelso's earlier grumble. "*Nothing else is going to fall.*"

So shaken he forgot to cow his detractor, Kelso looked at the small, swaying tree. "That thing coulda taken my head off."

"We've learned about these traps," Jake advised. "Mostly the hard way."

"Goddamn that Slocum," Kelso cursed for the hundredth time as he pulled himself uncomfortably to his feet.

"You know something?" Ollie Utting offered. "I'm beginning to think that maybe Slocum ain't anywhere around here. I think he set these traps and drifted on south through the canyon. Might have taken those fellers who disappeared along as prisoners."

"What gives you that idea?" Kelso challenged.

Utting furrowed his brow. Thinking logically wasn't his long suit. "Ever' time one of those things goes off, whoever gets it makes a whole lot of noise, right? An' some of us come runnin' to see what happened, ain't that so? Well, then, if Slocum wanted to finish us off, he'd be somewhere shootin' at us when we bunched up."

"And there hasn't been any shooting," Kelso concluded, warming to Utting's suggestion.

"That's right, he ain't fired a shot so far."

A second later, Ollie Utting's statement became invalid when a loud, meaty smack shattered the quiet and Jake flung his arms into the air, to fall over backward off his horse, one boot heel still caught in the stirrup. Kelso and the others stared in disbelief for three seconds before they heard the crack of the shot.

Slocum had heard the scream and reactive gunshots from a short distance away. He increased the pace of his lathered mount and rounded one turn in the main gorge to see ahead the haze of dust cloud that indicated fast-ridden horses headed into a side canyon. His terrain-savvy mind took in what his keen green eyes saw to one side. An animal trail led up along the slope of the steeper side of the draw. If he bent low, he could make it, he estimated.

True to nature, the pathway did not proceed in a straight line; rather, it meandered along below the spiney crest on the inward, or reverse, slope. The trail took him high up over the narrow gorge formed by a tributary of the Red River. At about the time Butch Kelso and Ollie Utting arrived at the deadfall, Slocum reached a spot that concealed him from observation below, but allowed him a clear view.

It would also provide a clear field of fire, he decided. Dismounting, Slocum took the long, narrow, wooden box from the pack rig and set in on the ground. He flipped up the brass hasps and raised the lid. Inside, nestled in fitted, velvet-covered padding, lay a brand-new Winchester .45–70–500 Express Rifle.

A special powder-and-bullet configuration gave the weapon an effective range of 800 to a thousand yards. Slocum estimated the range to be about 750 yards downhill to the men gathered on the floor of the small canyon below his position. A nice, easy shot. From a rectangular depression, he lifted a twenty-round cardboard ammunition box. One thick index finger slid the inner, partitioned portion outward, to reveal the pointed, soft gray lead tips and shiny brass casings.

Slocum carefully inserted five of the big cartridges through the loading gate on the right side of the receiver. Then he attached a long, brass scope to the preset mount and twisted the leather sling around his left arm. Eyes still fixed on the men below, he eased himself into a position covered by a jumble of large boulders. He rested the forestock of the rifle in a V-shaped notch between two lower rocks and sighted in.

Satisfied, Slocum worked the lever action and chambered a round. Again he peered into the scope, and set the cross hairs on the chest of one outlaw. He took a deep breath, raised the sight point to his shoulder joint, and exhaled half of the air. Settled into the scope again, Slocum squeezed gently on the trigger, taking up the slack.

The hammer fell, and the powerful rifle slammed into his shoulder. For a moment he lost his sight picture. Then Slocum steadied to see the man's arms fly upward. He arched his back and jerked backward out of the saddle.

"One down," Slocum breathed aloud softly as he cranked out the expended round and chambered another.

He sighted in on a second of the immobile rustlers and sent a 500-grain slug winging toward contact long before anyone in the canyon reacted. He recognized Kelso by his size and red hair. He purposefully selected others as targets; Kelso he wanted to take alive.

Slocum's bullet struck, and the following sound of the shot set the outlaws into action. They scattered, two of them abandoning their horses in favor of the security of thick tree trunks. They didn't move fast enough, though. Slocum's third round caught another rustler in the hip, slamming him forward to take a mouthful of pine needles.

Time to be going, Slocum reckoned. There'd be other moments and more targets to whittle away.

18

Slocum noted with interest that none of the rustlers had come out of the side canyon by the time he reached the main trail. It would take them some time to recover from the shock of his unexpected attack. Good enough, he reasoned. That would give him a chance to locate another gathering and visit them with his own brand of retribution.

They had tried to kill him only a few nights before. And, clearly, Kelso had had every intention of gunning him down at the saloon in Happy. By now the average member of the gang should be uneasy and uncertain enough that a few long-range shots would send them off to find greener pastures. Slocum had enough experience to be aware he could not hope to capture all of the cattle thieves. One man alone could not handle thirty-five.

If he corralled the ringleaders, the Rangers could sweat the identity of the rest out of them. That suited Slocum fine. He had enough scars from bullet holes, knife slashes, and other forms of mayhem. When the time came, he would enlist the aid of the Goodnight riders and those working for Carl Hartson of the Bar-C. For the time being, all he sought to do was keep the outlaws off balance.

Slocum picked his next site carefully. Like the last, it provided good cover and concealment, and afforded an excellent field of fire. It also gave him a generous pick of targets. Once more, he put the Winchester Express into action within five minutes of selecting his spot.

Dust rose to join the spreading puff of powder smoke when the big rifle went off. Slocum heard the echo walk along a fold in the draw before he saw his man fall. Another shot sent a large, blue granite coffeepot flying high, cartwheeling and spewing out a scalding hot brown wave. Faintly he heard the yells of pain and consternation from those soaked by the liquid.

Smiling grimly to himself, Slocum faded into the dark green vegetation on the slope above them. He picked his third location because of the size. Long ago in a side canyon, a wide valley had been formed that ended in a high rock wall and a waterfall. Slocum worked his way, unseen, around one side until he came to a stand of willows that would hide his horses. From there he went on foot to the fall.

Crystal clear, a thick gout of water tumbled over the lip from the higher plateau beyond. It set up a constant roar that made hearing anything else impossible. The noise would also disrupt the sound of the Express, Slocum reasoned. He worked his way out onto a flat shelf of rock, the far end of which was slick and glistening from the misty spray that boiled off the fall. This would do nicely, he decided.

Using field glasses first, Slocum scouted the terrain laid out below him. He located two small camps, with half a dozen men lounging in each. A rumble from his stomach reminded him that he had not eaten anything more solid than a few strips of jerky in a day and a half. While others searched, these rustlers wolfed down their midday meal. Slocum closed his mind to the demands of his body and traded the field glasses for the telescopic sight of the rifle, to spot his best targets.

He quickly found one that amused him. A grizzled older man bent over a fire, a large cast-iron skillet in one hand. Hot lead from the Express bulged the bottom of the skilled with a musical bong before the old-timer could settle it in place on a trivet. The impact shattered the bones in the outlaw's hand and brought a howl from deep in the beard that masked his mouth. Slocum already sought another target.

A younger hardcase had bolted to his feet in reaction to Slocum's first shot. He looked around in consternation, then flopped back in the dirt when a 500-grain slug punched through his left thigh. Slocum shifted to the second campsite.

He had no doubt the occupants had seen the results of the big rifle. Three men lay flat on the ground, weapons at the ready. Each faced a different direction. Slocum nodded with satisfaction. The waterfall served well to muffle, and confuse the direction from which the shots had come. Carefully he sighted in on the turn of quarter-inch rope around the bole of a stunted pine. His finger tightened on the trigger.

With another solid slam, the butt plate kissed Slocum's shoulder. A long moment later, the rope parted and five nervous horses pulled free of the picket line. The standing men rushed to intercept them before they bolted. Levering the action of the Winchester rapidly, Slocum put up a line of dust plumes only a foot ahead of one of them.

With an inaudible curse, the rustler dove to one side and rolled away from the walking line of incoming rounds. Slocum paused to insert more cartridges in the tubular magazine. By his reckoning, he had some fifty left in his pack. A couple more, he figured, and then he would move on to another site.

Sheriff Harlan Butcher had little confidence in sending Butch Kelso after Slocum. Accordingly, he closed out his unfinished details and left the office in Happy. He rode north, through Canyon and on to Amarillo. He reached his destination an hour after sundown.

Yates Harkness met the sheriff at the front door to his sprawling adobe ranch house. The wealthy rancher ushered Butcher into a small study that served as an office, poured bourbon for both of them, and settled behind the desk. His full, fleshy lips pursed, and he steepled sausage fingers over his growing potbelly.

"What brings you here, Harlan?" he asked, a note of irritation in his voice.

"Slocum," Butcher answered simply.

Harkness raised a bushy eyebrow over one hard, piercing blue eye. "I thought we had that under control. You know, of course, that it was necessary to deal with McClure. He had found out too much about my . . . uh . . . business connections."

"I always said you would have been smart to drop your name from that meat packing company in Chicago," Butcher admonished.

"All water down a badger hole now," Harkness said dismissively. "What really bothered me was learning from Bob that Slocum was the range detective sent from Fort

Worth. I had discounted the name," Harkness continued his explanation. "I figured he was just a fast gun on the prod after that run-in with Kelso in Happy. Then I got to thinking. A few years ago, Slocum brushed up against one of my operations in Montana. I don't even know if he remembers. But, if we'd met face-to-face in McClure's office, he might have recalled. Then, when I saw that letter from the Board of Trade at the Chicago Stockyard on McClure's desk, I had to take matters into my own hands."

"And now Slocum is on the loose," Butcher sighed out and drained his whiskey.

Harkness poured them another round. He handed Butcher his with a scowl. "How serious is that?"

"Deadly serious. Enough so that I think you should come with me to the canyon. We have to close out the operation and cover our tracks the best we can. I'm not certain how much Slocum knows, but he's threatened me with arrest as part of the rustling gang."

The scowl deepened into a worried frown that creased Harkness's forehead to his receeding hairline. "How many head do we currently hold there?"

"Around three hundred, all told," Butcher answered.

"Too many to move quickly," Harkness snapped. "What can we do about it?"

"That's why I want you to come with me. I sent Kelso after Slocum. But . . . Slocum has buffaloed him every time. You need to take direct charge of the gang, make some plan for getting rid of the cattle, and organize the search for Slocum."

"None of them . . . know my identity," Harkness protested.

"Too late to worry about that. My bet is Slocum has headed for the canyon. If he gets to meddling around in there, no telling what could come of it. The upshot is, we could find ourselves in Huntsville for a long time."

"Or on the gallows," Harkness amended with a shudder.

Shortly after sundown, Slocum located an isolated side canyon where five of the rustlers held some ninety-five head of cattle. Uncomfortable from two days without solid food, Slocum was drawn to the savory odor of meat roasting in a dutch oven, potatoes cooking in the coals, and coffee as a compass needle was drawn to the north pole. He decided on a bold tactic.

Tensed for instant action, he rode openly into the camp. H howdied the rustlers, and explained he was with another grou and had gotten separated while searching for "that damne Ranger." They welcomed him. Like most men who travele the vast frontier, Slocum and the outlaws weren't long o conversation.

They spoke little while they demolished the ample food with skillet cornbread to mop up the natural gravy produce in the cast-iron pot. After supper, Slocum sipped a final cup o coffee, got oriented on how to find his fictional confederates and thanked the self-appointed cook for his meal.

He tightened the cinch on his saddle and rode out unmolest ed. Beyond the mouth of the narrow draw that opened into th grassy box canyon, he retrieved his packhorse. He spent th rest of the night catching up on his long-missed sleep.

Early the next morning, Slocum went on the hunt again. H had noticed a distinct lack of morale among the outlaws wit whom he had dined. One had actually expressed a longing t leave the canyon and be shut of all they were involved in. / few more nudges, he opined to himself, and they would begi to desert.

Slocum picked his stand carefully. This time he lay low i the grass, the long barrel of the Winchester Express restin in a forked shooting stick. He relied on a brisk breeze t dispel the smoke from the weapon's discharge. His ambus ready, Slocum relaxed as best he could and waited for hi first customers.

Three of them came around a bend in the trail, ridin abreast. Slocum picked the one in the middle and put a bulle through his shoulder. He moved fast and cut the hat fron another rustler's head with his second round. Fright put som steam in their voices, and even at his extreme range, Slocun could hear enough fragments to make sense of what the said.

". . . hell with this."

"I . . . ay, we get . . . of this place."

"Curtis . . . ook a bad un . . . in the left shoulder," the hatles man declared.

"He can . . . ide can't he?"

"We . . . ot to . . . et past that damned rifle."

". . . etter than stayin' . . . an' bein' sh . . . down like dogs."

Slocum held his fire and watched while the pair dismounted and helped their companion into the saddle. With the wounded man hunched forward on his horse's neck, they started out at a quick trot. Slocum held his fire until they had ridden past his position on the trail below him. Then he sent a final reminder to crack over their heads and raise dust a dozen yards in front.

Mouth fixed in a grim smile, Slocum waited until they had ridden out of sight, then levered upright and set off for another spot.

Slocum rounded a bend on the main trail and blundered into a trio of rustlers. Made nervous by all the shooting, they had their weapons out and ready. Before even Slocum's finely tuned reflexes could respond, one of the outlaws fired a hasty shot in his direction.

A sharp pain, followed by sudden numbness, exploded in Slocum's left calf. The horse under him grunted at the impact of the nearly spent bullet. Slocum had his .45 Colt in action by then. His first round cleared the shooter from his saddle. The second detonated at the same time as one from the hardcase in the middle. Slocum's aim proved the better.

Screaming, the rustler clutched at his belly, blood seeping through his thick fingers. He slumped in the saddle and turned deathly pale. Slocum ignored him to deal with the remaining member of Kelso's gang. He punched a slug through the right side of the cattle thief's chest and sent the man sprawling on the ground. The temporary numbness had started to wear off, and the wound in his leg began to hurt Slocum like hellfire.

At least it hadn't put him entirely out of business, Slocum reasoned as he eased his way past the dead man and his wounded companions. He would have to find a place to hole up and get a bandage on his calf. Provided, Slocum reminded himself, the gang gave him enough time to do that.

"Good news, Boss," one of the gang reported to Butch Kelso.

"What's that? Do you have Slocum cornered?" Butch demanded eagerly.

"Better'n that. Artie put a slug in him. Slocum's leakin' blood along a trail that's easy to follow."

Kelso roused himself. "Then let's get at it." To those around him, still showing reluctance to chase after the elusive Slocum, he added, "You see? He ain't no ghost and he ain't bulletproof. Now move your butts."

Kelso could smell death when he and a dozen rustlers rode up to the scene where Slocum had taken out the three outlaws. Another man had died and lay stretched out beside the first. The one who had taken a round high in his chest sat against a large rock, gasping for breath, a wet neckerchief held against the sucking wound.

His complexion had grayed, and a tinge of green ringed his mouth. He spoke with difficulty. "H-he's the fastest son of a bitch I ever saw."

"Where did he go?" Kelso snarled at the wounded man.

"You . . . can see for yourself. Blood tracks. Artie pu-put one in him. I don't know where, but he's hit."

Their nerve restored by this, the gang showed signs of more willingness to pursue the heretofore invisible enemy. With Kelso in the lead, they started off after the trail of blood drops. It led them along the main trail, south and eastward, deeper into the Palo Duro.

Butch Kelso could feel the tension that hovered over them all as the red splatters began to darken. The darkening indicated that they were moving too slowly. Yet, Kelso reasoned, if they rode faster than a quick walk, they could lose the sign all together. When the droplets swung off the wide roadway, Kelso halted his men.

"Spread out. He's gone to ground somewhere. Close to the water, I'd say."

With worried expressions, the rustlers did as told. They dismounted and walked along in a single file, weapons in hand, headed for the distant gurgle of the Red River. Kelso urged them on from his place at the center of the line. He had Slocum now; he could taste it.

Slocum lay low over the final bank of the river, near a shallow ford. The water made a musical burble as it flowed over and around the smooth, rounded stones. He had walked his horse in the stream for half a mile from where he had left the road. Then he had stopped and tended to his wound. A strip of cheesecloth and some patching plaster formed a workable bandage. He then examined the animal and found the bullet wedged base-deep in the leather of the stirrup skirt. It had punched the sorrel in the ribs but failed to break the skin.

No sense in further tormenting the horse, he decided. Besides, he could use the beast's trail as a diversion. Slocum retained the Express rifle and all his spare ammunition and freed the Goodnight horse to find its way home.

After a long rest, he crossed the Red at the ford and struck out for the draw where he had left his packhorse. Walking proved uncomfortable, though not impossible. He made slow time. When he gained a little height over the main canyon floor, he looked back and, in the distance, saw Kelso's gang searching for him in the area around his last bloody traces.

Well and good, he decided. Let them waste time. He had scribbled a note to George Goodnight informing him of the situation. That should bring some help soon. Provided, of course, the horse had sense enough to go home.

Ollie Utting chucked a rock into the river. "There ain't no trace," he growled disgustedly. "Slocum's done disappeared on us again."

"That's not good enough, Ollie," Butch Kelso barked. "Use your eyes. Find that bastard. I want him here, on his knees, in front of me. I want to see him beg for his life before I shoot him."

"Then you'd best do something real smart about findin' him," Ollie groused back.

"Lip, Ollie. Watch that lip," Kelso warned. "We've got boys workin' up and down stream. They'll find something."

"I'm not so sure. What if he took off for the Goodnight spread? They say that ol' boy still hangs rustlers by himself."

Kelso eyed Utting a moment. "That sort of talk ain't good for the others to hear, Ollie. You'd be smart to keep it between us, hear?"

"Yeah, I hear you. But, what if that *is* what he did?"

Kelso considered that a minute. "Then we run like hell. No other choice."

"Why ain't Butcher doin' something to help?" Utting asked.

Kelso chewed on that a second. "Y'know, that's a good question. I think I'm gonna send a couple of the boys to get our good sheriff and Yates Harkness."

"You think the big boss will come?" Utting asked, doubtful.

"Oh, I think I can make it worth his while," Kelso hinted. "Now, for starters, get the boys together and we'll divide up the rest of the canyon to search. I mean to get Slocum and damned soon."

19

Slocum found a vantage point, high up on the wall of the main canyon. He had relocated his packhorse and sought out a location from which he could keep an eye on the activity of the outlaws without himself being seen. The exertion of his climb had reopened the wound in his leg.

Shortly before he'd settled into the cave-like depression, the wound had started once more to bleed profusely. Now Slocum crouched under the low overhang that had been carved out by a far more active river long ago. He redressed the through-and-through bullet hole and packed the entrance and exit wounds with moss scraped from a pine trunk, wetted with chill water from the Red River.

He had been weak and light-headed when he bathed himself in the icy water below and filled his two canteens. Carrying them, the ammunition, the Express rifle, and a cloth sack holding his dry rations had been an exhausting chore. He had nearly lost the rifle twice. Still feeling faint, he gnawed energetically on another strip of jerky.

Slocum reached the conclusion he should consume all of the dried meat to provide strength to recover. He would spend the afternoon watching the movements of the gang, then, if he felt better, he would climb down after dark. A short walk would retrieve his packhorse, and he would ride it to the Goodnight ranch. Debilitated by the wound, and unable to get about without leaving a clear trail, he admitted to himself that he needed help to finish out this nest of rustlers. A flicker caught in the corner of his left eye drew his attention.

Twelve members of the gang rode along the main trail, heads turning, alert for any sign of Slocum. Oddly, they never looked upward. Slocum watched them until they went out of sight, and then made a rough tally on a strip of creased, grease-stained paper. It appeared as though Kelso had concentrated the search on the south side of the river. That suited Slocum fine.

With plenty of water, and the regenerative power of the dried meat, he stood a fair chance of being able to pull off his plan to contact George Goodnight. Every minute he remained out of sight improved the odds. Still on watch for more of the gang, Slocum munched steadily on the dwindling pile of jerky. A distant rattle of gunfire brought a smile to his lips.

No doubt once more some of the gang had stumbled across a few of the others and started shooting instead of asking questions. Good. That wouldn't make too many of them happy about the situation. If that kept up, Slocum felt he could rely upon more desertions before long. Too bad he could do nothing more to encourage such a decision. Sleep beckoned to Slocum, and he welcomed the rest it would bring.

Three men from the gang met Sheriff Butcher and Yates Harkness at the upper entrance to the canyon near sundown. Harkness cursed hotly when he learned that Kelso had sent for him by name. Thoroughly demoralized by Slocum's unorthodox campaign against them, the rustlers remained unimpressed by the outburst. All they had been told to do was to deliver the messages.

"Butch says you've got to round up more men," Ike Baker repeated.

"What for?" Butcher demanded. "There's what in there, thirty-five or six?"

"No, sir. Only twenty-two, twenty-three left," Baker told him. "Seven of them is shot up like me," he added.

Butcher and Harkness exchanged glances. "Very well," Harkness relented. "I'd suggest you go in search of more men, Harlan." He sighed heavily. "I'll go try to put some fresh backbone in your top gunhand."

"It had best wait for morning, Boss," Baker suggested to Harkness. "Slocum has set up some deadly traps, an' in the dark you don't have a chance of getting clear of one."

"That's nonsense," Harkness blurted.

"No, Boss, it's jist *good* sense, believe me. We had to help pry a good friend off of a couple of wooden spikes stuck in a hunk of tree trunk that swung down out of the branches at us. It was plum messy." Baker gave a shudder of revulsion.

Harkness swallowed with difficulty and lighted a slim cigar. "Those drovers who took the last herd in to sale ought to be back by now," he prompted the sheriff.

"Right. I can be in Canyon within an hour. I'll look for them at the Branding Iron. You can be sure the first thing they'll do is hit a saloon."

"Do that. And bring them back at once. We'll camp right outside the canyon, and we can all go in together in the morning," Harkness said to put a cap on it.

Slocum awakened an hour after sundown. He felt more refreshed than he had even before he was shot. The next instant he cursed his vulnerability which had allowed him to miss a final check on the location of the rustlers. Time to be doing something, he urged his stiffened body.

Biting back the pain, Slocum compelled uncooperative joints to move. He secured all the loose objects around his body and began the strength-sapping descent from his hiding place. He had gone not more than thirty feet down the canyon wall when the sole of his boot came down on a loose rock.

When Slocum put his weight on it, the rounded stone gave way. His ankle twisted painfully and he lost his hold overhead. A cloud of dust and pebbles rose around his face as he shot downward, out of control.

New agony exploded in Slocum's leg as he plunged downward. In his imagination, he made enough noise to alarm the dead. His fingers encountered a snag of greasewood, and he clamped onto it in desperation. With a sudden shock that nearly disjointed his shoulder, Slocum came to an abrupt halt. He bit his lip to keep from shouting in pain and relief. Slowly the dust subsided and the rattle of rocks diminished.

His heart stopped pounding, and a rapid blink and natural tearing washed the grit from his eyes. Then, ever so slowly, the withered roots of the greasewood bush began to pull free. Slocum started to slide again. In spite of the misery in his wounded leg, he thrashed about for some foothold. He had descended half an arm's length when the toe of his right boot touched a tiny protrusion.

It proved enough to momentarily halt his plunge. With all his weight rested on his good leg, Slocum took quick stock of his condition. The scope-mounted rifle remained in place over his shoulder. To his left side he felt the round, canvas-covered shapes of the canteens. Slowly he reached outward in a descending arc with his left hand.

His arm felt weighted with lead as he slid his fingers over the rough, nearly vertical face to which he clung so precariously. After long, tension-stretched seconds, he discovered a wrist-thick branch or trunk. Carefully Slocum wound his fingers around it and gave a tentative yank.

To his relief, it did not budge. Now anchored above and below, Slocum edged his injured left leg sideways in search of another foothold. Sweat popped out in ridges of droplets on his forehead. Every five breaths, he held still and listened for any sign of an alarm. He was flooded with relief when none came each time. Still a stable platform eluded him.

At last he made tentative contact with an extension of the lip on which his right foot rested. Gingerly he let his weight shift and come to bear on the toe of his left boot. Nothing gave. Unfortunately, pain shot upward from the wounded calf to the base of his skull. It dizzied him and instantly invoked a nauseous surge.

Breathing deeply to recover, Slocum clung haphazardly like a fly to a ceiling. Gradually the wave of sick disorientation passed. He could only look upward and to one side. Already soft, silvery light frosted the rim of the canyon. The slightly less than half-moon had risen. He calculated how long before he would become an easy target for the hardcases below.

Not long enough, he decided. Rested, though still under a strain, Slocum turned his thoughts to the more pressing problem. How in hell would he get off this wall? He had obviously missed the goat path he had followed to the cave. Only, was it to his left or his right? If he chose incorrectly, Kelso would not have to worry about him. He would be dashed into a rag-covered pulp.

Slowly Slocum edged his left foot along the ledge. It somehow seemed familiar. He forced back the mental clamor for escape and turned his mind to a recollection of his climb.

About thirty feet below the cave, there had been a break in the outcropping, which had continued along the narrow trace all the way to the cave, where it became part of the roof.

That protrusion had been about shoulder height most of the way, Slocum remembered. With a tremendous effort of will, he eased his left leg over the edge of the lip and released his hold on the unsteady bush with his right hand. By inches he lowered his body, trying to will himself to see something, anything that would indicate his speculation had been correct.

A tiny twinge of pain followed contact of his boot sole with the wider ledge of the animal trace. Gusting out a too-long-held breath, Slocum hung by his left hand and let his body go. At the last moment, while he hung uncertainly over the canyon, he had to let go completely. It jarred his teeth when his right boot struck the ledge.

Safe at last, Slocum rejoiced. At least for the time being, the cynical corner of his brain reminded him.

Slocum negotiated the age-worn animal track by sidestepping his way, his back pressed to the canyon wall. He didn't breathe easily until his boots crunched on level ground. He made his way at once to the riverbank. The descent and his fall had opened the wound again. He needed to bathe and rebandage it. Trouble was he had run out of bandaging material up in the cave.

That meant he would have to wash out the existing wrappings and let the night air dry them. When the gurgle of water over the rocks announced his nearness to the slippery, red clay bank of the Red River, Slocum eased his burdens from his shoulders and sat on the grassy lip.

With discomfort, which he mentally suppressed below the screaming-in-agony level, Slocum removed his boots and woolen socks. Next came his gunbelt, which he laid at a calculated ready-to-hand position on the edge. His whipcord trousers, shirt, and short summer underdrawers followed. Wincing at the throbbing pain in his left leg, Slocum lowered himself into the chilly water.

Shock at first contact with the viscous, moving stream numbed the ache, and Slocum sank to his shoulders. His dust-clogged pores absorbed the water, and he felt the collection of effluvium lifting from his body. Having nothing else, he used his hands to clean himself, then located a suitable rock by starlight and eased up onto it. It took the help of his arms to lift Slocum's injured leg across the opposite one.

He unwound the bandage and sniffed of it. His nose registered only the scent of blood. At least the wound had not started to fester. Slocum bent low and washed the strip of cheesecloth. The clots of moss with which he had packed the bullet holes had come away with the binding. He noted with satisfaction that the bleeding had stopped. Perhaps it was the cold water, he speculated.

In any case, he would have to sit here until he and the bandage dried. No. He rejected the idea immediately. That would leave him entirely too exposed. Better to wrap the wounds and let the bandage dry on the bank. He could find cover in a low stand of willows that drooped over the river a short distance away.

To further that prospect, Slocum reached for a small pouch around his neck that contained the last of the moss he had gathered earlier. He packed that into both holes and wound the cloth around it. He would have to tear strips in the free end and tie them in place. Field surgeons on both sides in the War for Southern Independence had used that method, Slocum recalled. It would serve his purpose now.

With that accomplished, Slocum waded to shore and gathered up his clothing and weapons. Bent low, to avoid making a target of himself, he limped to the screening protection of the drooping willow limbs. The ground near the trees was bare under a layer of tiny brown leaves from last fall. Slocum settled in and draped his shirt over his shoulders to cut the chill. He would dry off soon enough. Then he could dress and wait to see what developed.

Drained of all energy by his ordeal, Slocum soon nodded off. He jerked awake at the echo in his head of the clop of a horse's hoof. Fisting his .45 Peacemaker, he shot a quick glance at the sky. From the moon's position, he judged it to be sometime after midnight, at least one-thirty. He heard another thump of shod feet on hard ground and saw a flash of spark from a iron shoe striking a stone. Slocum eased back the hammer of his Colt.

"Ranger?" came a low, tentative voice, muffled by the ripple of water. "Mr. Slocum, you there?"

Now, who in hell would be riding along doing something like that? Slocum mulled it over and decided certainly not one of the spooked rustlers. He moved slightly from his position and turned toward the near wall of the canyon.

"Over here." He spoke with enough force for the echo to carry across the river.

Immediately he moved back to his original position. Across the way the silhouette of the rider stiffened up, and the shoulder line elongated as the man turned in the saddle. A moment went by, and then his voice came somewhat louder.

"Where are you? Mr. George sent me. Ranger, are you all right?"

Slocum considered this a moment and decided it fit. "There's a ford a short ways up. Cross over, I'll meet you there."

"I know where it is. Be right there."

Slowed by his injuries, Slocum reached the ford after the Goodnight rider's horse had stopped dripping. He gave the area a careful once-over before showing himself. With instinctive concern, the cowboy leaned toward Slocum.

"You've been hurt."

"Yes. Nothing that won't heal," Slocum advised him.

"That sorrel you got from our string came in about sundown. Saddled, but no sign of you. Mr. George read your note and sent three of us out lookin'."

Slocum smiled in the darkness. "I thought he might. Now, listen close. There's about twenty or so of the rustling gang spread out in the canyon. They're hunting me. Actually, I've been hunting them," he added with a low chuckle. "Only the odds aren't good, now that I've taken a bullet. I want you to find your partners and ride fast as you can back to the ranch. Tell George Goodnight that I asked you to have him send all the men he can. We have a chance to round up the whole gang."

"Sounds good to me. Anything you need, Ranger?"

"I could stand some food."

"Oh, hell, I didn't bring any along."

"I'll manage," Slocum told him. "Now, get going."

● ● ●

Slocum rested for an hour. Then he made his way to where he had left the packhorse. The animal had grazed its fill on grass but welcomed a small ration of oats. That attended to, Slocum attached his rifle and the canteens to the pack frame and pulled himself atop the canvas-covered bundle. Picking his route carefully, he headed toward the Goodnight ranch.

He had covered what he estimated to be a third of the way when the pain in his leg and the dull throb of his bruised ribs forced Slocum to halt. He found a place from where he could watch the main road and still be out of sight. He put the packhorse farther away from the trail and settled in.

For all his efforts, his eyelids soon sagged like sash weights. Slocum's head bobbed and his body lost feeling, except for a dull pulsation of pain. With the moon still visible over the canyon rim, he drifted off into a deep, restorative sleep.

Kelso's gang had barely settled down for an early breakfast when Sheriff Butcher and ten men from Canyon rode into camp. Yates Harkness greeted him with a troubled expression.

"I've reminded Kelso of his probable reception in New Mexico. It doesn't seem to worry him as much as Slocum," Harkness explained.

"You mean he's going to end the hunt?"

"No, nothing like that. Though he suggested it at first. I recommend we wait for full daylight before setting out. Nothing Kelso or I could say would get any of these men out at night. Slocum has set traps that are murderous in the dark. I talked to some of those caught in them. I can't blame a one for not wanting a big wooden spike driven through his chest."

Butcher dismounted and walked to the cook fire. He helped himself to a tin plate of fatback and beans, two dense-looking biscuits, and a cup of coffee. "All right, we'll wait," he agreed. "Then we send these fresh men through the gorge right fast until they get beyond wherever Slocum might be holed up. That way we have him caught between us."

"Good thinking," Harkness agreed.

"I knew things would work out once you got here, Sheriff," Butch Kelso joined in. "That's a right smart idea. Now we've got Slocum by the balls."

20

A sledgehammer pounded the base of Slocum's skull, which awakened him to the new day. He examined his leg and saw only a slight seepage from both sides. The blood had clotted against the moss, he surmised. Barring any infection, even with the accompanying new pain, the clotting would let him get around a lot better. His stomach growled, to remind him he had not eaten properly in three days.

Lack of food made him light-headed. It caused him to miss the first, distant rumble of many hooves. He was filling his empty belly with the murky water of the Red when he noted them driving hard from the southeast. He had scant time to get closer to the road and show himself to the Goodnight hands as they cantered along the trail. The young rider from the previous night led the way.

He reined in and handed down a gunnysack that had been tied to his saddle horn. "Mr. Goodnight sent this along for you," he told Slocum.

Sincerely grateful, Slocum opened it without ceremony and delved inside. He came up with a pair of cold, fried pork chops wrapped in greasy paper, some of Lupe's sweet rolls, and a mason jar full of nearly warm beans. His belly rumbled in protest while he restrained himself long enough to brief the gun-toting cowboys.

"The rustlers are north of us. They should be coming this way, searching for me at any time. In fact I'm surprised they haven't been by here so far. You should spread out in numbers no less than five and keep out of sight until I give the signal. That will be two fast rounds followed by a pause and then a third shot. I'm beholdin' for the grub. Now, I'd better pay some attention to it before I fall over."

He began to gnaw the pork before the first of the cowhands rode out of sight.

Slocum finished half of the delicious, rich food and put the remainder aside. He set up for long shots, mobility being something he had to abandon. He had only settled in place when ten men he could not recall seeing before rode past his hiding spot. He decided to let them go and see what developed.

An hour later, the first recognizable faces in the gang showed up. They ambled their horses along, darting nervous glances from side to side. Slocum watched them out of sight. He tensed when seven more came into view a short time later. Good thing he had not given away his position by firing on the newcomers.

Slowly the day passed in the same manner. It became clear to Slocum that the outlaws had been unnerved enough that they stuck to the main trail. None seemed eager to investigate the side canyons. Several parties rode in both directions, reporting negative results to those they encountered going eastward.

Afternoon had painted long shadows on the northern wall when the riders with strange faces returned. They looked bored and discouraged. Voices drifted up to Slocum.

"What good are those cow nurses? I'll bet they didn't look in a single draw," one man said.

"If you'd seen some of those boys got busted up by the traps set by this Slocum, you wouldn't want to either," another answered him.

"Hell, he's only one man," the first man persisted.

"One mean son of a bitch," the second man pressed. "Ain't many men who'd leave it so you got smacked in the face with a bent tree."

"I figger some of them got drunked up and fell off their horses. D'you see the whiskey bottles piled up in that camp, Ez?"

"Sure did. Made my throat drier than a last year's corncob. Think we'll get some of that when we show up?" Ezra replied eagerly.

"Man huntin' an' panther piss don't mix."

"Says you. Now, me, I can take a jolt anytime."

"Don't we know, Ezra," the first man said, laughing.

Slocum watched them pass by, tested his left leg, and laid new plans.

Like the ghosts the rustlers were suspected of being, the Goodnight cowhands drifted in to the rendezvous selected by Slocum. Quickly he outlined his agenda for the night. Several older cowboys produced broad grins when they heard the details. He included directions to preselected spots around the main camp where they would have clear fields of fire. Others, greener cowpunchers, Slocum ordered to occupy static nightwatch positions. When he judged the time to be right, he sent them on their way and set out on a horse borrowed from the volunteer camp cook.

Slocum drifted silently toward the large, grassy box canyon that he had discovered the outlaws preferred for their main camp. The intense throbbing in his leg and head had reduced to a dull thud. He had changed the dressing on his wound at two-hour intervals, and although brightly pink, the ragged flesh around the holes did not reveal any of the angry red that would indicate infection. It hurt to walk, and most of the way he rode with his left leg out of the stirrup. When Slocum halted at last, he dismounted on the right-hand side.

At first he distrusted his ability to move silently. Slocum kept his .45 Colt in hand as a precaution against being surprised. He worked his way into the isolated canyon, along the edge of the trail ground into the earth by hundreds of head of stolen cattle. When the narrow entry widened into the grass-dotted floor of the canyon, he cut to his left and sought concealment in the tall mesquite scrub.

Quickly Slocum's ears became accustomed to the night sounds of the high-walled glen. Most prominent came the chittering and the buzz-saw drone of crickets and cicadas. Mosquitoes made their high-pitched whines as they dove to attack the exposed back of Slocum's neck. Gradually, over the forlorn croak of bullfrogs, Slocum discerned a soft purr of human speech.

"I don't like it on a quiet, peaceful night," one voice complained. "Let alone standin' guard with some crazy gunslick out there settin' traps and shootin' at us from hiding."

"Button that lip, an' get back on that horse," an older voice growled. "We've got another hour before we spell you off."

Slocum nodded in the darkness. Perfect. He slid toward the contentious rustlers as another youthful outlaw spoke up. "Yeah, Herbie, at least Kelso's let us ride two together since Mr. Harkness got here."

He took half the available time to move in on the unsuspecting men. He came upon them from behind. They sat close together, their backs supported by the thick branches of a mesquite bush. For a moment, Slocum wondered how they felt about the long thorns of the hostile shrub. One of them rose abruptly and stepped a few feet away. He spread his legs and a splash sounded from a growing puddle as he relieved himself.

That caused a change in Slocum's plan. He moved with all the swiftness he could muster to the other man, who instinctively looked away from his partner's chore. Slocum's Colt flashed silver-gray in the moonlight. With his powerful arm, he drove the barrel into the side of the outlaw's head.

The sound of its impact brought the other man around with a yellow spray shooting wide. He found himself looking into the muzzle of the .45.

"Come over here," Slocum commanded quietly.

Gaze fixed on the Colt's barrel, he obeyed. Slocum directed him to pull his partner upright and sit back-to-back with him. Then he brained the cooperative rustler and trussed them around the ankles with a lariat he took from one of their saddles. He slung the rope over a high, forearm-thick branch of the mesquite and took a dally around the horn of the saddle. The horse did the work.

When Slocum had the unconscious men upside down, their heads a foot off the ground, he halted the animal and dug inside the saddlebags for a ground anchor. The roan snuffled curiously as Slocum bent to screw the metal device into the turf. He tied off the reins and went back to inspect his handiwork.

Repeated coiling of the rope had put twists in it that caused the helpless pair to turn slowly in the air. Slocum used their neckerchiefs to fashion gags and fitted them in place. Now he needed only to wait for the two young gunhawks to return.

• • •

Charlie Goodnight's cowboys spent a busy night also. Following instructions, they waited until the last change of sentries then, as Slocum had done, they went to work. When morning found the bottom of the canyon, their efforts produced stunning results for the rustlers. Slocum watched with satisfaction from his chosen vantage point as alarm spread among the outlaws.

The cook was the first to notice that something had gone wrong. Not a one of the night guards drifted in with the dawn to get the relief of a cup of hot coffee and a brief, refreshing nap. Through his field glasses, Slocum observed the heated, unheard conversation between the cook and Butch Kelso. Their agitation decided him on his first target. By his calculation it would have to be their last usable coffee-pot.

"Gawdamnit, they run out on us," Butch Kelso growled when the cook reported no sign of the lookouts.

"I don't think so," the short, bowlegged old-timer opined. "You want me to rouse some of the boys to go have a look?"

"Damn right. I want to know what's goin' on," Kelso spat.

Within ten minutes, five of Kelso's gang had saddled up and ridden out to check on the missing men. They made a wide swing and found no sign of the riders or their horses. One rustler returned to report this.

Kelso had an uneasy feeling as he gave a new order. "Work closer in. There has to be something to show what happened."

Another fifteen minutes crept by with the same results. Then a shout of consternation came from near the mouth of the canyon. Kelso went out himself, along with four others. What they found left his jaw sagging.

A bulldog-faced rustler stated the obvious. "Someone strung them up on the mesquite."

Four very uncomfortable hardcases dangled from the higher limbs of a large mesquite bush. Dark red spots on their shirts and trouser legs showed where movement during the night had brought them into contact with the prickly thorns of the self-protective shrub.

"Get them down," Kelso said in a choked voice.

One of the older men had lost consciousness. After the gags had been removed from their mouths, the other three became frantically voluble. "It was Slocum. I swear it. He come on us without a sound."

Kelso thought that over. "He's been wounded. How did he manage this?"

"He just . . . up an' done it," one of the younger outlaws stated. "He didn't show no sign of bein' hurt that I could see."

Restored to their horses, the four gang members hastened to camp. They looked around for their friends who had been on watch the same shift. "Where's the others?"

"Gone," Kelso told them, uncomfortable with the fact.

"Didn't leave a trace," Ollie Utting added.

"None of them came past us," the young rustler called Eric declared. "If they had, we'd have heard them."

"You didn't hear Slocum," Kelso fired at them.

"That's different," Eric objected. "He was on foot. We would have heard horses, even if they was bein' walked."

"He's got a point," Ollie suggested.

"Then what happened to them?" Kelso demanded.

He didn't get an answer, because right then Slocum's slug sent the coffeepot flying noisily into the air. Two seconds of stunned silence followed before the gang heard the shot. By then another .45–70–500 bullet had shattered a dutch oven and upset the tripod from which it hung. Smoking hot beans flew in a wide spray, scalding the men they struck.

"Oh, shit, he's back," Kelso said as he hit the ground.

Slocum looked on as the outlaws recovered enough to try return fire. The rounds fell terribly short of his position. Shock being his intent, Slocum noted that with approval. He eased the Winchester Express into position again and sighted on a panicked rustler who had started to run for his horse.

The bullet cut the legs out from under the fleeing hardcase, who sprawled in the dirt. Before the impact, Slocum had pushed up from the ground and started off for his next position. His two quick shots followed by a later third had remained the signal for the Goodnight cowboys to close in. Slocum settled into the notch between two close-growing pines and lined up his fourth round.

Seen through the long, brass telescopic sight, the face of Johnny Tulip, grimacing in pain from his earlier wounds, hovered for a long, tempting time. Slocum lowered the cross hairs and centered them on the bulk of the holster at Tulip's hip. Gently he squeezed the trigger. The Winchester bucked and snorted. Seconds later, Slocum heard Tulip's howl of pain and fright.

Slocum looked up from the narrow field of the sight to see the already wounded outlaw dancing a jig under the trees, his holster, containing his revolver with a broken top strap, flopping against his right leg with every hop. By then, the Goodnight riders had thundered in among the outlaws, guns blazing. Slocum withdrew to his borrowed horse and pulled himself into the saddle.

His leg had begun a slow, heavy throb again. He dismissed it from his thoughts and secured the Express rifle. Then, with his .45 Colt in hand, he started off to the center of the fighting below. Slocum had crossed half the distance when four mounted rustlers broke clear and swung to attack the flank of the advancing cowboys. He put heels to the sorrel's ribs and hastened to close the range.

At seventy feet, Slocum got off a respectable shot that cleared one hardcase from his saddle. A quick look showed him that nearly half of both sides could no longer use their weapons for fear of hitting their own side. The fighting had turned to hand-to-hand. Slocum concluded that he would have to do something to break that deadlock.

Yates Harkness stood in the midst of a milling throng of confused and frightened rustlers. He cursed them for bunching up and cursed the unseen Slocum for bringing all his grand design to ruin. A cowboy crashed his horse into the human wall opposite him, and Harkness had a clear shot.

His bullet doubled the Goodnight rider over his saddle horn, and his horse bolted. That put some life and purpose back into the gang. Those on that side rallied and spread out to take better aim.

A second later, a dozen cowhands burst through the haze of dust and powder smoke, Slocum in the lead. Clearly outgunned, the demoralized rustlers threw down their weapons and raised arms above their heads.

"You cowardly bastards!" Yates Harkness raged. "Fight them." He looked about desperately and saw Sheriff Harlan Butcher making his way toward his saddled horse. With him went Butch Kelso. Then he heard a deep, resonate voice that sent ice sliding along his spine.

"Hold it there, Butcher," Slocum bellowed over the tumult.

Butcher recognized the voice and turned swiftly, hand streaking to his six-gun. Slocum had reined in, and he answered with his own weapon, only recently reloaded.

Butcher's first round cracked past Slocum's head, hastily fired and aimed too high. Slocum put a slug in the crooked lawman's left thigh. Butcher went to his right knee, a groan bitten back by his pale lips. He eared the hammer and let fly another bullet from his .44 Merwin and Hulbert.

Squealing, the sorrel reared as Butcher's slug cut skin on its right front quarter. With his weakened leg, Slocum was unable to control the pain-crazed animal. The violent rearing forced him to shuck free of the saddle. He landed hard, and a puff of grit teared his eyes. Slocum wiped furiously at his closed lids to clear his vision.

When he opened his eyes, he saw Butcher not twenty feet away. The sheriff raised his arm for another shot. Slocum snapped his cap a moment before Butcher could trigger the .44. Hot lead slammed into the corrupt sheriff's chest, and he flipped over backward, a red stain spreading on his shirt. A sudden, loud drumming of hooves drew Slocum's attention.

Butch Kelso and two men sprinted away from the battle, bent low over the stretched necks of their horses. Slocum raised his Colt and sent a bullet after them. It didn't find a mark, and the outlaws soon raced out of range. Slocum bit off a useless curse and suddenly became conscious that the gunfire around him had broken off.

He looked around to find rustlers with their hands held high, the Goodnight cowhands guarding them. In the middle of one cluster, Slocum saw a man he suspected was Yates Harkness. He pushed to his feet and walked over. His hard, angular face wore an expression devoid of compassion or lenience.

"You're Harkness?" He asked of the man crouched on his knees.

"Y-yes," the defeated man answered, lips and chin trembling.

"I have a few questions for you."

"I'll not give you the satisfaction of any answers."

Slocum nodded toward the cowboys. "They hang cattle rustlers, you know."

Harkness paled. "Look, I am a member of the Cattlemen's Association. I was brought here by force," he said, inventing this in a desperate effort to save his life. "It was the sheriff. He was behind this whole thing. I found out and confronted him. He and some of his men overpowered me and brought me here."

Only a single, harsh word passed Slocum's lips. "Bullshit."

Eyeing the cowhands, one of whom had begun to fashion a hangman's noose, Harkness lost the last small bit of his nerve. "All right, I'll tell you what you want to know."

"Who killed Bob McClure and why?" Slocum demanded.

"It was Sheriff Butcher."

"You can't blame everything on a dead man," Slocum countered. "Butcher wasn't even there until after I found the body."

Harkness nervously eyed the deadly knot. "McClure found out I owned half of a packinghouse in Chicago. It made him suspect I had something to do with the rustling. He confronted me with it that—that night when you were to come to the office. Butcher had sent one of his deputies with me. He shot McClure and you killed him in the hall. I hit you over the head when you came in the office and got rid of the body."

"Then Butcher knew all along that I was a range detective?"

"Yes. We decided to get you hanged for McClure's murder. That would have smoothed everything over. At first we didn't know your name, but after what you did to Kelso and two of his men, we considered you a danger. Then, when you showed up at McClure's office, it came clear."

Slocum shook his head in disgust. "Tie him up good, boys, and get ready to take all of the prisoners to Happy. They're going to stand trial for rustling and murder."

"What'll you be doin'?" Charlie Rorebaugh, Goodnight's range boss, asked.

"I'm going after Butch Kelso. I've got a good idea where he's heading," Slocum advised with a grim expression.

21

Having ridden through the day, Slocum reached Happy a quarter hour after sundown. He went directly to Ginny's house. From a distance of half a block, he could hear the sound of breaking glass and her screams. One of Kelso's henchmen rose up from the edge of the porch as the big, dark-featured Slocum approached.

Unwisely, the rustler rested his hand on the butt of his six-gun. Slocum reined in and pointed with the big index finger of his left hand. "Pull that or ease it to the ground."

Ollie Utting used only a half second of the scant time he had. "I've got no quarrel with you, Slocum." He undid his cartridge belt, pulled the tie-down thong, and let the rig slide to the ground.

Slocum stepped from the saddle with a set of manacles at the ready. He fastened Utting's hands behind him and frog marched him to the far side of the street. "Wait. I'll be back."

"Don't count on it," Utting found nerve enough to say with a sneer.

With the quickness and quiet of a panther, Slocum went up on the porch. He eased the Peacemaker from his holster and tried the knob. It turned freely and the door swung open.

Kelso's other man waited just inside. He caught the movement of the door and swung that way, .44 Colt tracking Slocum. Slocum shot him through the chest. He backpedaled and bounced off a wall. Eyes rolling up, he slid down to die in a sitting position. Slocum came all the way through the doorway.

Butch Kelso held a delicate side table in both hands, ready to smash it against the wall. Beyond him, eyes wide in fright,

Ginny Stuart looked on helplessly. Swearing a foul oath, Kelso destroyed the piece of furniture and swung a vicious back-hand at Ginny, who had screamed again at the loss of the small table.

Long strides brought Slocum close to the head rustler. Kelso seemed a man possessed. He had not reacted to the gunshot and continued to ignore Slocum until the big man with the Ranger badge planted a hard hand on his shoulder.

Slocum swung him, and Kelso surprised Slocum by leaping in the air. Legs scissored around Slocum's waist, Kelso hammered away with a fist at the end of an aching arm. Slocum bunched Kelso's shirt in his left hand and yanked forward, while he drove a hard right into his assailant's face.

Kelso's eyes crossed, and he slackened his grip on Slocum's hips. Ignoring the weakened blows to his chest, Slocum rammed another big-knuckled right into Kelso's face. Then he powered a third blow up under Kelso's chin and released his hold on the shirt. Kelso fell back into the litter of his earlier destructiveness. He gasped wildly, shuddered and went slack. Slocum eyed him a moment, then crossed to Ginny, who came sobbing into his arms.

"Oh, Lord, I'm glad to see you, Slocum," she blurted broken-ly. "He . . . he came a little while ago. I still haven't reopened the Virginia House, and I was keeping busy cleaning here. He kicked in the door and rushed at me."

"Did he . . . ?" Too painful to say, Slocum let the implica-tion hang.

"No. Kelso said that would come later, he wanted to destroy the h-house first."

Slocum had concentrated himself on Ginny so completely he did not hear Kelso rise to his feet. Groggy, his face battered, ears ringing, Kelso grabbed at the first thing he saw to use as a weapon. Ginny caught the motion of his descending arm and screamed a warning a second before the footstool crashed down on Slocum's head.

Slocum was driven to his knees, and pain and brightness exploded in his head. A warm trickle ran from the back of his head down his neck. He reached out to steady himself as he heard the clatter of the stool when Kelso released it. Slowly Kelso's reasoning power had returned enough that he recalled the hideout gun in the small of his back.

He reached for it, uttering an animal growl. "You're a dead man, Slocum," he grunted through mashed lips.

Ginny's scream cut through the daze and alerted Slocum to the danger. He half turned and drew the big seven-inch-barreled Colt .45 in a smooth, controlled motion. The hammer came back under the web of his hand, and he snapped the weapon forward to level on Kelso. The hammer free now, it dropped when Slocum's finger stroked the trigger.

Shatteringly loud in the confines of the small parlor, the muzzle blast stunned Ginny and brought a wince to Slocum's face. Kelso seemed not to be bothered by it as he stared stupidly at the hole in his chest, teetered for a breathless moment, then fell dead at Slocum's feet.

Out of gratitude and relief, the ranchers around Happy decreed a huge barbecue and hoedown to celebrate the end of the ghost rustlers. Slocum, naturally, became the hero of the hour. From somewhere, apparently close by, the town marshal returned to take up his duties. Slocum could not fault him, a gray-fringed man in his late sixties, for wanting to avoid a clash with the likes of Butch Kelso. Privately, though, he sincerely believed the elderly lawman should hang up his badge. Ginny, in straw hat and ribbons, attended the festivities on Slocum's arm.

"It's a lovely day," she said enthusiastically. "Everyone will be there."

"And I have a lot of prisoners to take to Fort Worth," the taciturn Slocum groused.

"They can wait. Besides, not all of them have been brought in by those cowboys of Charlie Goodnight's."

"They'll be here by tomorrow."

Ginny made a pouting moue. "Your bruises won't be gone by then."

"My leg won't be healed, either, but I have to take in these men."

"Oh, pooh, Slocum. You're spoiling all my plans."

"We'll talk about it after we eat," he said, stalling.

"And dance?" Ginny prompted.

Slocum produced a fleeting scowl. "I can't dance."

"You mean you're going to let a tiny little bullet hole stop you?" Ginny teased unmercifully.

"No. I mean I am about as graceful as a spavined cow pony on the dance floor," Slocum admitted uncomfortably.

Ginny's trill of laughter brightened Slocum's mood. "My dear, dear man, so am I. But we'll put blinders on everyone and dance to our hearts' content."

"We'll see," Slocum grumped.

When they reached the town park, applause and cheering broke out spontaneously. Men tussled with one another to shake Slocum's hand. Women batted eyes and fluttered fans, oohed and aahed. Arthur Canby bustled up and steered Slocum to a bunting-decorated buckboard. The whoops and hollers rose in volume as the mayor steadied Slocum while he climbed onto the wagon.

"This is a great day for Happy, a great day for Texas!" Canby began. "It's my privilege and honor to present to you the savior of the Panhandle, Ranger Slocum." The applause roared like a storm-tossed surf. Canby motioned for quiet, filled his chest, and then boomed in the best politician's manner, "Now, folks, we're gonna hear how this heroic Ranger, Mr. John Slocum, captured the villians who plundered us for so long."

Slocum looked peaked. He swallowed and tugged at the celluloid collar Ginny had badgered him into wearing. "There's not a lot to say," he began uncertainly, intensely disliking public speaking as he did. "The Association sent me to find out what was going on. I found out and stopped it. Thank you."

"More!" a portly man in the front called. "Speech!"

Slocum flushed in embarrassment. "I've made my speech. My thanks to you all for this fancy spread. The cowhands of the Goodnight ranch deserve it more than me. I only did my job."

Ginny hugged him when he hastily departed from the makeshift rostrum. The accolades continued after she released him and he stood with an arm possessively around her waist. His hand grew sore from innumerable firm shakes. He had whiskey and foaming schooners of beer pressed on him until he had to refuse all offers or become soddenly drunk.

Evening came, and the congratulations continued. Slocum had a warm glow about him, and the unformed thoughts snuck up on him without effort.

Yes, he decided, Happy, Texas, and Ginny Stuart made too unbeatable a combination for a fellow to turn down while he recuperated from his injuries. He glanced down at the shining auburn hair and lithe, lively body of Ginny and smiled broadly.

He'd go to Fort Worth, right enough, drop off the prisoners, and then stop back on his way north. Somehow, he thought, he'd get a warm welcome.